Death on an Autumn River

An Akitada Novel

I. J. Parker

I·J·P Books

Published 2013 by I.J.Parker and I·J·P Books, 428 Cedar
Lane, Virginia Beach, VA. 23452.
http://www.ijparker.com

First published electronically 2011.

Cover design by I. J. Parker;
Cover image by Matsunaga Tensho.

Book Layout ©2013 BookDesignTemplates.com

Death on an Autumn River/ I. J. Parker – 2nd Ed.
ISBN 978-1-491093634

Praise for I. J. Parker and the Akitada series

"Akitada is as rich a character as Robert Van Gulik's intriguing detective, Judge Dee." *The Dallas Morning News*

"Readers will be enchanted by Akitada." *Publishers Weekly* Starred Review

"A brisk and well-plotted mystery with a cast of regulars who become more fully developed with every episode." *Kirkus*

"Parker's research is extensive and she makes great use of the complex manners and relationships of feudal Japan." *Globe and Mail*

"The fast-moving, surprising plot and colorful writing will enthrall even those unfamiliar with the exotic setting." *Publishers Weekly,* Starred Review

". . .the author possesses both intimate knowledge of the time period and a fertile imagination as well. Combine that with an intriguing mystery and a fast-moving plot, and you've got a historical crime novel that anyone can love." *Chicago Sun-Times*

"Parker's series deserves a wide readership." *Historical Novel Society* ."

Characters:

Sugawara	Ministry of Justice official
Akitada	His clerk
Sadenari	His wife
Tamako	His little daughter
Yasuko	His elderly secretary
Seimei	Faithful retainers
Tora and Genba	Chief of the capital police
Kobe	

Characters in Eguchi:

Fujiwara Takeko	The lady of the River Mansion
Fukuda, Harima	Two poor, elderly people
Mrs. Wada	Owner of the Hananoya brothel
Warden Wada	Her husband
Nakagimi	The reigning queen of courtesans
Akogi	A young trainee in the Hananoya

Characters in Naniwa and Kawajiri:

Oga Sadazane	Governor of Settsu
Oga Yoshiyo	His son
Munata	The local prefect
Nakahara	Chief of the trade office
Nariyuki, Tameaki	His clerks
Otomo	A retired professor of Chinese
Watamaro	A local ship owner and merchant
Saburo	A severely disfigured former spy
Kunimitsu	Owner of a sailors' hostel.

In the Yodo's waters
The young Ayu fish
Cries out.
Pierced by the Cormorant's beak,
It writhes.
How pitiful!

(From the *Ryojin hisho*, a collection of the songs

of courtesans by Emperor Go-Shirakawa)

1

The River

Akitada watched the passing scenery through half-closed eyes. The river was as deep green as the wooded shoreline and flowed heavily toward the sea. Fish swam dimly in the glaucous depths of the water, shadows of silver in the shifting shades of green. On shore, the green curtain of the forest was broken here and there by a shimmer of gold or a touch of red. It was autumn, the "leaf-turning month."

Something he had read somewhere came to his mind: "Ceaselessly flows the river to the sea, never pausing, always changing, losing itself in eddies and rice paddies, gaining new life from streams and tributaries. Even so is man."

He had reached the middle of his life after almost losing himself on several occasions. His life's waters moved more calmly now, both in his official life and at home.

The boat rode low in the water, poled along by three half-naked men and guided by their master at the rudder. Under its reed covered midsection, the passengers drowsed in the late afternoon warmth. They huddled close together at a respectful distance. The motion of the boat had made them sleepy and their chatter desultory. Only the youngsters in front still chattered, bursting into laughter or song from time to time.

Akitada's clerk, Sadenari, was with them. The boy was nineteen and made him nervous with his awkward efforts to impress his superior. The young man was the son of a low-ranking official and had proved neither very capable nor useful. Being the newest member of the ministry, he was assigned to Akitada because he could be spared most easily.

As senior secretary in the Ministry of Justice, Akitada traveled on official business to the city of Naniwa on the Inland Sea. More elegant travel arrangements could have been made — he was entitled to them by rank and position — but he wanted to arrive with as little fanfare as possible. His true assignment, the delicate matter of finding out the truth about recent pirate attacks, must remain a secret. Ostensibly, he carried legal documents and instructions to the Naniwa office that handled matters of shipping goods from foreign countries and the western provinces to the capital.

Like most of the passengers, he was in a pleasant and soporific mood. Now and then a fish jumped in the distance, egrets made brilliant splashes of white against the dark green shoreline, and for a while seagulls had been circling overhead. Their boat would soon reach the coast. Soon enough he would have to deal with matters he knew little about. Anyone on this boat probably knew more about shipping and piracy than he did. The problem was that he could not ask questions and must learn from observation.

Pushing up a sleeve, he dipped his hand into the river. The water was cool on his wrist, and he instantly felt refreshed. They were turning into a bend of the river and the shore was coming closer. The curved roof of an elegant pavilion appeared among the trees.

There was a good deal of river traffic, coming and going between Naniwa and the inland towns and temples, but Akitada had not seen any villages or farms for a while. The pavilion had slender red-lacquered columns and a blue-tiled roof, and its veranda was suspended above the water. It was beautiful, almost other-worldly in its perfection. He watched it slowly gliding past, a dwelling fit for the heavenly beings in the western paradise.

Perhaps someday, he would build himself a small house on a river: a simple building of plain wood with a roof of pine bark so that squirrels and monkeys could play on it without sliding off. He would take his family there during the hottest weeks of summer. His little daughter Yasuko would like watching the animals. He would teach her how to fish, and they would sit side-by-side in their watery pavilion, letting their lines drift with the current until one of the bamboo rods would suddenly bend sharply, and Yasuko would cry, "I've caught one, father! I've caught one!"

And much later, when he was an old man and Yasuko had long since gone to be with her own family, he and his wife Tamako would live there and be at peace.

A shout from the front of the boat shattered the dream. The boatmen jumped about trying to stop the boat and turn it against the current. Some of the passengers asked questions but got no answers. Most got to their feet and craned their necks to see what was happening.

Akitada was as curious but restrained himself. Not so the young men in front. All five peered into the water over the shoulders of the boatmen. When the passengers went to join them, the boat began to list dangerously. The boat's master cursed them back to their places. Order restored, he and his men leaned over the side and dragged something sodden and heavy into the boat. A gasp went around, and excited babble broke out.

A drowned woman.

One of the passengers near him, a fat shopkeeper returning from a pilgrimage to Iwashimizu's Hachiman shrine, *tsked* and shook his head. "Happens all the time here," he announced. "The girls from the brothels are always killing themselves in the river."

A suicide?

"What brothels?" Akitada asked. "How did she get here?"

The boat's master explained, "We're almost in Eguchi."

Eguchi, along with Kamusaki and Kaya, adjoined the ancient capital Naniwa and the port city Kawajiri. The three smaller towns specialized in providing sailors and merchants with prostitutes.

Akitada protested, "But that's downriver."

"The currents and the river traffic can move bodies about quite a lot, sir," said the boat's master.

Perhaps. But still.

Akitada rose and went forward. He saw now that the river up ahead widened and another joined it. At their confluence, on the very tip of what appeared like a large island in a wide stream, lay a town.

He looked down at the body in the bottom of the boat. Curled on her side, she looked slight. Long black hair covered her face and much of her back. Her body was almost obscenely exposed under the wet silk of an undergown.

It was a beautiful body, not yet bloated from being in the river but shapely and flawless. Perhaps the river had washed away the trappings of her trade.

Someone was breathing heavily beside him. Sadenari was goggling at the dead woman, his face flushed and his mouth agape. When he caught Akitada's eyes, he swallowed hard.

Akitada snapped, "Sit down!" and then bent to examine the body more closely. The silk was very good quality, and the long hair, now tangled and full of small bits of vegetation and algae, had been cared for. He glanced at her small hands and feet and found them soft and the nails carefully trimmed.

"Let's turn her over to see if she has any wounds," he said to the boat's master.

They handled her with great gentleness for such rough men.

The body showed no wounds, but it astonished Akitada nevertheless. When he saw more of her face, she seemed far younger than he had assumed from her well-developed figure. Her face was slightly puffy on one side, perhaps from being in the water, and the eyes stared sightlessly, but even so she still had an extraordinary and childlike beauty. Some traces of make-up remained on the lips and around her eyes, but she had not needed it to improve her looks.

Given the innocence that her youth suggested, the other revelation shocked him more. The thin silk clinging to her pale skin left nothing to the imagination, and her body was perfectly hairless except for her head. She had shaved her pubic hair, a practice common among some prostitutes.

Akitada rose. "Cover her with something," he said to the boat's master, feeling some shame on behalf of the dead girl, though the boatmen were old enough to be fathers. "What is your normal procedure when you find drowning victims?"

"We take them to the warden in Eguchi."

Akitada nodded and returned to his seat. He was joined there by Sadenari, who was eager to make his apologies.

"It's just," he explained, blushing (the very young could still blush at such things), "that I'd never seen a dead woman. I know you must think it very unseemly of me, but we've been given eyes to look at the world, haven't we?"

He was an earnest youth, and Akitada relented. "True, but even the dead have some right to privacy."

Sadenari flushed more deeply. "Surely they don't care. And if the girl was a prostitute, many men must have seen her like that when she was alive." Akitada looked at him, and Sadenari positively flamed. He gulped. "At least . . . I think that must be what happens."

"Have you never visited a pleasure house?" Akitada asked, surprised.

Sadenari shook his head. "The others were talking about Eguchi. They've been there many times and say those places are full of beautiful women. A man may have several in one night." He blurted, "Oh, how I wish I might do so just once!"

Akitada snorted. "Nonsense. Your father wouldn't like it. Wait till you have a wife." Sadenari came from a very proper family. That probably accounted for the fact that at nineteen he was still a virgin.

"Yes, sir," Sadenari murmured, looking dejected.

Akitada felt a twinge of pity. The very young had their own worries, but having along a youth in the throes of lust could become a nuisance, perhaps even a danger, when one is tracking corrupt officials. The fact that their work would be so near the brothel towns was likely to keep Sadenari in a state of painful mental arousal and might lead him into mischief. Akitada toyed with the idea of letting him loose in Eguchi, but the youth probably did not have the money to purchase a woman. His father kept him very short. And advancing him the funds for a night of debauchery went against Akitada's grain.

He turned away to watch the approach to the Eguchi wharf, where other boats like theirs were moored. Already several small pleasure boats were coming toward them, their occupants holding large, brightly colored parasols. Prostitutes eager to snatch the first customers. He sighed and glanced at Sadenari. The boy watched the women hungrily. When the women in the first boat struck up a song, his face broke into a smile of delight.

"Oh," he breathed. "I had no idea they could be such artists."

Akitada snorted. Sadenari had a nice face, and he was young and a gentleman. Even the most mercenary female in the water trade might relent in such a case. Perhaps it was best to leave him to his own resources.

A lively exchange between passengers and boats sprang up as they maneuvered to the landing stage. One of the young men climbed into the boat with the rose-colored parasol and embraced its occupant.

When they had tied up, Akitada and Sadenari left the boat, but stopped to watch the unloading of the dead woman. Sadenari fidgeted.

The news of the drowned girl spread quickly, and a small crowd gathered to peer down at the reed mat covering the body. Most were women, young and older, anxious or merely curious.

After a short, tense wait, the local warden, a burly man with a paunch and a bristling mustache, pushed his way past them. He lifted the mat, looked, and shook his head. He singled out two middle-aged women and waved them over. "Take a look. Was she working here?" They peered and shook their heads. One said, "That one was a beauty, wasn't she?" The warden nodded and dropped the mat again. "Not one of ours," he called out to the onlookers, who dispersed.

Akitada, followed by Sadenari, approached the man and said, "I was on the boat. The boatmen found her upriver, near that bend." He pointed. "It seems too far for her to have come from Eguchi. It may not be a simple suicide of another prostitute. Besides, as the woman said, she was remarkably beautiful."

The warden eyed him, taking in the silk robe, and became deferential. "Very kind of you to take an interest, sir, but I assure you that our ladies are very superior. Our houses employ only the most talented and beautiful girls. There are many better looking than this one." He gave the body on the ground a dismissive shove with a booted foot. With a grin at Sadenari, he added, "I'm sure the gentlemen will enjoy checking out the truth of that while they're here."

Akitada was irritated. "Thank you, but we travel on official business. I noticed something tied around the girl's neck. Perhaps that will help you trace her." He bent to lift the mat again and pointed to a thin string of white silk braid that hid behind the long wet hair. It looped around the slender neck and disappeared under the folds of the robe.

The warden grasped it and pulled out a small brocade pouch. "Just an amulet," he said dismissively. "Most of the girls have them. We'll send word to Kamusaki and Kaya. She may have jumped into the water from one of the boats. Still, the best thing is to let the monks have her for cremation. She's been in the water, and those bodies don't keep long."

"That's all you're going to do? Aren't you even going to look at the amulet?" asked Sadenari angrily. "Lord Sugawara and I serve in the Ministry of Justice. It strikes me that you're very lax in your duties."

The warden flushed. He bent again and opened the little pouch, extracting a small gilded coin. "How about that? A piece of silver." He weighed the metal in his hand.

"Let me see that," Akitada demanded in a voice that allowed no argument.

The warden handed the coin over reluctantly. It was curiously made and appeared to be mostly silver, but with some decorative gold overlay. It had a square hole in the center, just like copper coinage. The holes in coppers were for a string so they could be carried more conveniently. But this was no copper coin. Both silver and gold coins were oblong and had no holes. Besides, this had an intricate design, so finely made that Akitada had to lift it closer to his eyes to make out the tiny Buddha figures and clouds. Most likely, this was meant as an amulet, the hole serving to tie it around the wearer's neck. Why then had the girl hidden it in a separate pouch?

"It's not a coin," said Akitada. "It's a Buddhist amulet, but not made in this country, I think. See." He showed the ornamentation to the warden.

"Doesn't matter," said the man said. "It's worth something. She got it from a customer, I expect. We get travelers from Korea and China. Even their monks have stopped in Eguchi." He chortled and gave Akitada a sly look. "You'd be surprised what monks can get up to, sir."

Akitada would not, but he tried to look disapproving. "I suppose it will go toward the young woman's funeral?"

"Right, sir." The warden held out his hand.

Akitada gazed at the medal. "Look here," he said, "it's a curious piece. I've a friend who would like it. What if I made a suitable donation, enough to cover the young woman's funeral, in exchange for this."

The warden frowned. "I don't know. It's evidence. How much did you have in mind, sir?"

Akitada reached into his sash and brought out a piece of gold. "Gold for silver?" He held both items up before the warden's greedy eyes. The gold piece was larger and shone in the setting sun. The amulet, its silver darkened by time, looked dull by comparison.

The warden reached for the gold. "Done, sir. And the poor girl will thank you from the other world." He caught Akitada's watchful eye as he stuffed the gold into his belt. "I'll see it gets to the monks, sir."

Akitada nodded and started for the town. Sadenari hung back, watching the warden and his men taking away the body of the drowned girl.

Then he hurried after Akitada. "That was kind, sir," he said, when he caught up, "but do you trust that warden? He looked like a thief to me."

"No doubt he is," said Akitada dryly. He glanced up and down the street of shops and eating places, all decorated with banners and paper lanterns. "I don't know about you, but I'm hungry. How about sampling the local food?"

They ate in a small place where they were unlikely to be bothered by women soliciting their business. Gauging Akitada's status nicely, an elderly waiter had bowed them to a recess where a few cushions rested on a raised section. They took off their shoes, sat down, and ordered food and wine.

The old waiter announced, "We have octopus balls," awaiting their reaction with a twinkle in his eyes.

Akitada chuckled dutifully. "By all means, bring us your balls, and whatever else you can recommend." The waiter wheezed with laughter and hobbled off.

It had been a juvenile bit of humor, but to Akitada's surprise, Sadenari had not even cracked a smile. He was subdued and silent. Akitada left him to his thoughts and looked around. Not all the guests were soberly dressed and quiet men, traveling on business and not for pleasure. There were also some of those who had clearly stopped in Eguchi for the courtesans and entertainers.

The wine arrived and was excellent. The waiter's hands trembled like Seimei's as he poured, and Akitada felt a pang of guilt. Seimei had become very frail. Recently, he had expressed a wish to visit his home village and worship at the family shrine. It seemed that his old friend was preparing to join his ancestors. He could not rid himself of uneasiness.

Sadenari broke into his thoughts. "You could have insisted on an investigation, sir," he said, looking at him fixedly. It sounded like a reproof.

"What?"

"That warden. He'll keep your gold and get rid of her body."

Akitada was irritated. "What is it to you?"

"I bet she was murdered. It isn't right. And you with your reputation for looking out for poor people." Sadenari seemed clearly upset. He gulped his wine – his second or third cup?

Before Akitada could respond, the waiter arrived with the food. The dishes looked and smelled appetizing. The octopus balls turned out to be fried rice cakes stuffed with octopus meat. Grilled eel and a stew of sea bream and vegetables made up the rest of the meal.

When they were alone again, Akitada said mildly, "What makes you think she was murdered?"

"She had a bruise, just here." Sadenari touched his hand to the left side of his face. "I have good eyes. Someone killed her and then threw her into the water."

Akitada sighed. "The bruise, if it was a bruise, was very recent. Most likely it happened after she was in the river." He sampled one of the octopus balls. "Or," he said, "it was an accident.

She fell overboard and hit her head. But you heard the boat's master and the warden. The women who work in these river towns often end their miserable lives in the river. Now eat, before the food gets cold." Akitada served himself some of the sea bream.

"It may be as you say, but she didn't look like a prostitute. She looked . . . innocent."

Akitada laughed. "Come on, Sadenari, not even you could have fallen in love with a drowned woman you'd never met."

The young man jumped up, knocking over his flask of wine. "Go ahead and have your little joke, sir. That girl was murdered, and nobody cares." To Akitada's embarrassment, the youngster's voice broke. "I was so proud of serving under you, but you're just like all the rest. You can't be bothered with a poor young woman's death, and you think I'm a fool."

It got quiet in the restaurant; eyes turned their way. The old waiter hobbled over with a cloth to mop up the wine.

"Sit down, Sadenari," said Akitada through clenched teeth. "You're making a scene." Louder, he added, "Come, let's eat this excellent food and then get a good night's rest. Tomorrow will be a busy day."

Sadenari looked around, flushed, and sat. The waiter cleaned up the wine and removed the empty flask. The other guests returned to their meals.

Akitada said, "I apologize for what I said. It was unkind and uncalled for. I don't think you a fool. In fact, it was perceptive of you to notice the bruise and to question the warden's verdict. You may be right, but we can't do anything about it."

Sadenari raised his head. There were tears of shame in his eyes, but his voice was steady again. "I don't understand."

"I suppose I owe you an explanation." Akitada lowered his voice. "You've been told that we're taking documents from the ministry to the trade office in Naniwa. What you don't know is that I'm seeking information concerning pirate attacks on private ships traveling between the Dazaifu and the capital. These ships carried priceless treasures in tribute gifts meant for the emperor. It may be that someone either in Naniwa or at the Dazaifu has been working with the pirates. Under the circumstances, we cannot get involved in local problems. It would attract undesirable attention."

Sadenari gaped. "You mean an official is involved? But that's a crime against the emperor." He brightened. "Oh, but it is exciting, sir! Thank you for bringing me along. I swear I'll be the soul of discretion. Just call on me for anything. I don't care how dangerous it is. I'd really like to get my hands on that traitor. And on those pirates, too." He flexed his hands.

"Thank you," Akitada said dryly. "I know I can count on you, but you mustn't tell anyone."

"Of course not. And I can see now our assignment is vastly more important than a case of drowning. I'll be more circumspect in the future."

"Good. Now let's eat."

Sadenari obeyed and Akitada had almost regained his good humor, when Sadenari remarked, "I really think I can be useful, sir. Please allow me to carry out the more dangerous parts of the investigation. I've had some training in wrestling and I'm very strong."

Akitada nearly choked on his last octopus ball. Clearly Sadenari thought him well past his prime. He swallowed, managed a "Thank you. I'll keep it in mind," and was preserved from further humiliations by a squabble breaking out in another part of the room.

Two middle-aged men in the dark robes and hats of officials were on their feet. Both shouted and one of them, with a spreading stain on the front of his robe, had the old waiter by the throat.

The owner of the restaurant rushed from the kitchen and tried to calm the officials while delivering kicks at the quailing waiter. Akitada felt sorry for the poor old man and instinctively disliked the officials. But the matter was settled quickly, and the owner bowed the irate guests out. The old waiter limped back to the kitchen, weeping.

"I wish they hadn't been so cruel," said Sadenari, and Akitada forgave him his earlier remark.

For that night, they stayed in a small monastery on the outskirts of Eguchi, away from the noise and the temptations of its brothels. Akitada fell asleep immediately, dreaming of casting his line into the water from the veranda of his river pavilion and dragging out an enormous fish. The fish changed into the shape of a dead young girl who had the features of his little daughter.

He came awake in a cold sweat and lay for a while looking up at the rafters. It had only been a nightmare, perhaps because he had been forced to ignore the case of the drowned girl. She had been so young, too young to end her life like that.

Something else nagged at him: the incident in the restaurant. Something had been wrong. Those officials were not what they seemed to be. Even at that distance, their robes had looked worn and the colored rank ribbons on their hats had been for the third and fourth rank respectively, far too high in the hierarchy for ordinary officials going about their business in a place like Eguchi.

He sat up and looked over to where Sadenari slept. His bedding seemed strangely flat in the dim moonlight that came through the shutters. Getting up, he went to check and found the quilts empty. Sadenari was gone, and he had taken his clothes, shoes, and money pouch with him.

2

The Old Couple

Akitada muttered under his breath as he dressed and gathered his belongings. He was very angry. Sadenari had managed to become a thorn in his side already.

The trick of arranging his bedding so that it would look occupied was juvenile. Common sense dictated ignoring this ruse and, if he did not make an appearance soon, continuing the journey alone. After all, the youth was nineteen and should know how to take care of himself.

On the other hand, he felt a responsibility for someone as naïve about the world as Sadenari was, and besides, the young man's father would hold him responsible if harm came to his child.

Sadenari had probably slipped out to sample the harlots, or possibly he had followed up on his obsession with the drowned girl. Either way, there was little to be done about it.

Akitada stepped outside the monastery gate and looked down the road toward Eguchi. In the east, the darkness was lifting, but the town was still asleep. The lights in the brothels had dimmed, and paper lanterns swayed ghostlike in the breeze from the river. Akitada sniffed. He could smell the open sea. The air was fresher here than in the capital, which was enclosed by mountains and tended to have stagnant summer days.

With an impatient sigh, he turned back into the monastery compound and sought out the dining hall for his breakfast. The monks had already been up for early morning lessons and now were chatting over their gruel. He ate what they ate, millet gruel with some vegetables added, and drank water. Two young monks sat near him, their shaved heads together, and whispered. He caught the word "drowned."

Belatedly, it occurred to Akitada that this must be the monastery in charge of the dead girl's funeral, and that she must have been brought here already.

When he asked the two monks, they flushed furiously. They were young and perhaps new to their vows, but it troubled him that, instead of sadness for a life lost so young, this death should cause prurient thoughts. Sadenari had also flushed because the nameless girl had aroused desire in him.

After his breakfast, he sought out the abbot, introduced himself, and asked if the warden had paid for the funeral.

"Oh, no," the elderly abbot said quickly. "We don't require payment. The poor young girl has no family and no money. But late last night a young woman from the town left some silver to have prayers read. They are very protective of each other."

Akitada did not mention the gold piece he had given the warden. Though he could not really afford it, he took out another one, saying, "Allow me to make a small contribution also." He asked for the name of the other donor—hoping that the girl had had a family after all—but the abbot did not know.

When he left the monastery, the sun was up, and still there was no sign of Sadenari.

He walked the entire length of Eguchi, passing several drunks sleeping in doorways, but none was Sadenari. At the wharf, the boats swayed gently in the river current, making soft bumping sounds. Here, too, he saw no one. The deep blue of the sky promised another fine day. Until the body of the girl had been discovered, the river journey had been very pleasant. Akitada decided to continue the short distance to Naniwa by water. He looked at the sun. There was time for a stroll before the first boat would leave.

Touching the drowned girl's amulet in his sash, he felt obscurely guilty for abandoning her to a crooked warden and a quick cremation by the monks. She had been too young to be in this profession, perhaps as young as twelve or thirteen.

It was a pity what happened to poor children— for the pleasure houses also provided boys to their customers.   Their parents frequently were too poor to feed them.   What a shocking life the dead girl must have found here.   He thought of his little daughter and shuddered.

He saw the first signs of life in the streets.   A woman opened shutters on one of the houses, a drunk staggered homeward holding his head, and the owner of the restaurant where they had eaten the night before was shouting at two maids who swept last night's dirt out into the street.   Akitada remembered the old waiter.

"Good morning," he called out to the owner. "My clerk and I happened to eat here last night." The man hurried over and bowed.   "You had an unpleasant incident," Akitada added.

"My deepest apologies.   I assure you, sir, that the worthless waiter has been dismissed.   We take pride in giving only the best service."

"I watched the incident. Your waiter was most likely innocent.   The two men who complained were not who they pretended to be.   I suspect they created the incident to get a free meal."

To his surprise, the man nodded.   "That is so, sir."

"You suspected them?"

"It's happened before.   In my business you have to keep your eyes and ears open."

"But in that case, why blame the waiter?"

"He was getting too old anyway.   I lost the payment for two meals and wine, but my customers think I got rid of a careless waiter."

Outraged, Akitada snapped, "What you did was unjust and heartless.   You should go and apologize to that old man and ask him to come back."

The restaurant owner started a laugh, turned it into a cough, and bowed. "Your pardon, sir, but my business waits." He disappeared into his establishment.

Akitada stared after him in helpless fury when one of the maids, an older woman sidled over with her broom and started sweeping. She murmured, "Fukuda lives behind the temple," and moved away.

Akitada bit his lip. Sadenari was still gone. Perhaps he should give him a bit more time and take the later boat. He walked to the small temple not far from the landing stage and found a narrow footpath leading through a bamboo grove. Within moments, the world became peaceful. A rabbit started and dove into the undergrowth, and very small birds fluttered up as he passed. The lush leaves above his head shut out the sky and were in a continuous rustling motion. From time to time, smaller footpaths crossed or led away from the one he was on until he feared he would become lost in this green world.

But the stems of bamboo thinned abruptly, and he found himself at the edge of a garden filled with vegetables and melon plants. A tiny house stood under a wide catalpa tree beyond the neat woven fencing that protected the garden from wildlife. And there an old woman was feeding a small flock of chickens and ducks.

He startled her when he called out, but she made him the most graceful bow. It would have done honor to an imperial princess, yet she was a frail white-haired creature, barefoot and in patched rags. For some obscure reason, he felt extremely flattered, and on his best behavior, he bowed also and said, "Please forgive me for startling you. I'm looking for a man called Fukuda. He is said to live nearby."

"He lives here, my Lord," she said, her voice still strong and quite beautiful. "May I announce you?"

Akitada glanced at the poor shack, the squawking fowl, the rows of vegetables. He felt silly, giving her his name as if he were calling on some great lord, but he did so anyway and watched her perform another flawless obeisance. She walked away from him as gracefully as a young woman, then ducked inside the hut.

It came to him that she must have been one of the courtesans at one time, perhaps even the ranking beauty. Her hair, twisted up in back, was still thick and long, though white as snow, and the wrinkled face retained some former beauty. Only the most rigorous training could have produced such perfect manners and posture.

She reappeared with two plain cushions. These she placed in the shade of the catalpa tree and invited him to sit. "It's a pleasant morning," she said. "Fukuda thought you would be more comfortable here than inside."

Akitada sat and smiled up at her. "An excellent idea."

"Please forgive this slow old woman," she said and tripped off into the vegetable patch to select a ripe melon. This she cut up with a knife she carried tied to a string around her waist. She presented it to him on a large cabbage leaf.

Akitada said, "Thank you. You take too much trouble. Please sit down and rest."

But Fukuda had appeared in the doorway of the hut. He was leaning on a stick and made his way painfully toward them. She went quickly to offer her arm for support and helped him down on the other cushion. Then she knelt behind him on the bare ground, much like a trained courtesan attending to her client.

Fukuda had a black eye and angry bruises on his scrawny neck. He bowed deeply to Akitada. "You're welcome here, sir. Please forgive this poor hospitality." Turning to the woman, he asked, "Is there no wine, my dear?"

Akitada said quickly, "Thank you, but it's far too early for wine for me." He reached for a slice of melon. "Your wife was kind enough to bring this fresh melon." He took a bite. The fruit was sweet and fragrant, better than any he had ever tasted. "Wonderful!" he said.

They smiled at him. Fukuda said, "Melons grow very well here. But Harima is not my wife, though I ask her often enough."

She raised a hand to cover her face and protested, "It would not be proper. I used to be an entertainer."

Fukuda looked at her with loving pride. "Harima was elected *choja* two years in a row. She was the most desired woman in Eguchi. I don't know why she puts up with a poor old stick like me."

She smiled and reached forward to touch his hand.

Akitada was moved. They were clearly very much in love, even at their advanced ages. And though Fukuda was only a waiter, and she had somehow missed her chance for a good marriage or for the wealth leading courtesans accumulated from the generous gifts of past lovers, they considered themselves fortunate in each other's affection.

He recalled his purpose.

"I was in the restaurant last night when you were treated so badly by your customers and your employer," he said to Fukuda.

Fukuda touched his swollen eye. "I should have been more careful," he said.

"I believe those two men created a scene to get a free meal."

Fukuda nodded. "Yes, I should have suspected as much and made it more difficult for them to cheat my employer. It was very good of you to come here to tell me, sir, but I knew quite well what was going on."

Harima interjected, "I think it was cruel and unjust of Master Wakita to dismiss you. And don't tell me he didn't give you that very nasty bruise on your leg."

Fukuda smiled a little. "She loves me," he said apologetically. "It makes me sad."

Akitada reached for another slice of melon. "Why do you say that? It should make you happy."

The old man shook his head. "Look at me. I'm an ugly old man, and now I've become a burden to Harima. How shall we eat? I'll die soon enough, but she? What will become of her?" He shuddered and put his head in his hands.

She shuffled forward on her knees and put an arm around him. Looking at Akitada, she said, "I shall not let him die. He won't get away so easily." She shook the old man a little. "Do you hear, Fukuda? You're not going to leave me."

Fukuda dropped his hands and sighed. "A long life accumulates shame. It's best for a man to die before he reaches forty."

By the waiter's count, Akitada had only another five years. Already his guilt and shame had accumulated. He cleared his throat. "Allow me to leave this small token of appreciation for your service last night. I did not have time to give it to you." He took another gold piece from his slash and placed it with a slight bow before Fukuda.

Fukuda blinked but did not touch it. Tears started down his wrinkled face. It was Harima who made Akitada a deep bow and said, "Your generosity is greatly appreciated, sir. Fukuda and I will say special prayers to the Buddha for you and yours. Happiness has returned to our poor hovel."

Akitada was embarrassed. He looked around. "You do your place an injustice. It's a hermitage rather than a hovel. A man, or woman, or both, may live contentedly here among the chickens and bees and tend a garden. And grow these superb melons." He took another slice and ate it, licking juice from his fingers.

She smiled behind her hand. "Exactly what I always tell Fukuda. He loves his garden, and now he will have more time to work in it."

Fukuda glanced toward the vegetable plot with a watery smile. "We cannot live on melons, no matter how delicious."

Akitada had an idea. "But you could grow your fine vegetables and melons to sell to the restaurants in town. And if you had more chickens and ducks, you could sell their eggs."

They looked at each other. Harima clapped her hands. "Of course. We could do that easily. I'm quite strong and still have good connections in town. What about it, Fukuda?"

Fukuda looked thoughtful, then nodded. "Perhaps. There's enough land to make the garden larger. Perhaps . . ."

As Akitada walked back through the bamboo grove, he wondered. Fukuda was unlike any waiter he had ever known. The man had sounded educated. How had these two found each other and ended up here? Surely, there was a story in that.

But he had no time to waste on the many mysteries of Eguchi, not even on the disappearance of Sadenari. He had to catch a boat for Naniwa.

.

3

Naniwa

The harbor at Naniwa was in the Yodo River delta. Here, Akitada saw many more ships, but the largest ones were at a distance at anchor out in the bay, leaving the wharves to smaller craft.

The boat's master, leaving the work of docking to his men, who performed the task several times each day, came to stand beside Akitada.

"It's silted up bad," he said, gesturing at the river delta. "The big ships go to Kawajiri on the Mikuni River. A new canal takes passengers and goods to the Yodo River and up to the capital."

Akitada saw that the bay widened into the Inland Sea. It was midmorning, and the sun cast an almost blinding light on the expanse of water. The distance to the horizon seemed immense. Above, in a cloudless sky, gulls whirled with raucous cries. It would have been hot, except for a wonderfully cooling breeze from the sea. "Is Kawajiri far from here?" he asked.

"You get there by boat within two hours, or you can rent a horse and be there even sooner."

Akitada studied the distant ships with their huge square sails. "And that's where all the shipping from the Inland Sea ends up?"

"Mostly. All the tribute ships from the western provinces and foreign ships from Korea and China. All the tax shipments twice a year, and all other merchant ships trading in the capital. It's a busy town."

Akitada turned to look at Naniwa. It had once been an imperial capital and the main port, but centuries had passed since then. There was little left of former splendor. Beyond the fishing boats tied up at the quay, gray-roofed wooden buildings on stilts stretched along the waterfront. The land was flat for half a mile or so, then began to rise slightly toward green hills. There, among the trees, he saw a few blue-tiled, curved roofs of more substantial buildings—temples, mansions, and administrative offices probably. A straight road led from the harbor.

He took a deep breath of the air filled with smells of saltwater and fish. The gulls swooped for fish entrails dropped overboard by fishermen who were readying their catch for market. On his left was a building flying the flags of an official post station. He left his and Sadenari's bags there and took the road into the city.

It took him past the housing of the poor and open fields and eventually brought him to the tree-shaded compounds of the well-to-do. He paused at a gate with flags and signs marking it as the district prefecture. The complex was well-maintained and included a number of large buildings, probably the jail and guards barrack. Across the street was the Foreign Trade Office. It was smaller in size but the compound also included several buildings.

The gatekeeper directed him to a hall that looked like a venerable building perhaps dating back to a time when Naniwa was an imperial capital. It was now in rather poor repair with the lacquer peeling from its columns. Akitada climbed the wide stone steps and walked through open double doors. The building appeared to be empty. He gave a shout, and after a moment, footsteps approached. A pale and serious young man in a black robe approached with a deep bow.

"Welcome, sir," he said, checking Akitada's rank ribbon with a glance. "His Lordship is in his office. May I announce you?"

"Secretary Sugawara from the Ministry of Justice. I left my baggage at the post station."

The young man looked momentarily startled, as well he might. Ranking imperial officials did not arrive on foot and alone. But he caught himself and bowed again. "You are expected, my Lord. Someone will bring your things. Please follow me."

He showed Akitada into a large room, containing numerous boxes, crates, and piles of bundles. The bundles were tied with ropes, and the wooden chests bound with metal and secured with enormous locks. An amazing assortment of loose odds and ends — casks, lacquer ware, scrolls, porcelain, piles of silk fabrics, and leather goods—was piled so high and wide that, at first, he thought he was in a large and poorly organized treasure house. He cleared his throat. That raised a grumble from beyond the pile.

A deep voice growled, "More interruptions! How many times do I have to tell you fools that I'm busy. What is it this time? Who's there?"

"Sugawara. From the Ministry of Justice," Akitada snapped back, irritated by the tone.

"What?"

A clatter, an "ouch," then quick steps. Given the voice, a surprisingly small man shot around the corner of the pile and peered at him. "Amida," he said, flapping his hands apologetically. "I thought those rascals were playing another joke on me. You really are Sugawara. At least, I take it that you are, because you said so. It must be so. Unless those rascals have hired one of those good-for-nothing actors." He laughed nervously. "You aren't an actor, are you?"

It was hardly a proper reception, but Akitada was amused. "No. And who are you?" he asked, suppressing a smile. This little man with the voice of a giant wore a green silk robe, somewhat stained across the chest. His head was nearly bald except for a thin braid twisted on top and tied with a large amount of silk ribbon, perhaps to give the few gray hairs more substance.

"Nakahara, at your service." The short man peered more closely at Akitada's face and said, "Hmm. Can't be too careful, you know. Everybody and his dog walks in here. So, you're here, Sugawara, and what d'you think of the place?

Ever been to Naniwa before? Know any of the local luminaries? Got connections?" He paused and moved quickly to look past Akitada. "You're alone? Tsk, tsk. Should've brought your people. You'll have to do your own work then or use my people. Well, let's not stand here. Come in, come in." Nakahara dashed back behind the pile of goods.

Akitada followed more slowly. This did not promise well. He had been told that Nakahara probably could be trusted, but this official seemed an oddly careless person and lacking in good sense.

On the other side of the pile of goods was a reasonably large area with Nakahara's desk and several smaller desks. Doors stood open to a courtyard. Nakahara grabbed one of the new silk cushions from the pile and dropped it on the floor beside his desk. The desk was large but barely visible underneath mounds of loose papers and open document boxes. An abacus balanced precariously on top.

Nakahara waved at the cushion. "Make yourself comfortable. It's a little cluttered here, but for all that, it's handy. Well, mostly. I think, I misplaced the lists of tribute goods from Chikuzen." He sat down and began to rummage. The abacus slipped and would have struck his head if Akitada had not caught it.

"Oh, Morito?" a youthful male voice called from beyond the pile of goods. A smiling young face looked around the boxes. "Dear me, you've got company. Hello, there. Morito, we're sending out for food. We thought Uzura's Crabhouse would be nice. Can we order something for you and your friend?"

Akitada's jaw nearly dropped at this young man's casual manner. Nakahara seemed to see nothing wrong with it. He smiled. "No, thank you, Yuki. This is Lord Sugawara. Just arrived from the ministry in the capital. You might tell Tameaki to find a room for him in my house. I expect we'll walk into town for a while. He'll want to have a look around." To Akitada, he added, "You never said if you've been here before."

Akitada shook his head, still speechless.

"Good," said Nakahara, rubbing his hands briskly. "That's what we'll do. But it was very good of you to ask, Yuki, and the crab rolls at Uzura's are very fine. Very fine." He licked his lips. " Perhaps we'll . . . but never mind, I'll leave it up to our guest. So run along, Yuki."

The youth grinned. "Well, if you're headed there, stay away from the sake. Uzura spikes it with something that'll curl your hair. You know what happened last time." His chuckle turned into a peal of laughter and he vanished.

Akitada found his voice. "Who was that?"

Nakahara looked a little shamefaced. "Oh, that's my senior clerk, Nariyuki. We call him Yuki. A very funny fellow. Likes to tease. You'll like him." He lowered his booming voice to a whisper, "Nothing like that stiff and proper black crow Tameaki. That one has no sense of humor or friendliness."

Akitada took it that Tameaki was the very serious young man who had shown him in. His opinion of Nakahara plummeted further. He took his papers and the documents from his sleeve and passed them across. "The Minister of the Right has asked me to deliver these letters and to assist you in any way I can. He has signed my credentials himself, as you will see."

Nakahara stared at the batch. "Did he now? You must be important, then." He flipped through them. "Where is it? Oh, never mind. I'll read it all later." He shuffled Akitada's documents together, found a loose piece of silk cord and tied them up. "Now, what do you say? Shall we walk into town?" Not waiting for an answer, he hopped up and headed past Akitada to the door.

Being accustomed to the bone-chilling formality of the court, Akitada was stunned. Far from reading the minister's missive after raising it reverently to his forehead, Nakahara had pushed it and the other papers under his piles of unfinished work. And now he was off, no doubt having crab rolls and sake on his mind. The man was not just eccentric; he must be demented. And what was more worrying, apparently any number of people had access to his documents. Even pirates might learn all about the richest shipments.

With a sigh, he got up again and followed Nakahara. Nakahara passed through the hall and out into the entrance courtyard, waving gaily to the guards and shouting that he would be gone for the rest of the afternoon.

Making things easy for spies, thought Akitada.

As they left his compound, Nakahara pointed to a building near the prefecture. "Look, over there is the government lodging house for couriers and those on official business. Of course, I hope you'll be my guest while you're here."

The government quarters looked adequate, and Akitada could have stayed there. There was much to be said for maintaining a neutral distance, but in this case it seemed better to meet the people around Nakahara. He accepted the invitation.

They walked back down to the harbor. Nakahara talked about the river and canal silting up and making shipping difficult, but the fate of the Naniwa harbor was of little interest to Akitada. The theft of imperial goods had taken place on the high seas, not here.

Akitada put up with the chatter for a while, then interrupted. "All of this is very interesting, sir, but the attention at court is on the recent piracies on the Inland Sea."

Nakahara stopped. "Do please call me Morito. Everybody does. It's friendlier."

"If you wish. I take it you're aware of the increased pirate activity?"

"Mmm, Yes. There has been talk." Nakahara avoided his eyes. "Are you certain that there is nothing else you would like to see? The old storehouses are this way, and we could have a look at Shitenno-ji. Everyone who comes here visits the temple.

Akitada declined the offer and returned to the issue of piracy. "It is the Dazaifu that dispatches the cargo from Kyushu to Naniwa. But apparently, that office has maintained the strictest secrecy. Besides, some tribute ships from the provinces have also been lost."

"Coincidence probably, but someone in the capital always gets worried about conspiracies. And usually they think it must be happening here."

Akitada suppressed a sarcastic comment. He was puzzled. According to his information, Naka-hara was above reproach. Why, then, was he stalling? "Perhaps it would be best to keep the matter between ourselves for the time being. And make sure that your documents are safe from curious eyes."

"You think I should?" Nakahara chewed his lower lip. "You may be right. The whole town seems to be in and out of my office lately."

"What makes the court suspect this area in particular?"

"The pirates have been attacking certain shipments and only on the last leg of their journey. They must be local. A cargo from China was carrying medicines and Buddhist scriptures and religious treasures for the Nara temple. The monks discovered that some of their goods had been sold to rival temples and are furious. Then two tribute ships for high-ranking officials disappeared. In all of the cases, official lists from the Dazaifu were sent to us weeks earlier." Seeing Akitada's surprise, Nakahara explained, "When the ships dock in Kawajiri, we check the cargo against those lists before they are transferred to smaller vessels. It cuts down on captains helping themselves to things. I think someone may have got hold of those lists. I must say, it's been somewhat embarrassing."

That was an understatement. Either Nakahara was covering up his own activities or he was incredibly incompetent. It occurred to Akitada, not for the first time, that someone at court had a personal interest in the matter.

Nakahara chewed his lip. "You should talk to Watamaro. He's a local merchant and ship owner. He knows all about shipping and is a very charitable man. I shall arrange a small dinner tonight so you can meet him and one or two other important men." The thought of entertaining apparently reminded Nakahara of his stomach, because he stopped and pointed down a narrow street. "Look! Uzura's is just a few steps from here."

Before Akitada could answer, he heard shouting. "Sir, sir! Wait up. Please."

The disheveled figure of Sadenari ran toward them, robe and trousers flapping, one hand holding onto his hat, the other waving frantically.

He had picked the perfect moment to show up. Akitada could hardly dress him down in front of their host. Seething,—Sadenari's clothes were sadly wrinkled and stained, and his eyes were bloodshot—Akitada made the introductions. At least Sadenari managed a decent bow and a courteous greeting.

Nakahara was all smiles. "Delighted to meet you, young man. You'll be right at home with my clerks. Young fellows know how to have a good time." He winked at Akitada. "Except Tameaki, perhaps. Come, you're just in time to join us. Best crab rolls you ever tasted."

The crab rolls were very good, and Sadenari refrained from discussing his night of debauchery in Eguchi. Instead, they talked about the capital. It was amazing to see the relief with which Nakahara dropped the piracy topic.

Akitada was sorry that he had taken Sadenari into his confidence about the assignment. At least he had not shared the details. While they were here, he would put Sadenari to feeling out the young clerks. That should keep him reasonably distracted while Akitada saw the local officials. The depredations had been of such size and profitability that it was unlikely youngsters were behind them, but they might have observed some irregularities in the office.

Sadenari made his humble apology later that day and in private. They had been assigned rooms in Nakahara's home, a comfortable residence in the compound of the foreign trade office.

His story was simple.

Unable to sleep, he had stepped outside. Curiosity had led him to stroll back into town to look around. That was where he had met again the young men from the boat, and they had taken him to a wine house.

"I meant to have just one cup with them," Sadenari said miserably. "I thought I would ask them about the poor girl. They are very experienced and were closer to her body." He gave Akitada a quick glance, perhaps to remind him that he had been ordered away from the dead girl. "They thought maybe she'd been drowned by a jealous wife or by a rival. I said, I didn't think so. We argued, and they kept refilling my cup, and then, of course, it was my turn to pay for wine, and the next thing I knew, I woke up in a backroom. There were women there . . . but they were with the others." This last was added in a murmur of shame.

Akitada almost felt sorry for him. All that frustrated desire, and in the end he had drunk too much to taste the pleasure. "Your behavior was reprehensible enough, but it seems to me you still had plenty of time to join me on the boat in the morning," he pointed out.

Sadenari hung his head. "I had no money left, sir, so I walked."

Well, it had been a salutary experience, and so Akitada said no more on the subject. "Go and take a bath and change out of those disgraceful clothes," he said, wrinkling his nose. "As for our assignment here, keep your eyes and ears open but don't talk about our real purpose."

Sadenari thanked him fervently and dashed out. Looking after him, Akitada shook his head.

4

A Sparrow among Cranes

Akitada's preference would have been to return immediately to the capital and report that Nakahara managed his office so carelessly that anyone could have consulted the lists of shipment and informed others. Nakahara would be replaced and the local authorities instructed to go after the pirates.

But he suspected that he was to produce a minor villain, a scapegoat if necessary, so that things could go on as they had. Someone was making big profits from piracy, and that someone had ties to the court.

His real problem was managing things in such a way that he would seem to have been following orders without actually stepping on the true culprit's toes. It struck Akitada that living here in quiet luxury might be preferable to maintaining a household close to the emperor. Court intrigue was dangerous when so many competed for positions of power.

It was a distasteful business he was engaged on.

After an afternoon of wandering around town, he returned without any brilliant ideas but pleasantly tired. With the prospect of Nakahara's dinner, he hurried to take a bath and change into his best robe, a dark blue figured silk, then presented himself in Nakahara's reception room.

Nakahara's residence sat on a small knoll that offered him views of the Inland Sea and the shoreline. The doors stood open to the veranda, and the sun was setting. The large room would soon be gloomy, even with the shutters still open, but Akitada saw a servant going around lighting candles and oil lamps. Outside, a blaze like burning embers marked the horizon between the silver sea and a sky the color of fading wisteria blossoms. Akitada could hardly take his eyes away. Sunsets over water always moved him deeply. He had seen them on his journey to Kazusa in his youth, and again later on Sado Island. Both times had marked close encounters with death.

There was no time to wonder about what might lie ahead this time. Other guests were waiting to meet him. Four men formed a casual group around Nakahara, and looked toward Akitada expectantly. He looked back no less curiously. The heavy-set, clean-shaven man in his fifties in the very costly gray robe was clearly someone of high rank, but a white-haired pole of a man in sober brown could be anyone. The jovially smiling giant with the trimmed beard and a rather dashing hunting coat looked like a local landowner, while the black-robed, short man with the mustache and goatee was clearly an official of sorts. Akitada guessed he might be the prefect.

His host's deep voice boomed. "There you are, Sugawara. Come in, come in." He skipped over to take Akitada's arm and lead him toward the large man in gray, saying, "Excellency, meet Sugawara Akitada, the famous investigator of crimes. He's fresh from the capital. We'll have to watch ourselves, or he'll discover all of our nasty little secrets." His laugh was a little forced, and Akitada cringed as he bowed.

Nakahara continued, "Oga Sadazane is our governor. Isn't it a wonderful coincidence that he should be here the very day you arrive?"

"A fortunate turn of events," Akitada said, inclining his head. "I'm afraid our host exaggerates my abilities, governor. I'm a mere messenger on this occasion. Some documents needed signatures, and I decided to pay a visit to your beautiful province. Paperwork day in and day out can make for a dull life."

Oga smiled and bowed, but his eyes were watchful.

Nakahara made the other introductions more quickly. The cheerful bearded man in the fine hunting robe was the ship owner Watamaro; the small, pale fellow in black was indeed the local prefect Munata; and the elderly gentleman with the white hair and beard turned out to be a Professor Otomo.

Akitada found himself beside the governor when they took their seats and wine was being passed around. The governor said, "This is indeed a beautiful province, though very little happens here. I'm afraid you may have a dull visit. Still, Nakahara can be a very entertaining fellow. No doubt, he'll introduce you to the lovely ladies of our river towns. Their beauty and skills are equally legendary."

The fleshpots on the Yodo River were famous in the capital, and Oga might well be one of those senior officials who led licentious lives and assumed everyone else did also. Akitada disapproved and said pointedly, "Well, my plan was to visit Shitenoji temple and see some other sights, but perhaps you can instruct me about these attractions. I'm not familiar with them myself."

He knew he had made a mistake as soon as the words were out. Oga flushed and turned away. Akitada reminded himself that he might need this man in his investigations.

Nakahara on Akitada's other side said with a laugh, "The ladies are pretty creatures, but sometimes taking care of one's soul outweighs other temptations. What say you, Watamaro?"

The merchant was a commoner, but he certainly seemed to know his place. His voice was low and apologetic. "I, too, visit Shitenoji frequently to look westward toward the Buddha's paradise. In my business, one becomes mindful of the closeness of the other world."

Why? Was a merchant closer to death than a governor? No doubt, the man was nervous because he felt like a fish out of water here. Akitada had learned to admire men who had risen in the world without being nobly born. Trying to make up for his earlier gaffe with Oga, he engaged Watamaro in questions about places worth seeing in Naniwa. Though Watamaro would know much about pirates, Akitada avoided the subject.

The two other guests hung back and did not join the conversation. Akitada found an excuse to draw the prefect into the conversation, but Munata had little to say beyond the hope that Akitada would find his visit pleasant.

The talk next turned to the former regent Fujiwara Michinaga, who had just disowned his son Yorimichi, the chancellor. Michinaga had made this surprising gesture to show his displeasure with the laziness of court officials serving under Yorimichi. The topic was uncomfortable for Akitada, who was a court official, though of a much lower rank and position than those who had given offense. He saw that the professor had stepped out onto the veranda to admire the view and joined him.

The colors of the sunset were fading but still incredibly beautiful. Akitada said, "Such beauty is very moving, isn't it?" and gestured at the rapidly darkening sky. "No wonder, our ancestors believed that the place where the sun sets is where we'll find paradise."

Otomo gave him a shrewd look and a smile. "Do I take it that you don't believe in the Buddha, Lord Sugawara?"

Akitada did not, but Buddhism was the court-approved faith and he avoided an answer. "We must believe in something," he said vaguely. "Otherwise death would be too hard to bear."

The old man nodded. "Forgive me. I shouldn't probe into your beliefs. The fact is that I was looking at the western horizon for a different reason. My people came from there, you see. From Koryo, as you call it."

Since no foreign settlers from either Korea or China had been admitted to the nation for a century or more, Akitada was surprised. "Surely that must have been a long time ago."

"Oh, yes. They were my great-grandparents. And even then, an exception was being made for them. My great-grandfather took a Japanese name and earned his living teaching Chinese literature. It was a skill that was considered useful then. As you see, I follow the example of my forebears."

"Your ancestral background turns out to be a perfect coincidence." Akitada took out the dead girl's silver amulet from his sash. "I had hoped someone could tell me about this. I think it may have come from Koryo, or perhaps Silla. What do you think, and do you have any idea what it signifies?"

The professor's bushy white eyebrows rose. He seemed to freeze as he peered at the silver piece, turning it this way and that. "Where did you get it?" he asked in a tight voice.

The transaction with the warden suddenly seemed tasteless, and Akitada said only, "I bought it in Eguchi because it looked like exceptionally fine work even though it's only silver."

"In Eguchi? How extraordinary." The professor frowned, then returned the piece reluctantly. "It is an amulet and finely made, as you recognized. Such a thing would have been given to a noble daughter at birth. My people never thought of giving girls a dagger, as they do here. They felt women needed to be treasured and protected."

Akitada thanked him, and thought of his own little daughter. He had given her the traditional dagger without much thought that it was meant to end her life if she should suffer dishonor. Of course, he treasured her and wanted to protect her so that nothing so awful should ever befall her. He would have asked more questions about the amulet, but the servants began to serve the food and he tucked it away again.

Since the governor outranked Akitada by two degrees, the seating arrangement was problematic. Nakahara solved it by placing his guests in a circle with Oga on his right and Akitada on his left. As it turned out, it prevented Akitada from conversing with Oga, and that was a relief. It was Watamaro who sat on Akitada's other side.

Akitada glanced around the room. The furnishings were modest, but good. Thick mats covered the dark wood floor where they were seated, and a painted screen of rugged cliffs with wind-tossed pines and foaming ocean waves protected them from drafts. In the *tokonoma* niche, a single large ink painting of a detailed landscape hung behind a copper bowl of white chrysanthemums. He would have liked a better look at the painting because it was unlike anything he had ever seen, but dinner began and comments about the wine and various dishes passed back and forth. Nakahara evidently had a talented cook and was himself very knowledgeable about local delicacies. Akitada, who paid little attention to food as a rule, found things edible, if a little salty, and gave polite praise. He drank liberally because he was thirsty and the wine was particularly refreshing, having been chilled rather than heated.

Watamaro shared Nakahara's appreciation for food, and talk went smoothly, but when the final delicacy had been consumed and discussed, it stalled.

Nakahara broke into the sudden silence with the words, "I heard from your clerk that your journey yesterday was marred by an unpleasantness, Sugawara. What exactly happened? A body bumped against your boat near Eguchi?"

Before Akitada could answer, Oga gasped and went quite white. This caused a fuss, with Nakahara calling for more wine and Oga drinking deeply, choking, gasping for air. The color returned to his face, and he made a dismissive remark that it had been nothing, a matter of swallowing awkwardly. Taking a deep breath, he asked Akitada, "Did you find out who the dead man was?"

"It was a woman, or perhaps a child. In any case, she was very young and very pretty," said Akitada. He was unusually thirsty after the salty food and drinking too much wine. The servants kept refilling his cup, and he had lost track of how many he had had. "I'm told suicides are common among the courtesans," he added. It was not a windy day, but Nakahara's scroll painting seemed to move in a breeze. He blinked and found that he had been mistaken.

Oga heaved a breath and nodded. "Yes, that's very true. A great pity when they are young and attractive. I hope you were not too upset by the incident."

Akitada did not like the remark but said only, "No. I've seen many dead bodies in my work. This one was merely remarkable for her youth."

The professor, who had remained quiet during the meal, now said, "If I may ask, are you certain it was a suicide?"

This touched a nerve. Akitada was increasingly troubled about the manner of the young woman's death and the hurried way the Eguchi warden had disposed of the body. Otomo's interest disconcerted him. Having been so far a detached observer at this party, the professor looked at him intently, leaning forward and fixing Akitada with such a sharp gaze that he was taken aback.

"No," he said honestly. "I have no proof, though I saw no wounds on the body. I suppose, it could have been an accident." He paused. "I confess it weighs on my mind. I should have insisted on a proper investigation."

Nakahara teased, "Why the interest, Professor? Have you broken someone's heart in Eguchi?"

This broke the tension, but Otomo only smiled and shook his head.

Watamaro put his hand on the professor's shoulder. "Come, there's no shame in loving the beauties of Eguchi or in having some fun talking about them."

Otomo quoted, "'Don't go singing the song of the Willow Branches when there's no one here with a heart for you to break.' One of the great Chinese poets wrote that when he had reached my age and was being teased by a pretty girl of fifteen. I'm well past my spring and summer, and even my autumn is nearly past."

Watamaro chuckled and fell to quoting other lines of poetry. The rest joined in, and the wine cups were kept full. Akitada sank into a melancholy mood, pondering his own lost youth, and drank his host's excellent wine.

When Akitada returned to their room, Sadenari was already there, wide awake and eager.

"Wait till you hear what I found out, sir," he cried.

Akitada, his head muddled with wine and his eyes full of sand, said, "What?" as he took off his good silk robe.

"Our host is the very man we're seeking! How about that?"

Akitada frowned and draped the robe somewhat crookedly over the curtain stand. "An' how d'you know that?" he asked, staggering a little as he stepped out of his full trousers. He tossed them toward the curtain stand and missed. Swaying a little, he considered that he was setting a poor example for Sadenari—especially after the lecture he had read him earlier.

Sadahira chattered on. "I introduced myself to Director Nakahara's clerks. They were helpful in finding a small room with a desk and writing materials for us. I thought we should try to look as businesslike as possible so there won't be any suspicions about our real assignment. I hope I did right, sir?"

"Mmm, yes." Akitada flopped down on his bedding and pulled off his socks. He was surprised and gratified that he managed this very well.

"Well, the one they call Yuki is a very nice fellow. His family is in the capital, and he invited me to come for a visit when we get back. They keep horses and go hunting. It's a family tradition since ancient days. I've always wanted to hunt."

Akitada lay down and pulled the quilt up to his nose. Nakahara's bedding was deliciously comfortable. "Go on," he murmured and closed his eyes.

"Yuki says that his boss is pretty easy-going, so they have lots of time for local outings. I thought he could show me around and introduce me to the pirates."

Akitada opened one eye and mumbled, "What?" He hoped he had not heard correctly. Two irresponsible youths running around town asking questions about pirates? But he was too tired and woozy, so he said only, "Better wait till morning," and fell asleep.

5

The Ugly Man

Akitada woke to a vicious headache and blurred vision. He sat up, groaned, and then staggered to the veranda to vomit into the shrubbery. His head pounding, he returned to his room and gulped water from the earthenware pitcher the maid had left.

To his relief, Sadenari was gone, but then the sun was already high. Akitada sat back down and held his throbbing head. He had no recall of the later part of the evening. Had he drunk too much, or had there been something wrong with the wine or the food? A vague memory surfaced of Sadenari telling him something last night, but he could not recall what it had been.

With more groans, he got up and dressed in his plain robe and trousers. Last night's finery looked badly creased and stained. As he bent to pick up the silk trousers to hang them on the clothes stand, a blinding pain stabbed at his eyes from inside his skull. He reeled and suppressed another bout of nausea.

He clapped his hands for one of the maids and asked for hot water. When it came, he washed his face and hands, and retied his topknot. The maid took his good clothes away to have them cleaned.

Feeling slightly better, he went in search of Sadenari. Tea would have been welcome, but most people did not make it part of their diet, and he could not stomach more wine, or even gruel. He headed for the main hall and Nakahara's office.

Nakahara was not there yet, a fact that cheered Akitada a little. His clerk Tameaki was arranging the mass of papers and documents into neat piles and writing small notes to place on top of them.

When he saw Akitada, he bowed. "I regret that the director is not available yet, sir. Can I be of assistance?"

"I wondered what had happened to my clerk."

"He left early this morning with Nariyuki. I assumed it was on your business."

Akitada frowned. What was it that Sadenari had babbled about last night? He had been very tired—and very drunk, if he was honest—but surely in that condition he would not have sent the boy on an assignment.

Tameaki read the puzzlement in his face and smirked. "I may well have jumped to conclusions, sir. Nariyuki likes any excuse to visit the wine shops in the city. I did hear the word "pirates." Does that suggest anything?"

It did, and most unpleasantly. Akitada still had no idea what they had talked about, but he was nearly sure now that pirates had figured in it. He sat down and held his aching head again. What damage was the impossible youth doing now?

Ever solicitous, Tameaki asked, "Are you unwell, sir? Can I send for someone or perhaps offer you some wine?"

Akitada shuddered. "No, nothing. Thank you. There was most likely some misunderstanding. Sadenari should return eventually." He glanced at the desk with its newly neat stacks of papers and added, "I've interrupted your work. What are you doing?"

Tameaki sat down. "I try to keep things in their proper places, and I write notes to remind the director of the subjects and which is most urgent."

"I see." Akitada felt that this was something that should not be left to a young clerk. Here was another example of Nakahara's carelessness with classified materials and private letters. Somewhere in those stacks were the documents he had delivered yesterday. "You must have earned your superior's confidence. That speaks highly of your abilities."

Tameaki looked modest. "It is very kind of you, sir, but I'm afraid it's more a matter of who is available to do the work." He shot Akitada a glance. "Not that I don't enjoy the work and feel the greatest gratitude to Director Nakahara for allowing me to help."

It all sounded very praiseworthy, but Akitada felt uneasy about the industrious Tameaki. Perhaps it had to do with his real errand here. Anyone working here could be passing information to the pirates. He looked around.

"I assume Director Nakahara keeps some documents securely locked away?"

"Oh, yes." Tameaki patted a wooden box on the desk. It had the metal bands and lock of a small money chest. Its key was in the lock.

At that moment, Nakahara himself trailed in. His skin looked pasty, and his eyes were blood-shot and puffy. Akitada hoped he looked better than that.

"Oh," Nakahara said. "Very sorry to be late. Something I ate didn't agree with me. I hope you slept well, Sugawara?"

"Yes. Thank you. Our quarters are very com-fortable. Allow me to thank you for the fine enter-tainment last night."

Nakahara blinked. "Was it fine? I don't re-member much. They had to carry out Watamaro. He and the governor went home in the governor's carriage." He shook his head and winced. "That wine was very strong. How are you, Tameaki? All bright-eyed and eager, as usual?"

"Yes, sir," said Tameaki, getting up and bow-ing. "I straightened your desk. Do you have any other work for me?"

The director made it to his seat and waved Tameaki away. "No, nothing. Go do some filing or whatever." He collapsed on his cushion and groaned.

Tameaki's footsteps faded. Akitada got up and looked behind the piles of goods. But Tameaki was really gone, and Akitada closed the door to the hallway. When he was seated again, he said, "It was very good of you to introduce me to the local notables last night. Do you suspect one of them of being involved with the pirates?"

Nakahara looked shocked. "Good heavens, no! The governor happened to be in town. He usually stays on his estate upcountry. Watamaro, of course, I invited because he can be useful to you. He knows all there is to know about shipping routes. Munata was included because the governor stays at his house when he's here, and the professor knows a lot about foreigners. He's descended from them himself, you know."

Akitada took this for proof that his fellow countrymen did not accept immigrants readily or forget the origin of their descendants. He said nothing about it, however. Instead he asked again, "So you trust them all?"

Nakahara twitched uncomfortably. "I don't know that I trust you," he said, half-joking. He rubbed his face. "I beg your pardon. This has been a worrisome business. What exactly are you going to do about it?"

Akitada did not know and ignored the question. He said, "I'm anxious to get to work on the reports. It was good of you to make a room available, but my clerk seems to have disappeared again. I suppose, I'll have to write them myself. Perhaps you can let me have the lists requested by the controller's office."

"Oh, you can borrow Tameaki," Nakahara said generously. "He's irritating but efficient."

"Thanks, but I like to keep myself informed. Perhaps later, if Sadenari hasn't returned by then."

The reports of foreign goods shipped from the Dazaifu, the clearing office in Kyushu, and of tribute goods from the western provinces were the ostensible reason Akitada was sent here. The government was mired in paperwork, and in this case only a legal expert could understand the tangled laws, permits, authorizations, shares paid to local administrations, and special exceptions. Akitada did not look forward to this work, especially since he fully expected a lax administrator like Nakahara to have mislaid crucial documents.

Somewhat to his surprise, Nakahara came up with most of the required information, perhaps thanks to the orderliness of the underappreciated Tameaki.

"What do you plan to do about the other matter?" Nakahara asked again, though his expression suggested that he would rather not know.

"Nothing for the time being," said Akitada. "I have a job to do. Perhaps your documents will provide some insight on who benefits from the pirate attacks."

Nakahara shuddered. "I doubt it. A very unpleasant business."

Akitada spent the rest of the morning in a small eave chamber on Nakahara's papers. Apart from the totally absent shipments that had fallen to the pirates, they seemed to be mostly correct. There was the usual pilfering by ships' captains and warehouse supervisors, but this was normal and the government did not concern itself with it. Nothing he had read suggested who was behind the pirate attacks.

The sun was past its zenith, and his back was stiff when it struck him that Sadenari had not yet returned. He got up to stretch. Really, he must send the youth back in disgrace and request a replacement. Angrily, he strode down the hallway to Nakahara's office. Nakahara was dictating to Tameaki while the other clerk, Yuki, sat nearby transcribing something.

"Forgive me for interrupting," Akitada said, "but I'm still looking for my clerk. I was told that he left early this morning with, er, Yuki. And I see Yuki has returned."

The friendly Yuki jumped up and bowed. "Sadenari only required my help for a little while. Once I had explained about the harbors and how to get to Kawajiri, he said he was able to handle his assignment alone and sent me back."

"Kawajiri? Assignment?" Akitada asked blankly, getting a hollow feeling in his stomach.

"He wished to gather information about the pirates, sir. I told him about the docks and the wine shops frequented by sailors."

Nakahara cleared his throat. "Was that entirely wise, Yuki? There are some very rough characters on the waterfront."

Tameaki sniggered.

Yuki looked at Akitada uneasily. "He insisted he was acting under your instructions, sir. I tried to be helpful. I hope I haven't done wrong."

Tameaki said snidely, "And Yuki is very knowledgeable about those low places. Sadenari asked my help also, but I left it to Yuki's expertise to give him assistance."

Akitada found his tongue. "Thank you. There may have been a misunderstanding. I'd better go after him."

Yuki cried, "Oh, allow me, sir. That is, if Director Nakahara can spare me?"

Nakahara said, "Of course."

But Akitada was already heading for the door. "No, thank you. We have taken up too much of your time. I understand it isn't far. I believe I shall manage. No doubt we'll both be back by nightfall."

To avoid further argument, he left quickly. He did not want witnesses to the dressing-down he intended to give Sadenari before packing him off on the next homeward-bound boat.

Down at the dock, he found a boatman eager to take him to Kawajiri. Once the fee was agreed upon, he went about his business of poling them along efficiently enough, but because the labor was hard for one man, he was disinclined for conversation.

The journey took them along several canals through a flat landscape of reeds, marshes, and swamps. The reeds were tall and golden this time of year. Akitada gazed at this confusing watery world and felt out of his depth. People engaged in the water trade lived here in this warren of marshes, small islands, sandbanks, and fishermen's huts hidden deep in the reed beds. They navigated the obscure waterways the way farmers knew the tracks and byways of their villages. They were desperately poor people, the men working as sailors or fishermen. It was likely that poverty drove them to piracy and prostitution. Piracy was the local equivalent of highway robbery. Pirates attacked the big ships in the open waters of Naniwa Bay and the Inland Sea beyond, and then hurried back into their hideaways. Still, no desperately poor man could afford a ship. Someone was financing the attacks.

Here and there on a river bank, a group of fishermen's huts appeared and disappeared. Once he saw that the land rose in the distance, and ordinary farm houses appeared on higher ground, shaded by groves of trees. Then the landscape changed. The waterway widened and bridges crossed it. There were more boats boat and barges.

Sweat poured off the boatman's back as he maneuvered expertly between other vessels. Buildings crept closer to the shores, and in the distance pagodas above roofs. Before Akitada's eyes, the scene opened up to the bay again. Many large ships lay at anchor, their square sails white against the immense blue of sea and sky.

Lumber yards encroached on the shoreline. Barges carried boards and beams, and large rafts of tree trunks, tied together with vines or hemp ropes, bobbed on the river.

In the harbor, several large ships were tied up at docks. On land, warehouses stood in rows, many more than in Naniwa, also built on tall stilts to protect the goods from storm tides. A steady flow of porters went between them and the docks, loading or unloading cargo.

Akitada felt a surge of pride at the sight of so much healthy commerce. His was a great nation, and his people were surely the most industrious on this earth.

Goods used by the court, fine utensils and art works displayed in the great temples, the sustenance of nobles and commoners came this way. Kawajiri was the end of the sea route from Kyushu and the western provinces. Tribute and tax goods, as well as goods and people from foreign countries sailed across the waters of the Inland Sea to this place.

When he set him ashore, his boatman looked exhausted. Akitada paid him with the agreed upon government token and a handful of coins from his own funds. The man bowed deeply and raised his hands to his forehead, then jumped back into his boat to pick up another customer for the return trip. Akitada looked after him and marveled at how hard the man worked for a few coins.

He walked along the crowded harbor, stopping from time to time to ask if anyone had seen Sadenari. Not surprisingly, he had no luck at all. One of the ships had the colorful name Black Dragon and a painted carving of a black dragon with red eyes, white teeth, and red flames shooting from its body at its bow. He admired more ships with names like Great Phoenix, Flying Crane, Cloud Falcon, and Curling Wave. Sailors had poetic souls, it seemed, but he detected signs of hostility whenever he asked his question. Tora would have handled this better. Akitada felt humble.

When he had his fill of the smells of tar and fish and the often incomprehensible language, he turned inland. Bales and cases were stacked along the docks, and two-wheeled carts waited to be loaded. The warehouses stood in enclosures, no doubt for security. He noted watchmen and red-coated police at the open gates. Clearly, theft was much easier before the ship reached this port.

"Who owns all the warehouses?" he asked a porter, who stood waiting beside his cart.

"The ones with the flags belong to the emperor," he said in a broad dialect. "It's part of the palace storehouses. The others are mostly Master Watamaro's or belong to temples."

"Watamaro? He must be a rich man if he owns so much."

The man rolled his eyes. "He's very rich. Richer than the emperor maybe, but a lot more generous to the poor."

Akitada was taken aback by the comparison but let it go. It was past the time of the midday rice and his stomach growled. Turning his back on the harbor, he took one of the narrow streets beside the customs house. It led into town and was crowded with signs and paper lanterns belonging to small wine shops and eating places. They were much smaller and more modest than the crab restaurant Nakahara had taken him to, but Akitada was ravenous. He chose a restaurant that seemed busier than the rest, perhaps because of the delectable smell of fried fish and a sign that promised "delicacies to make the gods smile".

Inside, he found a wooden platform extending toward the back where a fat cook dipped into a large cauldron for golden nuggets of fish. Nobody seemed to mind the heat. A number of guests sat near the open doors singly or in small groups. They looked like small tradesmen and travelers. He threaded his way past them and found an open space where a slight breeze from the doorway made the heat seem less oppressive. It was too warm for comfort, and the smells coming from the cauldron made him slightly nauseous .

A waitress came with wine and recited a selection of seafood. Akitada turned down the wine with a shudder and asked for something simple, soup for example. The waitress frowned but said they had noodle soup with fish and vegetables. Good enough.

She left and returned with a large bowl of soup. Akitada paid a modest sum and tasted the broth. It was good and settled his delicate stomach wonderfully. He wolfed down the rest, using his fingers to catch the slippery noodles and chunks of fish.

The cook had watched him, and when Akitada put down the empty bowl, he caught the man's eyes and gave him a nod, holding up a finger for another serving. The cook's sweating red face broke into a wide smile. The next bowl arrived with particularly large and tasty bits of fish.

At that moment, a group of men got up to leave, and Akitada's gaze fell on a strange-looking creature who huddled in a dark corner some ten feet away. He was about fifty, thin to emaciation, and poorly dressed. When he turned his head, Akitada almost recoiled. He was horribly disfigured. One of his eyes looked upward, showing the white of the eyeball, and a scar carved a jagged cicatrice across his face, having taken part of his nose. The wound had been deep and when it healed, it had caused his thin-lipped mouth to twist downwards in a permanent sneer.

The ugly man was also staring, but his eyes were on Akitada's bowl of noodle soup. He licked his lips, then caught Akitada's glance and looked away quickly. Akitada saw the man's threadbare, patched gown and felt pity.

After a moment, the other man glanced back and read Akitada's expression. The scar on his face darkened. He inclined his head and got up to leave.

On an impulse, Akitada called out, "Could you spare me a moment of your time?"

The other man, even thinner than before now that he was upright, glanced over his shoulder to see if someone else was meant, then approached slowly. "Were you addressing me, sir?"

The formal words did not match his appearance. Akitada adjusted his own tone. "Yes. If you would have the goodness to join me, I need some information. Perhaps you would allow me to order you some wine?"

The scarred man bowed, then knelt. He hesitated. The scar flamed red again, and he said, "No wine, thank you. But I could join you in a bowl of noodles."

"You would do me an honor." Akitada gestured to the waitress.

The ugly man bowed again. "Thank you. My name is Saburo. I'm at your service, sir."

Close up, the face was even more frightful. The scar was puckered and pitted. Normally nearly white against the dark tan, it seemed to change colors with the man's moods. Akitada wondered how he had become so disfigured. The eye, of course, he might have been born with, though more small scars suggested an accident of some sort. Such disfigurements were not uncommon among the poor, but they frightened small children and made adults look away.

Life was often unfair.

Akitada smiled at his guest. "My name is Sugawara. I'm not from here, and you look like a local man who knows his way around this part of town."

Saburo's soup arrived, set down so carelessly by the waitress that some of the broth splashed on Saburo's patched robe.

Akitada paid and snapped, "Next time watch what you're doing." The waitress slunk off with an apology.

Saburo brushed at the stain. "They would rather not serve me here. I make the guests uncomfortable."

"Nonsense."

Saburo gave Akitada a lopsided grin and raised the bowl to his mouth. He took a small bite, chewed, then set the soup back down. "I'm not from here either," he said, "but I've stayed long enough. Please feel free to ask me whatever you please."

By now Akitada had such trouble putting the man's appearance together with his educated speech and courteous manner, that his first question was, "What happened to you?"

Saburo lowered his head and studied the food in his bowl.

Ashamed, Akitada said quickly, "Forgive me. I had no right to ask." He recalled the old waiter in Eguchi. He, too, had been shockingly reduced to poverty and abuse.

The ugly man's face contorted into a grimace. "There is nothing to forgive. I made a mistake and bad things happened. They say when the gods want to send disaster, they first give a man some good luck to confuse him and blind him to what is to come. I was too sure of myself."

It was no answer, but Akitada accepted it. The man's bitterness did not astonish him. He must have fallen far indeed from his good luck. He gestured at the half-filled bowl, and said, "Please eat or this good soup will get cold. Meanwhile I'll explain. I came to Naniwa yesterday on business for my ministry. My young clerk disappeared this morning. Apparently he came here for a visit. He is rather young, and he told another clerk that he could manage on his own. I'm worried about him and need to find him quickly. What is your advice? Where should I look? Whom should I ask? He takes an interest in ships and sailors, but I had no luck in the harbor."

Saburo had been eating and listening. Now he put down his bowl again. It was empty. "Why do you need to find him quickly?"

Akitada prevaricated. "Well, he's away from his home in the capital for the first time and very inexperienced. I lost him once before in Eguchi. There he just got drunk and spent all his money."

The other man nodded. "Frustrating. But it's only afternoon. Why the urgency?"

Akitada could not tell this stranger the truth about his assignment and his fears that Sadenari would talk too much. He said lamely, "He may run into serious trouble in a port city. And it will soon be night."

Saburo cocked his head and regarded him thoughtfully. "Or he may return on his own. In fact he may be back in Naniwa already. But if you don't think so, I could try to find him or ask questions for you. I know the dives where sailors spend their money, and as you say, a young gentleman may indeed encounter trouble there. Will you trust me to do that for you?"

It was a reasonable proposition, but Akitada could not avail himself of the offer — even in the unlikely event that it was free. In truth, the ugly man did not inspire trust. He had made an impulsive mistake. With a little laugh, he said, "Thank you, but I think you must be right. I expect the young rascal's gone back already and I'd better do the same. Thank you for your offer, Saburo." Reaching into his sash, he extracted a small piece of silver and laid it down between them. Then he got up.

Saburo was not looking at him. "I'm in your debt, sir," he said softly and bowed.

And then, when Akitada was already a few steps away, he added, "Be careful!"

6

The Dead End

Akitada had no intention of returning to Naniwa without making another effort at finding Sadenari himself. Even if the rascal had returned from this excursion, Akitada might at least learn how much of their purpose he had given away and to whom.

He left the restaurant quickly and explored the side streets close to the harbor. Narrow and dirty, they were apparently inhabited by the rough men who worked as porters or did menial labor. His appearance marked him as an alien presence there, and women and children stared as he passed. When he stopped to ask about Sadenari, they just shook their heads. Either Sadenari had not passed this way, or they had no intention of telling him anything.

Eventually even these poor quarters deteriorated. More men were about, but they wore ragged clothing and their eyes were hard and hungry.

Be careful!

The ugly man's warning was ridiculous, of course. It was still daylight, and he was physically fit. Besides, they lived in a law-abiding nation, and he had seen many policemen around the harbor.

Still, he was not getting any information and retreated toward the harbor again. The sun was sinking, and it was time to take a boat back. By now he wished Sadenari to the devil and hoped he got at least a good drubbing for his foolish excursion.

Just as he was about to approach one of the boatmen, he saw a tall fellow with a tattoo on his leg who looked like a seafaring man. He paused, wondering if there was any point in asking his question one more time, when the other man spoke to him. "Are you lost, sir?"

Akitada gave him a grateful smile. "No, I'm not lost, but I've been looking for someone. A young clerk who was visiting the port. He's tall and may have been asking about pirates. It's a fixed idea of his."

"Oh, that one." The seafaring man laughed. "We sent him to the sailors' hostel. The men are full of stories. He may still be there. Would you like me to show you the way?"

Finally! Akitada felt vindicated in his conviction that he could find Sadenari on his own. "I don't want to trouble you," he said.

"No trouble. I'm going that way."

Chatting about local attractions and young men's enthusiasms, they walked together into the warren of streets and alleys that made up the slums of Naniwa. As before, hot, hungry eyes followed them, and Akitada was glad to be with this tall, strong companion. He had begun to think that he should have brought his sword with him. A slattern of a woman exposed her breasts and called out an invitation. The man with him ignored her. At the corner of a narrow street, little more than an alleyway, he stopped. "I have to leave here," he said, "but the hostel's at the end of this street." He pointed. "It's the large building you can see over the rooftops."

Akitada thanked him and walked down the narrow, winding road. He did not much like his surroundings, but sailors needed cheap accommodations. The few houses on either side looked empty and shuttered. No doubt, their inhabitants worked elsewhere during the day. In the silence, he could hear the echo of his footfall.

Or perhaps someone else was walking the same way. He stopped and turned, but he saw no one. The sun had set, and the narrow street lay in deep shadow.

He reached remnants of a tall fence and thick shrubberies, but a footpath turned the corner to the hostel. It was a mere track between leaning fences and tall weeds. Uncertain, Akitada stopped again, and this time he heard the steps clearly.

He hurried forward. The hostel was just ahead; he could reach it before his shadow caught up with him.

He was wrong.

The footpath led to a dead end. Between him and the hostel rose a high wall. He stood in a mere patch of weedy dirt that was being used for cast-off utensils and waste.

And he knew in an instant that he was in trouble. The helpful man had lied to him and sent him down a blind alley and he was about to find out what trap he had walked into.

He was looking down the path, when two burly men suddenly appeared on either side of him. Akitada dashed toward the wall. He saw they had knives — knives with long and sharp blades. Being unarmed, Akitada had no hope of fighting them.

There was also no point in shouting for help. In this area, it would do no good at all. He tried reasoning with them.

"Come, you don't want trouble, do you?" he said. "I'm an official from the capital. Attacking me will bring down the wrath of the government on your entire neighborhood."

They were big, and the one with the pock-marked face was also heavy and muscular. The other was thinner but moved like a practiced fighter. Their faces were dirty and covered with stubble, and their greasy hair hung loose. They were probably Akitada's age or a bit younger, but such men lived and fought rough every day of their lives.

And they had knives.

And they were not reasonable men.

They kept coming, slowly, a step at a time. Warily, but with a predatory gleam in their eyes. Enjoying themselves.

Akitada pulled all his money from his sash and threw it on the dusty ground in front of them. "There, take it!"

They did not even glance at it.

He backed away a little farther.

The heavier man on the right grinned, his teeth a brief gleam in the twilight.

"What do you want?" shouted Akitada.

No answer, but they kept coming. They meant to kill him here in this weed-overgrown, forgotten corner of Naniwa.

Glancing around for something he could use as a weapon among the debris, he realized that he could not reach it in time. He had only moments, but in that small space of time, memories of his wife and of their little daughter, of Tora and Seimei, of Genba, and even of the dog Trouble flashed through his mind. They seemed incredibly precious because they were about to be lost forever. And for what? A foolish young man's mistake? Another ridiculous assignment from his superiors? Or his own careless exploration of the slums of Kawajiri?

From among these tangled thoughts, one crystallized: even in a hopeless situation, a man must try to defend himself, must make at least an effort to escape. He must fight the two killers with their long knives who had waited for him here. And in the unlikely event that he got past these two, he must fight or evade at least one more. Because those footsteps that had followed him meant that there was at least one more.

Akitada moved suddenly, putting the tall attacker between himself and the other man. Then he jumped. He meant to twist the knife out of his hand, then slip past and run.

It did not work.

The big man cursed and veered aside as he snatched for the knife, and Akitada fell. He fell hard, on his face and right shoulder and nearly passed out from the sudden pain that shot through his arm and across his back. At first he thought he had a knife in his back. The relief that he did not was short-lived. He was down and expected to be killed. But the expected blow from the knife did not come. Instead there were shouts and grunts. He raised his head a little and blinked dirt out of his eyes. Three pairs of legs moved before him. He got to his knees.

The thin robber stood quite still with a ludicrous expression of astonishment on his face, while the big man was falling to his knees, clutching at his neck. Blood seeped from between his fingers. A third man was moving between them like a grey ghost.

Akitada stumbled to his feet. His right shoulder and arm were stiff with pain and he was confused. The thin man made a choking sound and collapsed. Both of his attackers were on the ground.

None of it made sense.

Beyond the failed attack on the big man, he had done nothing to account for the defeat of the two ruffians, and yet there was blood. He had not touched the second man, yet he lay dead or unconscious on the ground, bleeding from his throat.

Akitada looked at the third man. His eyes still watered and the third man was a thin grey shape against the background of weathered fencing. He moved to the fallen men and bent to feel their necks.

Recognition came, and with it more confusion. What the devil was he doing here?

The ugly man from the restaurant pushed one of the bodies out of the way and bent to pick up an object which he put inside his patched robe.

Then he finally met Akitada's eyes and said calmly, "We'd better leave before someone comes."

Akitada still gaped. "You? You followed me?"

The ugly man took his elbow to pull him away. Akitada gasped with pain.

"Sorry. Are you hurt?"

"It's nothing. I fell." Akitada found his feet and started walking

"Can you run?"

They ran back the way he had come, Akitada cradling his arm and gritting his teeth. For a while, he followed the man Saburo blindly. He was about twenty years younger than his savior, but catching up with him took all of his strength.

They were both gasping by then. Akitada managed, "Thank you for that," and the ugly man gave him a grimace that might have been a smile.

Eventually, they saw the masts of the ships ahead. It was nearly dark by then, but the restaurants had their lanterns lit, and people moved about. Akitada slowed down.

"Thank the gods," he said with feeling when he had caught his breath. "I don't know what would have happened if you hadn't come in time." There was no answer, and he turned.

The ugly man was gone.

7

The Amulet

kitada returned to Naniwa at sunset. As before, the boatman maneuvered his craft skillfully, though much of the trip was up-stream and it took longer. But he was a young man, and Akitada paid him little attention, being preoccupied with assorted aches and a sense of confusion and anger.

As he trudged back to the Foreign Trade Of-fice, he was still trying to understand what had just happened. The best he had come up with was that Sadenari's questioning of the people in Naniwa must have alerted someone involved in the piracies, and Akitada's presence had become a threat. In other words, someone had given or-ders to eliminate him, and perhaps the foolish Sadenari had met the same fate.

The role of the ugly man was completely in-comprehensible. Why had he taken the trouble to shadow Akitada, and then saved his life? And how had he done it? Akitada had not expected an ally and was distracted at the time, but whatever weapon the ugly man had used, he had been incredibly quick and silent. And what had been his weapon? A knife long enough to do much damage was not easily hidden.

Akitada had meant to ask, but the man had disappeared again.

There was something very peculiar about him.

In the end, all these considerations were overshadowed by a furious anger that the villains — whoever they were — had dared make this attack on an imperial official. Holding his painful arm, he stormed into Nakahara's office.

"I want the chief of the police and the prefect alerted," he told the startled Nakahara. "Two hired killers attacked me with knives, and I'm almost certain that Sadenari has been murdered."

The clerk Yuki goggled at him. Nakahara's mouth sagged open. When he found speech, he said, "The police. Yes, we must call the police and report this. First thing tomorrow. But the prefect? Surely . . ." He noticed Akitada supporting his arm, and started to his feet. "Are you hurt? There's blood on your face. Shall we send for a physician?"

Akitada brushed a hand across his forehead and encountered a cut, but he ignored the question. "As soon as there is daylight, I want a complete sweep made of the Kawajiri waterfront and slums. We must find Sadenari and question people about the attack on me. I want every man on and near the ships or working at the harbor interrogated. My clerk must be found. Dead or alive. That will take a large force, Nakahara, and to get this organized, we need the prefect. In fact, you may as well inform the governor also. The provincial guard may be needed if those involved decide to fight. Furthermore, since my real purpose here seems to be no longer a secret, you must immediately begin an official investigation. Someone in Naniwa is working with the pirates."

Nakahara had paled and slumped back down. The clerks looked alarmed and waited to let the director respond. But Nakahara was bereft of words, and it was Tameaki who rose and bowed to Akitada. There was a gleam of excitement in his sharp eyes. "Please allow me to notify the proper authorities, sir. May I suggest that we send word tonight to the harbor police and to the warden of the quarter where you were attacked?"

Trust Tameaki to be the only useful person here. "Yes, thank you," said Akitada and glowered at the stupefied Nakahara.

"Where did the attack take place, and what did the criminals look like?" Tameaki asked, reaching for brush and paper.

Akitada sat down abruptly. He was asking too much of Nakahara, and it was already night. He said, "I'm not sure what the area is called. It was a derelict spot. I saw poor tenements, mostly shuttered, a great deal of debris, and one large building behind a tall wall. I was cornered by two rough men in a blind alley just behind this building. It must be about half a mile from the harbor."

Tameaki frowned. "I don't know . . . "

Yuki finally woke from his astonishment. "That might me near the Hostel of the Flying Cranes. It's a bit run down, but it has a tall wall in back.

They keep the wall repaired to keep out the riffraff from the other side."

Akitada cheered up and nodded. Perhaps his "guide" had at least told the truth about the hostel. But he wrestled with another problem. He did not know how badly hurt the two thugs had been. What if the police found two dead men and wanted to know what had happened? It could not be helped. He said, "Tell the police and the warden that the two men were tall and about my age. One was heavy-set and muscular. The other was lean. I did not have time to look for any distinguishing characteristics. Their clothes were ordinary jackets and pants. What a laborer might wear."

"That'll be enough." Tameaki ran out, black robe flying.

"Umm," said Nakahara, "should we rush into this? Your clerk has not been gone so very long. Calling up so many people . . . well, it will upset things."

Akitada felt no pity. All authority had been taken out of the man's hands. His junior clerk had made the decision for him and sprung into action. "Things are already upset," he said. "In your position, it's advisable to seem in control."

Nakahara ran a shaking hand over his face. "Is that why they sent you? Because they think I'm not doing my job? What do they want from me?"

Yuki had been following this, gnawing his lower lip. Now he said loyally, "The director couldn't have known that Sadenari would get lost and that you, sir, would run into those thugs. The waterfront is full of rough people. Surely that's all it was. All this talk of pirates! I told Sadenari there have always been pirates. Pirates are normal on the Inland Sea."

Nakahara nodded eagerly. "That's right. As long as things don't reach the point of that Suitomo thing, it's really just a matter of ship captains being more careful."

Suitomo had been a Fujiwara governor of one of the western provinces who had decided that he could enrich himself more quickly by becoming a pirate chief. The court had tried to appease him with gifts and honors until it had no choice but to raise an army against him.

Akitada gave Nakahara a look, and he subsided into silence. The lackadaisical attitude he expressed toward the depredations by pirates was either due to stupidity, or the man was in this up to his neck. Akitada's eyes went to the goods piled nearly to the rafters of Nakahara's office, and he got angry again.

"What is all this stuff?" he asked, pointing at it.

Nakahara flushed. "It should have been warehoused, but this way it's more convenient. It saves the clerks and servants running back and forth."

"That isn't what I asked you."

Nakahara sighed. "We do inspections of all ships that pass through Kawajiri and continue inland. Any goods that aren't listed on their manifests or that seem otherwise suspicious are confiscated and brought here."

Walking over to the piles, Akitada inspected them. "Some of these look foreign, and if I'm not mistaken, there are valuable art objects among them."

"I know. Maybe they were stolen, or else people are making private purchases from Chinese and Korean merchants. All I can say is that they were found on ships with otherwise legitimate cargo."

"Either way, it is illegal."

Nakahara raised his chin. "Exactly. And we confiscate them for that reason."

Ignoring the fact that he had finally made his host angry, Akitada held up a carved lacquer vase and blew a thick cloud of dust from it. "It looks as though most of these things have been here for a long time. Should they not have been shipped to their proper owners?"

"I'll do so gladly if you tell me who their owners are," Nakahara snapped, looking daggers.

"You haven't checked them against the lists of stolen items?"

"The lists are not specific. What we find is single pieces. And when we question the captains of the ships about such goods, they always claim they have no idea where they came from."

Akitada sat down again and thought this over. It was all very careless and improper, but perhaps not criminal. "What did you mean when you said you keep these things here to save the servants steps?" he asked after a moment.

To his surprise, Nakahara did not meet his eyes this time. There was a brief silence, then he said, "Sometimes it becomes necessary to use this or that to pay for a service." No longer belligerent, he sounded defeated.

Raising his brows, Akitada asked, "How do you mean?"

Nakahara shifted in his seat. "I don't know if you're aware of it, but this office has not received any funds for a number of years. My own salary is arrears."

"I was not aware of it." It was likely, and it would explain much. "I'm sorry if I've sounded harsh," Akitada added. "Such irregularities happen sometimes, but I wasn't informed in your case. So you've sold some of the confiscated goods in order to cover expenses?"

Nakahara nodded miserably.

They sat in silence, contemplating the dilemma faced by officials who were not given the means to carry out their duties. Akitada had once been in the same position.

Tameaki returned at this point and said, "Begging your pardon, but as I was leaving the building, I ran into Professor Otomo. He wishes to have a word with Lord Sugawara."

Akitada, embarrassed about his accusations of Nakahara, welcomed the interruption. With an apology, he rose and followed Tameaki to a small anteroom on the east side of the main hall.

He found the white-bearded Otomo pacing nervously, his hands clasped behind his back.

"Ah, Lord Sugawara," he said, bowing. "Please forgive this rude and unannounced visit, but the burden on my conscience is getting too heavy. I had to come and speak to you."

Akitada gestured to cushions placed side by side near a small writing desk. He wondered what this was all about. Could Otomo, with his

Korean ancestry, have become involved in piracy? Most of the foreign merchants who brought goods to Naniwa these days were Koreans, but they carried shipping permits. Still, the sea between the two countries was treacherous because of Korean pirate ships.

Otomo sat and looked down at his clenched hands. He sighed deeply. When he raised his head, his eyes widened. "I do beg your pardon, sir. You've been injured?"

"It's nothing. I took a tumble. Please go on."

Another sigh. "You may recall showing me the amulet last night? You said you purchased it in Eguchi."

Still mystified, Akitada nodded.

"And I told you it was the sort of thing bestowed on a treasured daughter in our culture. That is true, but I did not mention another matter. It is that which brings me here. Forgive me, but I'm about to betray a confidence."

Akitada said cautiously, "You may speak freely unless the matter is criminal or a threat to the nation."

Otomo sighed again. "May I ask if the amulet is in any way connected with the young girl that drowned?"

A little embarrassed, Akitada nodded. "Yes. She was wearing it. How did you know?"

"You see," the professor said, his voice brittle with emotion, "I suspect that young girls from Koryo may have been brought here and forced into service in the brothels of Eguchi and elsewhere."

Akitada raised his brows. "I would have thought that we have enough willing females to follow the trade."

"I know it sounds very strange, and I don't blame you for doubting me. When you showed me the amulet and later mentioned the dead girl found in the river, I was afraid that another poor child had chosen death. She's not the first one. There were two others, also drowned and called suicides. A month ago, a friend of mine — forgive me if don't mention his name — wrote me an anxious letter, saying that he had met a Korean girl in Eguchi, but when he went back and asked for her again, he was told that she had committed suicide. He was very upset."

"That could have been a coincidence. There probably aren't many girls of Korean descent in the business, but such things happen. Apparently, suicides are frequent."

"But that's the point, sir. Think about the misery suffered by girls who've been brought from Korea. They don't speak your language. And they're very unhappy."

"Yes, I see. And you think my dead girl is one of those?"

"Yes, I do. When you showed me the amulet and mentioned the drowned girl, I found I could not remain silent."

Silence fell. Otomo sat with his head bowed, waiting. Akitada was troubled by Otomo's tale. On the whole, he was inclined to believe him, but many things argued against it. How had the young women been brought all this way? Such a thing might have happened in Kyushu, which was much closer to the Korean peninsula. There was a constant coming and going of merchants and fishermen between both countries. But the Inland Sea was closed to all but their own ships and a few well-known merchant ships from Koryo. These had applied for and received special permission to travel to the capital, but their ships would have been most carefully inspected in Kyushu and again at Naniwa. Could the pirates be involved in this?

He asked the obvious question. "Why? Why bring Korean women here when hiding them from the authorities must be very difficult and dangerous? I am told brothel towns are very carefully supervised."

Otomo shook his head. "I do not know."

Akitada thought. "This amulet—you said it would only be given to girls of rank."

"Ah, yes. My friend claimed his girl was well educated. She knew Korean poetry and songs, and she could read and write. The singing . . . it's possible that they like young girls who have a special talent like that. I wonder, could you let me have the amulet long enough to make some inquiries?"

Akitada reached into his sash and froze.

"What's the matter, sir?"

There was no amulet in Akitada's sash. He realized what had happened. He must have thrown it in the dirt along with his money when the two ruffians confronted him in the blind alley. He got up. "I would like to but seem to have misplaced it. You must forgive me. My clerk has gone missing, and I'm worried. I promise, I'll look for the amulet and think about your story."

Otomo rose immediately and bowed deeply. "Thank you. I thought I should speak to you and offer an explanation for the poor girl's death. Please pardon my arrival at such an inconvenient moment."

"Not at all," said Akitada as they walked out together. When they reached the entrance doors, he paused. "Do you think there could be an organization smuggling in foreign women?"

"I hope not, sir, but I admit I have wondered about the same thing."

Perhaps the pirates engaged not only in robbery and murder on the high seas but also had a lucrative side business dealing in human beings. His encounter in the blind alley in Kawajiri and young Sadenari's fate took on a more ominous significance.

8

The Hostel of the Flying Cranes

Akitada's first thought had been to rush back to the place where he had been attacked to look for the amulet and his few gold and silver pieces. A foolish notion and proof that events had addled his usual common sense. Not only was it night and he did not know the way, but his very sore arm was a reminder that he had barely escaped from that neighborhood with his life. Besides, Sadenari was still gone, and that was beginning to weigh heavily on his conscience. The boy must be found before anything else.

Otomo's idea that someone had been kidnapping Korean girls for prostitution he put away for the time being. Still, if his story was indeed true, it would have to be followed up. Quite apart from the sheer viciousness of such crimes, they could lead to serious problems with a neighboring nation they were mercifully at peace with at the moment.

He felt suddenly exhausted. Nothing else could be done this day. He went to his room without meeting anyone. There, he took off his outer clothes, unrolled the bedding, and fell asleep the moment he lay down.

Early the next morning he was on his way to Nakahara's office when he saw the prefect coming across the courtyard. Apparently Munata had been alerted by Nakahara, or more likely by the efficient Tameaki.

Munata looked flushed, perhaps from his dash across the road. He sounded breathless as he bowed to Akitada. "I just heard. Can it be true, sir? You were hurt? This is outrageous. I assure you the culprits will be found and punished severely."

Akitada's arm and shoulder felt much better this morning, and he had washed the blood from his face and found only scratches underneath. "Thank you. I only have a few scrapes, as it happens. Someone distracted the villains, and I made my escape. Come inside. We must put our heads together and decide how to find my clerk."

Nakahara and Yuki were having an argument. Nakahara waved his finger in front of Yuki's face, and Yuki looked stubborn. He said, "You should have warned me, Morito. How was I to know that they'd send someone important to catch us out?"

Nakahara caught sight of them. "Shshhh!" he hissed at Yuki and rearranged his face into a smile. "Ah, Munata. Very good of you to come so quickly. I suppose, Lord Sugawara told you what happened?"

"Not in so many words," said Munata, glancing at Akitada. "I hoped that he would fill me in on the details. Your clerk said that I was to call out the guard and send for Lieutenant Saeki and his men. Do I understand that His Lordship had an unpleasant encounter with hoodlums in Kawajiri and has misplaced his young companion?"

Akitada thought he detected a sneer and nearly growled. Gritting his teeth, he said, "Two ruffians attacked me with long knives, and there's a good chance that the same thing happened to Sadenari. He's a mere youngster and has been gone for a day and a night."

Munata stared at him. "I see. Yes. How shocking . . . if true. I had no idea matters were so serious. Allow me to apologize for the prefecture. I shall look into it immediately." He made a motion toward the door, but Akitada lost his temper and grabbed his sleeve.

"Not so fast, Munata. You'll do more than 'look into it', as you put it. Sit down. There is also the matter of treason."

Munata gaped at him. "Treason?" Akitada glared back. The prefect went to sit down.

Akitada sat down himself. "Nakahara will confirm that my real assignment here involved the recent pirate activity. It appears that someone has been passing confidential information to these pirates."

"I find it hard to believe . . ."

Akitada cut in curtly, "I don't care what you believe, Prefect. You will take your orders from me and stop arguing."

Munata drew himself up. "I take my orders from the governor," he said stiffly.

"Where is Oga anyway?" demanded Akitada, pointedly skipping the honorifics. Munata needed a reminder that Akitada's standing in this instance was equivalent to Oga's. He was here under direct orders from the Minister of the Right. Besides the Sugawara name was older and more respected than the governor's. "I understood that he was staying with you. Surely Nakahara's clerk included him in the call for a meeting."

"My home is on the outskirts of Naniwa," said Munata. "I dispatched a messenger. Frankly, I hope this won't make him angry."

Akitada swallowed his disgust. "You will go to Kawajiri with soldiers to organize the local police there. Take however many people you have at your command. I want a ship-by-ship and house-by-house search made for my clerk. No ships or boats are to leave, and traffic on the roads must be inspected. I also want an armed escort to accompany me to the place where I was attacked. I plan to have a look at this Hostel of the Flying Cranes."

Munata shot Nakahara a look, then got up with a bow, and left the room. Akitada looked after him. The prefect's opposition was troubling.

The door closed, and silence fell.

After a moment, Akitada turned back to Nakahara. "Why is Munata so hostile?"

Nakahara shifted nervously. Perhaps he recalled his own flare-up the night before. "Munata is a strange man," he said. "He's perfectly agreeable until his ability is questioned. I think he feels strongly that you are doing so now."

Such behavior by a lower-grade official would not be tolerated in the capital, but Akitada was not in the capital and in a place like Naniwa different rules might apply. That, of course, made his work harder. If he could not make people like Munata and Nakahara obey him, he would hardly do so with the governor, a man of rank, privilege, and power.

"What exactly is Munata's relationship to the governor?" he asked.

"His is the most important district of the state. Governor Oga appointed him, and he is loyal to the governor. The Munatas have also been overseers of the Oga estates here. That's why the governor stays at Munata's country residence whenever he is here."

This threw an interesting light on the division of power and the bonds of personal relationships. Akitada was becoming very curious about both men. "And you? How do you feel about them? I know they were your guests last night, but I assumed they were invited as a courtesy to me and to the governor. Perhaps you, too, have closer ties?"

Nakahara flushed. "You have an extraordinary way of accusing me of impropriety. Apparently you think that I've been plotting against my emperor, stealing government property, and aiding the pirates. Frankly, I resent your manner, sir.

You're an official visitor, carrying powers from the Minister of the Right, so I cannot very well bid you be gone, but if you find Munata's manners wanting, what should I say about yours?"

The director bristled with belligerence. It almost seemed as if each of his sparse hairs were trying to stand up. Akitada was tempted to laugh, but of course that would have made matters even worse, and he was in fact Nakahara's guest. Besides, perhaps he should have controlled his temper better with both officials.

He sighed and said, "Calm down. Put yourself in my position. I was sent here to find out who is behind the pirate attacks. Within a day, my clerk disappears, and I'm lured into the slums of Kawajiri to be assassinated. It seems to me I'm no longer dealing with a minor leak of information, but with a conspiracy which may include everyone who has any power in this state. And you have been sitting at the very center of this web, pretending not to know what is going on. How can I possibly trust you, or believe anything you tell me?"

Nakahara did not answer. He had turned his head away.

Akitada got up with a grunt of impatience. "I have to go now to find the foolish young man who thought he could solve this case on his own. May your conscience forgive you if I find him dead."

When he stepped from the boat in Kawajiri harbor, a contingent of police in their red coats was assembling. In the brilliant sunlight reflected by the sea, they appeared to be bathed in blood.

Akitada pictured the torn corpse of young Sadenari and shuddered.

The commander, a grey-haired Lieutenant Saeki, who looked like an ex-military man, was mounted, and a second horse was waiting.

Akitada introduced himself, and swung himself into the saddle. They set off at a moderate trot, the policemen jogging along behind them. Apparently the lieutenant had been given instructions. He led the way to the dead end of the alleyway where Akitada had encountered the two thugs.

There was no sign that the fight had taken place. The dirt was scuffed about, and his coins and the amulet were gone. There were also no blood stains or bodies. Someone had cleaned up, and if there had been corpses or wounded men here, they had been moved. He would have liked proof of the attack, but then he would be hard pressed to explain how he had wounded or killed two armed men without a weapon of his own.

Akitada did not like losing his money, but he had additional funds in his baggage and could send for more. What troubled him more was the loss of the amulet. It felt as if another veil had been drawn across the death of the young Korean girl. He said nothing about all this to the police, however.

On the command of Lieutenant Saeki, the men spread out and searched. They found nothing that pointed to the attackers, but it appeared that a narrow footpath wound through the shrubbery to a breach in the wall where the plaster and mud had crumbled, leaving a mound of rubble and easy passage to the back of the Hostel of the Flying Cranes.

"So," said the lieutenant, "the criminals came from there. Not surprising. Let's take a look."

They left the horses with one of the constables and climbed over the pile of rubble. On the other side, they found a storage shed in the back of the hostel. Given the long and imposing roofline of the building, the lower level looked pathetic. The boards were rotting away in places, and doorways and windows were covered with torn and dirty fabric. Part of the shed was a makeshift kitchen. A nasty stench came from barrels of refuse.

Lieutenant Saeki gave orders for some of his men to station themselves at the doors and windows. Then he and Akitada, accompanied by four of his burliest constables, walked around the corner to the front door.

This stood invitingly open, and they marched in, the police in front and Akitada trailing behind.

The interior was primitive and simple. The ground floor was earth, long since compacted and turned a shiny black from many feet, bare or sandaled. Huge timbers rose from the floor to support the roof. Here and there, a second level had been made by linking crossbeams and covering them with boards. Simple ladders reached up to those sleeping lofts. Below, there were few room dividers. Most spaces were open and served many guests. Dirty covers lay rolled up against walls or were stacked up in convenient piles along with headrests. A few simple sea chests probably held the belongings of current guests. The smell of dirt, sweat, and unwashed bodies lingered. In one corner, a man snored rhythmically.

From the back came the sound of voices, the clacking of dice, and clinking of coins. Gambling was illegal, and the policemen smiled with anticipation. Grasping their clubs and metal prongs more firmly, they advanced silently.

Suddenly there was sharp whistling sound from the corner where the snoring had stopped abruptly. The policemen cursed and rushed forward. Akitada turned to look at the sleeper. He was sitting up, a grin on his bearded face. He winked at Akitada, who shook his head and hurried after the police.

The constables had gathered in a circle around five middle-aged men who sat on the floor, trying to look innocent. There was no sign of dice or money anywhere. The oldest of them, a stoop-shouldered fellow with a ragged gray beard and long hair tied up in a piece of black cloth blustered, "What's this? I run a respectable establishment here."

That raised some appreciative murmurs from his companions and caused one of the constables to kick him in the side.

The lieutenant said, "Up, scum. Bow to your betters."

The man turned stubborn. He took his time getting to his feet, then searched their faces one by one. "My betters? I don't see them," he said defiantly. "You've got no right, busting in on a private citizen entertaining his friends."

The constable retracted his foot again, but Akitada said sharply, "Leave him be!" He stepped closer. They had had no time to hide their gambling pieces properly. If the policemen took it into their heads to search them, they could all be arrested. In that case, they would certainly not part with any information. He said to the bearded man, "I'm sorry for the interruption, but we're searching for a young friend of mine. He was said to have come here earlier today. I'm very worried, because there is a rumor that someone was murdered behind your hostel. If any of you men have information to give me, speak up and we'll be off."

They looked at each other, suddenly dead serious.

The bearded man cleared his throat. "At least someone has some manners," he said, making Akitada a small bow. "I'm Kunimitsu. I'm in charge here. This relative of yours, was he a young kid, acting important?"

"That sounds like him. His name is Sadenari. He's a stranger in Naniwa and thinks he can handle himself in any situation."

Kunimitsu snorted. "Wet behind his ears like a newborn kitten, if you ask me. He didn't think twice about walking in and asking questions. We get some rough customers here. As to what happened to him, I can't say, but he was alive and well when he left here. I got busy collecting from the crew of the Black Dragon before they rushed off to their ship. When I remembered him, he'd gone." He glanced at his companions. "Any of you see him leave?"

They shook their heads in unison. Akitada decided that they were neighbors rather than guests of the hostel. They had the look of small tradesmen and were probably fairly honest. None seemed the type to take violent action, but one man was a tall, skinny fellow with sharp features and shifty eyes.

"The Black Dragon?" Akitada asked.

Saeki said, "A large ship from Kyushu. It arrived two days ago, unloaded its cargo and left again this morning."

"It has left?" This was worrisome. What if Sadenari had been abducted and was now somewhere on the Inland Sea?

Akitada thanked Kunimitsu, adding, "If you should hear anything, will you let me know? I'm staying in Naniwa. You can reach me at the foreign trade office. There's a piece of gold in it for you." Turning to the lieutenant, he said, "Come. We must look elsewhere."

Lieutenant Saeki cast a longing look around. "We should search the place. He runs a gambling den and is a money lender on the side. I bet we'd find dice and money."

This set his constables to grumbling. No doubt they had hoped to pocket the haul.

Akitada said firmly, "We have no time for that now. You can make your raid another time."

He was still afraid that a search might turn up the bodies of his attackers. The Hostel of the Flying Cranes was a likely shelter for thieves and robbers. He wanted to explore it a little more without the heavy-handed police along and told Saeki, "Have your men question the people who live on this street if anyone saw Sadenari leave, if he was alone, and which way he was going."

Lieutenant Saeki rounded up his constables. No one had tried to leave the hostel by the back way. He gave his instructions and took them on their house-to-house visits.

Akitada watched them for a while, then went back into the hostel. As before, the "sleeper" gave his sharp whistle, and as before all the dice had disappeared, and the men sat with Kunimitsu, acting innocent. It would have been amusing, but Sadenari's fate was beginning to hang on Akitada like some monstrous burden of guilt.

"Sorry for the interruption," he said. "I didn't want to ask my questions while the police were here in case they started searching the premises. I didn't think you would welcome that. Earlier this day I ran into two robbers on the other side of the wall behind the hostel. One was tall and muscular, the other slim. They carried unusually long knives and came from the footpath that passes through your broken wall. I'm afraid they got hurt in the encounter. Have you seen any wounded men pass by here?"

They stared at him and looked at each other, then shook their heads. Kunimitsu said cautiously, "A lot of people take that shortcut. And people get into fights." He paused. "Was it you who wounded them?"

"Never mind what happened. Do I take it that you know nothing of these two?"

Kunimitsu frowned. "As I said, this is a legal establishment. I don't allow weapons here. You'll have to look elsewhere for your robbers."

It had been a long shot and Kunimitsu's answer might or might not be true. Akitada was almost certain that the man knew the two thugs, though he might not have knowledge of the attack or had a hand in getting them away. He looked at Kunimitsu's companions. All but one looked back at him with blank faces. The one who was preoccupied with picking a scab on one of his feet, was the small one with the sharp features of a weasel.

Akitada missed Tora more than ever and decided that he would send for him. Experience had taught him painful lessons about meddling in the affairs of violent men. The last time he had taken matters into his own hands, he had angered a gang in the capital. They had buried him alive.

A shout outside made up his mind for him. With a nod to Kunimitsu, he hurried from the hostel.

Lieutenant Saeki stood in the street, looking around. When he saw Akitada leave the hostel, he came quickly.

"Thank heaven," he said, adding sternly, "I've been looking everywhere for you, sir. It's not safe for you to go about alone. Especially not after what happened to you earlier."

The man was right, but the remark chafed. Akitada hated being thought of as a helpless official. He snapped, "Never mind that. Have you found out anything?"

The lieutenant looked offended, but he nodded. "An old crone in the house at the end of the street claims she saw something."

9

The Black Dragon

The old one received them, enthroned on a barrel in front of her tiny home. She was surrounded by a group of women and children, their eyes wide with curiosity. Dressed in a plain brown cotton dress and barefoot, she had thrown a piece of old quilted bedding around her shoulders and from the distance, the colorful fabric looked a little like the costly, embroidered Chinese jackets worn by highborn ladies at court. Her long white hair hung loose and added to the aristocratic impression.

She watched them as they walked toward her and maintained a noble reserve when they arrived, but her eyes were quick and bright with interest.

Lieutenant Saeki addressed her. "Tell this gentleman what you told me, auntie."

She studied Akitada's tall figure in a leisurely fashion. He had the odd fancy that she searched for outward signs of depravity in his face, proof of physical weakness in his body, and bad taste in his clothes. When he cleared his throat, her eyes came back to his face, and she cackled.

He said, "Please, grandmother, if you have any news of the young man I lost, tell me. He is my responsibility. I must account for his welfare to his parents."

She nodded. "Good! Parents should take care of their children. Children should take care of their parents. The Ancient One teaches this." Her voice was high and strident, and she spoke in a singsong rhythm.

He said, "I also admire Master Kung-Fu-tse. I see you are a wise woman."

She pursed her lips. "He didn't have any liking for women, the Ancient One."

"Possibly his only mistake," said Akitada politely.

He must have passed the test, for she decided to answer his question. "I sit here most days. I like to watch the sailor boys come and go." She cackled again. "Such bodies! Young. Strong. Such muscles. Give me a muscular man any day. They make the best lovers because they don't get tired."

The women around her squealed and giggled. One of them covered her face and said, "Mother, please don't say such things."

The old one opened a toothless mouth and burst into more cackling laughter. "Stupid girl," she told her daughter. "You with that weakling of a husband, what do you know?" She looked Akitada up and down again. "You're tall for one of the good people. Do you please your wives in bed?"

Akitada kept a straight face. He had only one wife, who had ideas of her own on the subject. "As often as I possibly can."

"Hehehe!" She slapped her thighs, then got serious again. "Well, I was sitting here when the boys from the Black Dragon passed by. Time for them to go home to Kyushu. I know them all. We pass comments as they walk by." She grinned. "They like to show off to the women, even old ones like me. Those thighs and buttocks!" Her hands made grasping motions and she smacked her lips. "Sailors use those legs and hindquarters extra hard on a ship." She winked at Akitada. "And elsewhere, too."

The women covered their mouths and giggled again.

The old woman shot them a glance. "You know what I mean, don't you girls? Hehehe. So long as your husbands are at work, what do they know?" Her daughter pulled her sleeve and muttered, "Please, Mother!"

Lieutenant Saeki was getting impatient. "Never mind all that. Get on with what you saw."

The old woman glared at him. "Thighs and buttocks! That's what counts in a man," she said firmly, giving the lieutenant's a disparaging glance. But she relented and turned back to Akitada. "There was a youngster with them. A city boy, wearing a prissy robe and hat, like you." She grinned. "Couldn't see his thighs and buttocks, but he was young and tall and eager. The kind of boy a woman can teach a thing or two."

It must have been Sadenari. Akitada asked the lieutenant, "Where is the Black Dragon now?"

"It left hours ago."

Akitada thanked the old woman, and took Saeki aside. "We must go after that ship. I believe my clerk was tricked and is on board."

Saeki shook his head. "Can't be done, sir. If he's really on the Black Dragon, and there's no proof of that, he's on his way to Kyushu. You can't catch that ship. It's one of the fastest. And on its homeward journey, it'll be even faster."

Akitada bit his lip. What if the Black Dragon was run by pirates? Otherwise, surely they would have brought Sadenari back. He said, "Perhaps Watamaro could help us."

Saeki grinned. "The Black Dragon's not a pirate ship. It belongs to Watamaro, sir."

Akitada and the lieutenant stopped at the Kawajiri harbor to ask if a young man of Sadenari's description had been seen climbing into a boat with some sailors returning to the Black Dragon. They found no witnesses, perhaps because the ship was already in the channel and on the point of departure.

It was after dark before he reached Naniwa again. Although he was tired and his arm throbbed again, he went straight to Nakahara's office. He almost did not recognize the room. Someone had removed the disordered piles of confiscated goods, and the space was now large, spare, and businesslike. All the empty space and the flickering light of candles and oil lamps emphasized the impression that he was walking into a court session. Governor Oga, Nakahara, and Munata awaited him, seated side by side like judges of the underworld awaiting the souls of wrongdoers.

Oga, his corpulence compressed in a stiff brown brocade robe and his double chins nearly strangled by the collar, sat in the middle and addressed him coldly and without preamble.

"Finally! Whatever the details and circumstances of your assignment, sir, it seems to me that it should have been handled differently. I don't hold with secretiveness and prevarication. You should have reported to me when you first arrived here."

He had a point. Courtesy as much as proper protocol required that the highest ranking official be apprised of problems immediately. But Akitada's instructions had been to speak with Nakahara and investigate the matter quietly. The trouble was that it had not remained quiet.

Akitada bowed. "My apologies, Governor. I arrived here with specific instructions from the Ministry of the Right to check out an internal matter connected with the foreign trade office. Since that office is separate from the provincial administration and operates directly under the Ministry of the Right, I was not required to notify you. Things got out of hand when my clerk was abducted and I was attacked while searching for him in Kawajiri."

Oga huffed rudely.

Akitada ignored this and continued, "I'm afraid the situation has become dangerous. I thought it best to notify you. Provincial forces may be needed to arrest and punish the guilty. It turns out that Sadenari may have been taken away on a ship and must be rescued. His father is a court official who is much respected. I think any indifference shown by the province or the prefecture would not sit at all well with his friends or the central government."

This was an exaggeration. Sadenari's family was of very minor importance, but Oga might not know that. More importantly, Akitada had reminded Oga of his authority in the investigation.

Oga hooted his derision. "The young fool probably just went off on a little jaunt. It's ridiculous to link his going on board a ship with some sort of conspiracy or with pirates. Ever since the Sumitomo rebellion, certain people have nursed unreasonable fears about a few ambitious fishermen who try to improve their lot by stealing small items from careless skippers. There have always been cases of piracy on the Inland Sea. It's our version of the thieves and robbers in the capital who terrify the courtiers in their very offices."

It did not help that the comment about the lack of security in the capital was deserved. Akitada fully agreed with Oga that flagrant crimes committed in the very heart of the government enclosure were a shameful sign of a lack of control. But a far bigger problem for the emperor and his ministers was the threat of an uprising in the provinces. That might topple the government and cost thousands of lives.

Munata and Nakahara, their faces were stiff with disapproval, agreed with Oga. Akitada's anger and his worry about Sadenari had caused him to speak much too harshly to Nakahara and Munata earlier. It had got him nothing but stubborn non-cooperation and hostility. Now the governor had joined their faction. He felt defeated.

"What is it that you recommend doing, Governor?" he asked after a moment.

"Nothing at all. The police have done all that needed to be done. Your clerk has gone on a sea voyage. The young have an adventurous spirit and get carried away by foolish notions. My own son . . ." He stopped himself. "When your clerk gets tired of his explorations, he'll return. And you were careless and tangled with some rough men from the waterfront. Fortunately, nothing much happened. As for the notion of someone selling shipping information to the pirates, it seems to me if that were the case, the information would have come from Hakata in Kyushu where the ships originate, and not from here. I propose informing His Gracious Excellency, the Minister of the Right, that we have met, discussed the situation, and found that the reports were mistaken. No doubt, you will wish to return to your duties in the capital."

Akitada struggled to keep his temper. "You'll forgive me, Governor," he said, his voice shaking a little, "but the report is mine to make, and I will certainly not put my name to what you propose. What is more, if you impede my investigation, I shall make my own report to His Excellency. I suggest you offer some cooperation instead. His Excellency specifically required the local administration to do so in his letter to Nakahara. Perhaps Nakahara would be good enough to show His Excellency's instructions to you?"

Nakahara gulped and reached into a document box that stood before him. He handed Oga the minister's letter. Akitada was fairly certain that he had shared its content with the other two men already.

Oga barely glanced at it. "Bah, what is this besides the usual court language on every document? It means nothing."

Such disrespect was profoundly shocking. Akitada looked at Munata and Nakahara to see if he had heard correctly. Munata's face was expressionless, but Nakahara squirmed a little and avoided his eyes.

"In that case," Akitada said coldly, "we have nothing else to discuss. My thanks for your hospitality, Nakahara, but I shall move to the official hostel for the remainder of my stay. Someone will come for our things." He barely nodded to the others.

Nakahara made some sputtering protest. Akitada had reached the door when it opened and Yuki stood there with Watamaro.

For once the burly ship owner was not smiling. He bowed to Akitada and said, "Forgive me. I was just coming to see you, sir. Lieutenant Saeki told me that your clerk has been taken aboard the Black Dragon. Is this true?"

"Don't believe a word of it, Watamaro," cried the governor before Akitada could speak. "Come in, and let's try to unravel this ridiculous story."

Akitada turned to give Oga a look. Then he took Watamaro's arm. "Thank you for coming so promptly, Watamaro. If you don't mind, I'd like a word in private. Let's go outside."

Watamaro hesitated. He bowed deeply to the governor, but Akitada was firm. Either this man was about the plot against him and Sadenari, or he was innocent. Akitada intended to find out.

As they walked down the hallway, Watamaro asked, "What was that about, sir? Has anything else happened? Why are we talking in private?"

"In a moment."

They gained the veranda and took the stairs into the courtyard. The governor's entourage milled about by the light of torches, but Akitada found a dimly lit and quiet corner where they could not be overheard.

"I've sent another ship after the Black Dragon and several messengers overland to various ports where the captain may stop," Watamaro said. "If your clerk is on board, we'll get him back."

"Thank you. But there's also another matter. I very much need assistance from a man like yourself. It seems the pirates on the Inland Sea have been getting help from someone here in Naniwa. I came to find out who that is. My clerk was abducted because he was asking too many questions, and shortly afterwards I was lured to a deserted street in Kawajiri and attacked. I think someone is taking steps to halt my investigation. And it seems I cannot expect any help from the local officials."

Watamaro looked dumbfounded. Gradually the dismay and shock gave way to acute embarrassment. "I hardly know what to do or say, sir. This has put me into a very difficult position. Forgive me, my Lord, but I'm only an ordinary man. The local authorities can make an end of my business if they take it into their heads that I'm acting against them. The governor can have me arrested and my property confiscated, and Munata and Nakahara can make it impossible for my ships to dock here or to get shipping permits."

It was true enough. Watamaro could not take his side. Akitada nodded. "Yes. I'm sorry I asked. I don't insist that you show your support publicly. But I'm grateful that you're helping me to get my foolish young clerk back."

Watamaro bowed. "Yes, of course. You have my word. And I'll try to keep you informed if I learn anything about the other matter."

"Thank you. Where is the ship taking him?"

"The Black Dragon is Kyushu-bound and a fast ship. I don't think any of my people are corrupt. Perhaps the youngster went on board and was forgotten in the activities of departure. The ships have to take advantage of wind and tide, you see, and the ships' masters are not going to turn around once under way."

That might have happened, but Akitada did not think so. Still, he nodded. "I don't want to keep you. Thank you again. You'd best make some explanation to the governor and the others. I'll be staying in the government hostelry."

Akitada watched Watamaro hurry back inside before setting out for the government accommodations. He still did not know anything. Before him lay the night, and the vast Inland Sea shimmered like a tarnished silver mirror in the moonlight.

10

The Ugly Man Returns

The hostel for government personnel was near the prefecture. Akitada walked in, found a man dozing over his guestbook, and clapped his hands sharply. The man was hugely fat and slow to wake or move. Eventually, he raised a round and greasy face to Akitada, blinked eyes that sat deep in the flesh of his face, and asked, "What do you want?"

This did not promise well, and the accommodations lived up to the promise. When Akitada had communicated his wish for a room and handed over his government chit to prove that he was entitled to it, the fat man pushed the guest ledger his way and rubbed water on a mangy bit of ink stone. Akitada used the worn-out brush to write his name under that day's date. He saw that he was joining only two other guests. The fat man shouted, and a skinny little girl appeared.

"The second eastern chamber," he growled, and the little girl lit a small oil lamp and headed for a hallway leading off to the right.

"You'll need to send a servant for two bags," Akitada said. "They are at Director Nakahara's house. My name is Sugawara, but there will be two bags. One is mine, the other belongs to my clerk Sadenari." The manager grunted and Akitada followed the little girl.

She looked to be about eight or nine years old and should have been skipping along. Instead, she crept forward silently until she reached a door. This she opened and stepped aside for him to enter.

The room was small and mean, the rafters bare to the roof as they had been in the Flying Crane, but it had walls and a wooden floor. Solid sliding doors led to the outside but were closed. Akitada went to open them and found a strip of veranda without railing. The moon shone fitfully among moving clouds but showed a narrow space of weeds and beyond it a wooden fence in poor repair. Roofs of other buildings blocked the rest of the view.

He turned back to look around. The little girl had followed him in and had lit another oil lamp. Now she was struggling with a roll of bedding almost larger than she was. He went to help her. The bedding was plain cotton, worn, but clean. Akitada noted that the room contained also a small writing desk, a water container, and a small brazier. With the bedding spread out, there was little space left.

It would do until he could return to the capital.

The little girl stood near the door and watched him with lackluster eyes that seemed too large for her narrow face. Akitada became uncomfortably aware that he was without money. He said gently, "Thank you, my dear. You shall have a copper later."

She bowed and crept out, closing the door behind her.

Akitada stepped onto the narrow strip of veranda and stared at the tall fence a few feet away. He had stormed out of the meeting in Nakahara's office without wasting much thought on his immediate future. Now he could do nothing until the inn's servant came with his bags. His own contained a small amount of money, though hardly enough for an extended stay. At least he had a roof over his head, and that expense was covered by the government.

A cricket's strident song broke into his thoughts. The night was hot and oppressive, but the autumn crickets signaled cooler days. Sadness crept into his heart. As always, autumn brought sadness.

But his greatest loss had come to him in early summer a few years ago. He had lost his little son to smallpox and grieved into that fall, a dark and hopeless time.

Sitting down on the veranda, he let his legs dangle, listened to the cricket, and wished for his flute. The sky was clouding over; there would soon be a thunderstorm. Already, the hot air was moving.

He missed his family: his wife, Tamako, who was a part of him, and his little daughter who always put her small arms around his neck and planted wet kisses on his face. He missed old Seimei, too. On this dark night far away from them, the cricket's call reminded him that Seimei, too, might soon leave him. Life held as many certainties as uncertainties.

He blinked away the moisture, and cursed the cricket. There was no time for foolish fancies. He must consider his options. But every way he turned his mind, circumstances seemed against him. The governor and Munata had flatly refused his request for help and mocked his investigation. Offended, Nakahara — the only man he had power over — had joined them. The ministry's instructions had spelled out clearly that the director and his staff were to give him every assistance. Nakahara would be in trouble as soon as Akitada reported him, but even so he had made his choice.

Of course, turning in Nakahara also meant admitting his own failure. Not only had he not discovered the spy, but he had lost his clerk and angered the local authorities. He could not remember a time when he had felt more inadequate.

The first large raindrops drove him inside. Akitada closed the doors against the storm. He must send for Tora. He also needed money, supplies, his sword, and another clerk. But above all, he needed Tora.

Thunder cracked, and the cricket fell silent. Then the rain came drumming and gushing down. The night turned noisy with the storm.

Someone scratched at the inner door, and Akitada opened it. Outside stood the little girl, drenched and clutching one of the bags. This she dragged inside and disappeared. Akitada went after her and caught her at the front door of the hostelry. She was struggling with the other bag, Sadenari's. The fat man sat and watched.

"What's the matter with you, you oaf?" Akitada asked him, taking the heavy bag from the girl's wet hand. "Can't you see she's too small to carry this?"

The fat man looked at him blankly. "She's strong," he said. "She carried both of them all the way from Nakahara's place."

Akitada's hand itched to slap that fat complacent face. He looked down at the girl. She was wet and looked exhausted. "Thank you," he said. "Come and you shall have something for your trouble."

In his room, Akitada found the rest of his funds where he had tucked them into his spare clothing, and counted off ten coppers. This generous sum he gave to the little girl, who received it with a bow and no other sign of gratification before slipping from the room. It occurred to Akitada that the fat man would probably collect the money from her. Perhaps he was her father.

With a sigh, he took off his outer robe, folded it carefully on top of his bag, and lay down on the thin bedding.

In spite of the storm, he fell asleep instantly. When he woke, there was daylight in the room.

Akitada stretched, remembered where he was, and sat up.

He stared at the doors. They stood open. Cool, moist air came in after the night's storm. He recalled closing those doors before going to sleep. The hostelry had not struck him as the sort that would wake patrons with light and fresh air.

He turned his head to check the door to the hallway but stopped at the sight of a half-naked man sitting on the floor. He was hunched over and seemed engaged in prayer or meditation. Akitada drew in a breath sharply and jumped up. "Who the devil are you? What are you doing in my room?"

The man's head came up. "Oh, forgive me, sir. I did not mean to startle you. I came late last night, but you were asleep, so I waited."

The ugly man had returned.

Akitada was outraged at the intrusion. "Why? And how did you get in?"

The ugly man smiled a crooked smile and gestured up. Akitada raised his eyes but saw nothing beyond the bare rafters and the darkness of the roof above. He frowned. "I don't understand. How did you know I was here, and where are your clothes?" His initial panic subsided, but he was still very uneasy about this visitor.

The ugly man chuckled. "I came through the roof. It seemed best not to announce my presence to the fat bastard at the front door. And I took off my clothes to dry them. There was a terrible storm earlier. As for how I knew you were here, I followed you."

Akitada peered around the room and now saw that a gray shirt and a pair of short pants lay spread on the floor boards. The ugly man wore only a loincloth. Akitada sat down and said, "I see," though he did not really see anything at all. "What do you want, er . . ."

"Saburo," said the ugly man helpfully.

"Why are you following me, Saburo?"

"I have information that may be useful to you and an offer that may benefit both of us. I thought this way we could meet unobserved."

Akitada looked at the man in silence. He really wished he had brought his sword. While this strange creature had indubitably saved his life, his behavior had been and remained suspicious. But there was nothing to be gained from throwing him out. At the present state of his affairs, he might as well listen to what Saburo had to say.

"What information?"

"Everyone knows you're looking for the young man who traveled with you." He gave Akitada his crooked smile and recited, "'The sailing clouds understand the traveler's dreams, but the setting sun must go away like parting friends.' Young men are full of enthusiasm and care little about the worry they cause their friends. Though perhaps this parting is more of an inconvenience than a grief?"

The man was astounding. The poem he quoted sounded familiar. Akitada had taken him for a common man, and a vagrant at that. "An inconvenience is putting it mildly. He may already be dead. Go on."

"Oh, but he may also be alive. I came to offer you my help in finding him."

Akitada waved that away as a mere ploy to get money. "Thank you, but the matter is in good hands. He was seen going on board of one of the ships. He'll be brought back . . . if he is alive. And even if he's dead, I shall know what happened to him."

Saburo cocked his head. The damaged eye leered horribly at Akitada. "What if I told you he's not on the Black Dragon?"

Akitada sat up. "How do you know that?"

The ugly man chuckled. "I had no other work to occupy me and decided to do some work for you . . . on account, so to speak. In other words, I kept my eyes and ears open."

Akitada said quickly, "I cannot pay for information that isn't verified."

The other man nodded. "I only mentioned it to prove I can be useful. You need not pay me a copper coin if you're not satisfied with the information."

Narrowing his eyes suspiciously, Akitada asked, "Who are you exactly? What is your profession?"

Saburo hesitated a moment. "I'm nobody now, but once I was a monk, a warrior, and an informer."

"A full life," commented Akitada, raising his brows. "Those two men who attacked me. Did you kill them?"

The ugly man shook his head. "The first one bled badly, but that was an accident. Call it age and lack of practice. The angle wasn't right and I had no time to move. His friend must've helped him away. Anyway, their tracks showed they walked."

"I'm relieved," Akitada said dryly. "The police could have blamed me. So you went back after you left me?"

Saburo nodded.

"You didn't by any chance find the silver I threw to the robbers?"

"No. Just footsteps and blood, and I got rid of those."

It might be a lie, but considering that the man had saved his life, Akitada did not persist. Still, the amulet was another matter. "The money can be replaced, but I accidentally dropped a small amulet, a family heirloom. It's important to me."

"Sorry. They must've found it." Saburo paused, giving him a sideways glance something like an evil leer. "I could try to get it back for you."

Aha, thought Akitada, so he does have it. He said, "Surely that would be difficult, even impossible."

The other man grinned crookedly. "Perhaps not. I shall try."

"Good. It's worth two pieces of silver to me."

The ugly man waved the offer away grandly. "Don't mention it. It's all part of the job."

"How did you manage to overcome two armed men so quickly? They were younger and stronger than you and armed. It almost looked like a magic trick."

Saburo smirked and shoved a hand into the jacket that was drying on the floor near him. He brought out a curious metal disk with prongs around its circumference. It was about the size of an orange. This he handed to Akitada. The disk was quite heavy and the prongs were sharp.

"What is it?"

"A *shuriken*. It is thrown like a knife. It isn't as efficient as a knife, but then no one takes it for a weapon. That's useful when a man is caught and searched."

Akitada gave back the disk and glanced up at the beams. Saburo reminded him of the clever thief Tora had rescued from a vicious gang of youths a few years back. "You mean you're a thief?"

Saburo smiled. "Never a common thief. I was a *shinobi-mono*. These days, I'm getting too old for such work."

"What brought down the second man?"

Saburo reached again into his wet jacket and drew out two slender black sticks about a foot long. "This," he said, taking them apart to show that they were connected at one end by a thin chain.

"How?"

Saburo chuckled. "It's a *nunchaku*." He held one of the sticks and whirled the other through the air. It made a strange humming noise, and the cricket outside answered. Catching the flying stick deftly, he passed both to Akitada. They were surprisingly heavy.

"Steel," said Saburo. "Small enough to hide inside my sleeve, but deadly when they strike a man's head. Also useful for strangling."

Akitada dropped the sticks. "So you're a killer," he said flatly. "Why did you save my life?"

Saburo sighed and tucked the *nunchaku* away. "I'm not a killer. Those two who attacked you were the killers. I did not kill them."

Akitada grunted in disbelief, but the sound reminded him of the governor's insulting huffing, and he cleared his throat. "Perhaps you'd better explain yourself."

"I told you I was a monk once. It was the time when the great monasteries were jealous of each other. I was very young then and an acolyte."

Since he did not regard the Buddhist faith with the same reverence as the court did, Akitada was not favorably impressed by this, but he said nothing.

"My monastery trained its own warriors. I wasn't big and strong enough for battle, but I was quick and agile, so they sent me to Mount Koya."

This did not help either. Akitada thought that the arming of monks in order to kill other monks was disgusting behavior for someone who professed to live by the Buddha's teachings. The existence of heavily armed monks furthermore was dangerous to maintaining peace and harmony among the people and posed a threat to the government.

Saburo must have read his face, because he said apologetically, "I was very young and found the excitement of this training very much more to my taste than the constant round of praying, instruction, and meditation."

Akitada nodded. "To become a *shinobu-mono*, a shadow warrior?"

"Yes. The monks taught me the skills. I was a scout."

"You mean you were a spy," Akitada snapped. Many people considered spying a particularly cowardly way to fight in a war. As an agent for Fujiwara Hidesato, the young Koharumaru had spied out Taira Masakado's sleeping quarters in order to let his enemies surprise him. Masakado discovered the plot in time, won the battle, and then hunted Koharomaru down and cut off his head.

Saburo leered at him with his crooked smile. "We don't all have choices in what we do. I was very good once, but I had to give up spying after I was caught." He gestured to his face.

As the daylight outside grew stronger, Akitada could see his visitor more clearly. Since he wore nothing but his loincloth, he also saw that many scars made odd patterns across his narrow chest and belly. Shocked, Akitada said, "You were tortured. Did you talk?"

Saburo looked away. "Oh, yes. Eventually. It made them even angrier. That's when they popped out my eye. After that, I was no longer any use to my monastery as a scout, and I certainly didn't relish becoming an ordinary monk."

"But you still carry those strange weapons, climb into people's houses, and, if I'm not mistaken, you offer to work for me."

The ugly man looked at him. "A man must eat," he said. "And you need help. I thought I'd offer, but I see I was wrong about you." He reached for his shirt, felt it, made a face, and put it on. Getting up, he reached for his pants.

Akitada faced a dilemma. He despised men like Saburo and wanted nothing to do with them, but he had been left without an attendant, and — more importantly — Saburo had saved his life. "Hmm," he said reluctantly, "what do you propose to do for me?"

The ugly man paused for a moment to glance at Akitada. "I made a mistake," he said dully. "The fact that you offered me food made me forget how the good people regard us. I may have given up my past life, but it appears it clings to me like pitch. As far as you're concerned, I'm as much an untouchable as if I'd been born one."

He sounded bitter, perhaps resentful, and this added to Akitada's sense of having repaid a gift (that of his life) with insult and rejection. He softened his manner. "Look, I did not mean to offend you, and I'm deeply in your debt, of course, but I cannot represent the Emperor and the Ministry of Justice if I hire men with a criminal past."

This was not quite true. He had done so before. Three of his retainers had had a criminal past when he had taken them on. Tora had been arrested with a gang of highway robbers, and Genba and Hitomaro had both killed men to avenge great wrongs done to them. But surely that was a far cry from this man, who had devoted his life to nefarious doings.

Saburo finished putting on his pants, then made him a mocking bow. "Good luck, my Lord. May you find your clerk and also the man who betrays secrets to the pirates. Setting a thief to catch a thief may be clever, but unfortunately it offends your sense of righteousness."

He used one of the shutters for a toehold and swung himself up to a crossbeam like a cat.

Chafing under the other man's ridicule, Akitada watched him run along the beam like a tightrope walker at a temple fair and disappear into the darkness under the eaves.

He wondered if he had made another bad mistake.

11

Ducks

Akitada dressed, tucked his remaining money into his sash, and wrote a letter home. He asked that Tora come to join him, added greetings to the rest of his family, and a poem for his wife Tamako: "Hardly parted, I long to see you again, like the white waves making for the shore." Pleased with himself, he walked to the post station where he paid for a mounted courier to take his letter to the capital. Tora should reach Naniwa late that night or by morning.

After that, he stopped at the nearest bath house where he bathed and had himself shaved. A modest breakfast of a bowl of noodles, purchased at a stand followed, and he returned to Kawajiri to check with the harbor authorities for news of Sadenari. To his shock, they informed him that a body had been fished out of the river and that the dead man's appearance tallied with Akitada's description of his clerk.

Afraid of what he would find, Akitada trudged to the small building they used as a morgue. The corpse was covered with a reed mat. When the custodian turned this back, Akitada saw a stranger who had died from a knife wound in the chest. He heaved a sigh of relief. There was still hope. The custodian waited, and Akitada shook his head. A mild curiosity made him ask, "Do the police have any idea who murdered this man?"

"I doubt it," said the man, dropping the mat back into place. "This happens all the time. A fight in a wine shop or someone is tossed overboard from one of the ships."

"But doesn't anyone investigate?"

"When it gets bad and the bodies pile up, the prefect orders a sweep of the wine shops and whore houses."

"What about currents? Can they tell where the body entered the water?"

The man looked blank. "Here? Where there's tides and river currents and ship traffic? Impossible. Besides, nobody cares."

It was a lawless environment. And yet both the governor and Prefect Munata had seemed reasonably responsible administrators—even if they objected to Akitada sticking his nose into their business when it came to piracy. He thanked the man and returned to Naniwa. Until he got word from Watamaro, he could do little. For that matter, he was beginning to doubt that man's probity again. Watamaro was too perfectly placed for deals with pirates or for engaging in piracy himself. He decided to spend the rest of the day writing his report for the office of the Minister of the Right.

Back in his cheerless room, he opened the doors to the small courtyard—someone had put away his bedding and closed the doors in his absence—and carried his small writing box outside. The narrow strip of veranda had dried in the sunshine, and the air was still pleasant after the rain. He spread out a sheet of paper, got a little water from the pitcher inside, and rubbed ink. After a while, the cricket started its song again.

Perhaps an hour later he was done with the report. He still hoped he would not have to send it. Blaming his difficulties on Oga, Munata, and Nakahara made him look incompetent. He started on his letter to his own superior. Sadenari's parents would have to be informed of their son's disappearance. This letter was even harder to write.

He was staring at the fence across the way, pondering the next phrase, when someone called from the corridor outside his room. He got up and let in Professor Otomo.

The professor wore a sober black robe that had the effect of making his white hair and eyebrows contrast sharply in the dim corridor. He bowed, murmuring an apology and a greeting. When he took in his surroundings, his jaw sagged. "Umm," he said, flushed, and went on quickly, "They sent me here from the trade office." His eyes went to the veranda and the writing utensils. "But I see you're working. I can come another time, or . . .?" He looked nervously at Akitada, who smiled and shook his head.

"I moved here because I thought it best to separate my work from that of the trade office. It's only for the short time I'll be staying in Naniwa. And I'm almost done with a letter. What gives me the pleasure of your visit?" Otomo looked about him again and shuffled his feet. There was no place to sit. Akitada gestured toward the veranda. "If you don't mind sitting outside, I'll put away my papers and ink."

"I don't mind," said Otomo, "but please don't let me interrupt. Perhaps I could come back in a little while?"

"Very well, if you're sure."

Otomo fled, and Akitada went back to his letter, shaking his head a little. The room must look pretty bad if not even a poorly paid academic found it tolerable. He added a few more sentences to his letter, dated, and signed it, and impressed his seal. Then, he put everything back into his writing case, and went in search of Otomo.

He found him outside the hostelry, playing rock, scissors, paper with the thin little girl. His heart warmed to the elderly man when he heard a gurgling laugh escape from the sad little child. He went to join them.

"I see this little lady had the courtesy to entertain my guest," he said, smiling at her as he fished out a penny. She took it, bowed, and dashed away. "Can she speak?" he asked Otomo.

The professor nodded. "Oh, yes. But she has little enough to say about her world, poor little flower. Her parents, or whoever has her care, mistreat her. There are always new bruises on the child. And she doesn't get enough to eat."

"I see you know her. I suspected as much. It's hard to know what to do."

Otomo sighed and glanced at the hostelry. "Young girls are vulnerable."

It was clear what dangers the professor foresaw for the little girl. Soon she would be old enough to sell her body to travelers passing through. Akitada thought of his own little girl and shuddered. The professor was probably thinking of the Korean girls who had died in Eguchi. If what Otomo suspected was true, they were not much older than this child. It was very wrong that children should become the playthings of spoiled older men who took their pleasure in initiating them into the world of the clouds and the rain, a poetic term that had little in common with the realities of a life of prostitution. He felt guilty that he could not offer Otomo his help.

Perhaps reading his mind, Otomo said, "I came to see you about the young girl in Eguchi. And I'd like to put my very humble home at your disposal. Whatever its shortcomings, it's surely more comfortable than your current quarters. I hope you will forgive me for making such an offer."

Akitada hesitated. It was a kind gesture, but he did not like to move again. He said, "You are very generous, but my stay will not be long. I hope my clerk turns up today. If he doesn't, I shall have to return to the capital." It occurred to him that Otomo must wonder about the real reason for his move. Perhaps he had been given a highly colored account by Nakahara when he had called there.

The professor cleared his throat. "Since I'm here, forgive me for troubling you again in the other matter. Perhaps we could talk at my house?" He smiled a little nervously. "You could see it that way. It might be to your taste after all."

Akitada weakened. "I have a little spare time just now. But I'm not at all particular about my lodging."

The weather had warmed again, but the sun was getting low. Their walk turned out to be pleasant. Otomo explained the sights as he led the way from the center of town. They crossed several canals and passed through some quiet streets with many trees. The land rose gently, and eventually they reached a longer bridge crossing a sizable river.

"My house is just on the other side." Otomo pointed to a roof rising among pines and other trees. It was a small building surrounded by a charming wilderness and high on the bank of the river.

"Where are we?" Akitada asked. "This is surely not the Yodo River?"

"It's a smaller branch. The Yodo has many arms reaching for the sea. My father liked the quiet here, and so do I."

The troubled world of violent men and scheming officials did seem far removed. Through the trees, Akitada could see some fishermen casting nets. He gazed with pleasure. "How pleasant this is! You are a fortunate man." The memory of that elegant pavilion overhanging the Yodo River came back to him. He decided that this was much better for a simple life.

"Oh, it's very modest," said the professor, "and the land is mostly wild. I'm afraid neither my father nor I have any garden-making talents. I had some trees removed so I could see the river from the house, but that's about all. Come, let me show you the ducks."

As they walked down toward the shimmering water, Akitada realized that Sadenari need not have been taken away on one of the big ships. Boat journeys in this huge river delta could begin and end anywhere.

Somewhere a monkey chattered in the trees, and from the river came the busy quacking of ducks. In a small cove, the ducks, some twenty of them, swam about chittering softly. One of them set up loud warning cries, and a violent flapping of wings and splashing ensued.

Otomo made clucking sounds, and after a moment they calmed down and swam back. "I feed them," he said to Akitada, adding, slightly embarrassed. "They are such trusting and gentle creatures. There is much to be said for the Buddha's prohibition against taking the lives of helpless creatures. I'm afraid my neighbors hunt them down for food, and so they have become shy."

Akitada really liked the man. He needed a friend, and his heart warmed to Otomo.

Back at the house, they encountered a startled white-haired lady. She was slender and soberly dressed in dark green silk, her long white hair twisted into a knot at her neck.

Otomo smiled at her and said simply, "My wife. My dear, this is Lord Sugawara from the capital."

She must have been very pretty once, Akitada thought, with even features and large luminous eyes. At the moment, she was flustered, greeting an unexpected nobleman, and without her fan. She bowed and withdrew quickly, murmuring something about refreshments.

"There are just the two of us now," said Otomo. "My wife's maid is also our cook, and I hire occasional help for the heavy work. "Only one of our daughters lives. She is married to an official in Kyushu. We don't see them often." He sighed.

"Children and grandchildren are a great blessing." It was a conventional retort, but these days Akitada felt its truth deeply.

The professor showed Akitada into his study. "You see how we live," he said. "You really would honor us greatly if you would accept our hospitality."

The house was just large enough for a guest or two, even if it had none of the outbuildings and pavilions customary in noble houses. Several rooms had covered verandas overlooking the river. It was very tempting to stay here for a few days, and Akitada liked the Otomos.

"I truly wish I could accept your generous offer," he said, "but I doubt I'll spend another night in Naniwa. Watamaro has sent a ship or ships after the one Sadenari is supposed to be on. If there's no news today, I must return to the capital and report his disappearance."

Otomo looked surprised. "But you will return?" He added, "You may come any time and you'll be welcomed."

"Thank you." Such generosity was almost embarrassing. "What a fine library you have." The room reminded Akitada of the one that had belonged to Tamako's father, who had also been a professor. There were just as many books here, some on stands, others stacked against the walls or used to support shelves which held more books and scrolls.

Otomo said, "I've deprived my family in order to buy books. No doubt there is a special punishment in hell for such self-indulgence. Perhaps I shall be struck with blindness among the rarest works known to men." He laughed nervously.

"Surely searching for knowledge is a good thing."

An elderly maid brought wine, pickled plums, and nuts. They sat on cushions near doors that stood open to a view of the distant river. Here, too, the crickets were chirping. The sadness of autumn seized Akitada again. Perhaps it was his worry about Sadenari, or the memory of the poor young drowned girl, but thoughts of death seemed never far away lately.

Otomo poured wine and offered the nuts and plums. "Knowledge lays obligations on a man," he said. "Your own ancestor wrote movingly about our duty." He quoted in Chinese: "'Even if one turns away from harmony for just one night, suffering ensues.' How very true that is." He sighed deeply. "I'm afraid I have troubled you with my concerns."

The Chinese quote came from one of Michizane's poems. He felt a little resentful that Otomo had used the words of that most moral of men and statesmen to remind him of a man's obligations, but he swallowed his displeasure. "I, too, must seek to reestablish harmony by returning a lost young man to his family. I see you're still troubled by the death of the young girl?"

Otomo looked down at his folded hands. "Yes, it troubles me so much that I cannot sleep at night. It is difficult to know what to do. When one asks awkward questions of those in power, one is bound to cause more trouble. And in this case . . ." He paused, searching for words. "Perhaps I'd better tell you what I did. I took a boat to Eguchi and walked from brothel to brothel, asking if they employed foreign girls and if any had committed suicide. In the last house at the western edge of town, one of the young women said they had had a suicide recently. I sent for the owner of the house. She was very short with me when I told her why I had come. I persisted. Finally, she admitted that a girl had drowned herself and that the body of the girl had been taken away by her family. She said they had not been foreigners. When I tried to question her more closely, she became really angry. She snapped at me that she had no foreign girls and that I should stop listening to gossip and learn to appreciate our local beauties." The professor blushed a little.

Akitada chuckled. "Awkward. But it need not mean anything except patriotic pride in her own girls."

"Possibly, except for what happened next. I left, but I hadn't walked very far when the girl I had spoken to called after me. She was nervous, but she offered to sell me information. It was dear, but I paid. She told me the girl who died had been so unhappy that she couldn't bear her life any longer, and that there had been others."

"Do you mean other foreigners or other suicides?"

Otomo admitted, "I didn't ask. She seemed a little resentful of the dead girl."

Akitada's interest was aroused by this. Very wealthy men with certain sexual obsessions might make it worthwhile for the owner to provide them with a particular kind of female. If the girls had been foreign and very young and pretty, the brothel keeper might have supplied a special demand. "Did she say anything about who the clients were?"

"Oh, no. . . er . . . she didn't know."

"I really wish I had the time to look into this. If your suspicions are correct, it sounds like a very unsavory situation. But there is nothing to say how the girl died, or that she wasn't sold into the trade legitimately by her parents."

"There was the amulet," Otomo said sadly. "A family who gives such a thing to their daughter doesn't sell her."

There was no answer to that. Akitada emptied his cup and sighed. "Forgive me. I must seem very uncaring to you, but I have my own obligations. Perhaps when my clerk is found and my assignment is finished, I can stop in Eguchi on my homeward journey and ask a few questions."

Otomo did not persist. "You're very generous. Even the fact that you have listened to me is a great encouragement. Sometimes one feels so helpless."

The feeling of helplessness Akitada could well relate to. It was dark by the time he got back to the hostel. There was still no news of Sadenari, but he found a message from Watamaro that the Black Dragon was headed for Bizen province, and that he hoped to catch up with it there. He did not say how long that would take.

Akitada's conviction that the youngster was dead increased, and he shuddered at the thought that he must tell his parents. He had made arrangements with the fat manager to leave Sadenari's bag there for him to pick up when or if he returned. He let the man think that the young man's absence was no more than a sightseeing trip. The manager nodded, then said, "There was a fellow here, looking for you. I said you'd gone to the harbor."

Hoping it was Sadenari after all this time, Akitada asked, "What sort of fellow?"

The fat man made a face. "Young and big. A proper thug. He threatened me. Best watch out for that one, sir."

Not Sadenari then. Could one of the men who had attacked him be so foolhardy as to attack him again? He decided it was not impossible, given the attitude of the local authorities. After all he had been through, it even seemed possible that the governor, the prefect, or Nakahara, singly or in concert, had hired killers to get rid of him.

He thanked the man and went in search of his evening meal while keeping his eyes open against trouble.

He had not gone far when he heard a shout, "Sir, sir!" and turned.

"Tora?" Surprise and pleasure gave way to puzzlement. He could not have made the trip quite this quickly. "Has anything happened?"

Stopping before him, Tora grinned. "All's well. I was here earlier but you were out. Her ladyship sent me to check up on you." He chuckled. "I didn't object. A trip to see the beauties of the river towns was just what I wanted."

"I'm very glad to see you, but does Hanae know why you're so eager to be here?"

"No, but don't worry. I'm a faithful husband these days. Still, no harm in looking, right?"

Akitada gave up. "As it happens, I did send for you this morning. You must have missed my letter. My clerk has disappeared, and I've run into trouble in Kawajiri. I should have brought an armed escort, but you'll do."

12

A Flea between a Dog's Teeth

They had almost reached the restaurant where they planned to eat their evening rice when someone hailed them. Akitada's heart sank. It was Otomo again. He glanced at Tora. "It's the professor I mentioned," he said.

Tora's eyes lit up.

No wonder, Akitada thought. A case of a drowned courtesan in Eguchi was just what Tora would like to investigate. Heaven forbid that Sadenari's fascination with the drowned girl should be reborn in Tora. He could not afford to have another assistant take off and possibly disappear. "Let's hope he won't detain us," he added.

Otomo made his bow and Akitada made introductions.

Tora said immediately, "My master told me the story of the drowned girl, sir. I think we should investigate, find out who she is, and who killed her."

Otomo blinked at so much enthusiasm. "Your honored master thinks it was an ordinary suicide," he said cautiously. "I agree. The brothel keeper is married to the local warden. That explains why they don't want to talk about it. It's bad for business to have too many suicides."

Tora said darkly, "I bet that female's up to no good. I can see it now. Young girls are stolen and forced to work in brothels, and the law does nothing about it because the warden is in the business, too. It's the perfect set-up. For all we know, there may be hundreds of young women like that in the other towns just like Eguchi. And what happens if the girls don't obey? Most likely they're killed. There's nobody to ask questions because their families don't know what happened to them."

Akitada cleared his throat. "We don't know that, Tora. What we have is one drowning victim and rumors of two or three girls that may have come from Koryo."

Otomo hung his head and said, "I cannot help feeling a sense of responsibility, but perhaps I have become too involved. Please forget what I said before."

Akitada could not allow anything to detract him from his assignment, but Tora's theory had sounded reasonable. He wished he could ask questions about the mansion on the river and about the drowned girl, but he must not encourage Tora and Otomo. He said, "It does you credit that you care, Professor, but as you know, we're here on duty."

Otomo nodded. "Yes, of course. Tora's interest somehow gave me the notion that you would be looking into the case after all. Please don't concern yourself. I blush to think that you should feel the least obligation. No, no. We shall say no more about it. May I look forward to sharing my evening rice with both of you?"

Akitada thanked him but claimed business. He thought Otomo looked relieved.

Later, over a leisurely dinner at the restaurant, Akitada filled Tora in on all that had happened. He proposed that they work separately to start with.

"While you're still a stranger here, you can move about and ask your questions without making people suspicious. And you're more likely to get answers than I."

Tora had a faraway look on his face. "That goes for Eguchi, too. Someone there knows about those girls. It's the sort of investigation I'm good at."

Akitada snapped, "Absolutely not. I have an assignment, and finding Sadenari is more important than enjoying yourself among the harlots of Eguchi. Besides, a drowning in Eguchi is none of our business. I want you here or in Kawajiri. Start at the post station. Ask if they remember Sadenari. He may have arranged to take a boat to Kawajiri. Perhaps he wasn't alone. If you cannot follow up on that trail, go on to Kawajiri, to the Hostel of the Flying Cranes. It's the last place where Sadenari was seen and a likely hide-out for pirates."

After their meal, they walked back to the government hostel to arrange for Tora's lodging. The fat man raised no objections.

Later, Tora asked Akitada, "Doesn't that fat bastard feed his daughter? I've seen healthier kids among the beggars in the capital."

"It worries me, too. He makes her work, carrying heavy bags for guests and then, I think, he collects her tips. Poor child."

"Hah! I'll see about that while I'm here."

"No, Tora. Get some sleep and then look into Sadenari's whereabouts. Besides, we cannot interfere between a parent and child."

Tora nodded, but he had his familiar stubborn look that told Akitada that he would find ways to do both.

Early the following morning, Akitada went to speak to Nakahara again. Apparently, apart from removing the confiscated goods from Nakahara's office, business was conducted in the same casual manner. No one stopped him, and he walked in unannounced.

Nakahara was dictating. Typically, it was Tameaki who sat beside him, taking down the letter while Nariyuki lounged nearby, looking bored.

Nakahara started up like a frightened rabbit. "You're back," he gasped, flinging out an arm that upset Tameaki's ink stone and scattered papers.

Akitada eyed him suspiciously. "Yes, I'm back. Sorry to interrupt, but as you know, I'm under orders from the Minister of the Right. I keep hoping you'll take his Excellency's instructions to heart. Dismiss your clerks."

Tameaki and Nariyuki left with bows to Akitada. As Akitada sat down on a cushion, Nariyuki's voice could be heard from the corridor, proposing a quick visit to the market for a bowl of noodles.

Nakahara's hands were shaking.

Good, thought Akitada. He deserves to tremble. That is what happens to officials who shift their allegiance to local strong men and ignore the wishes of the court. He looked into the other man's face, saw the flush of shame, the tightening of the lips and said, "I have made my report to His Excellency. He will be displeased that I met with obstruction from you and the local officials when I attempted to carry out my orders."

Nakahara made a jerky gesture of entreaty. "You must understand that I find myself in a difficult situation here. The court is a good distance away. Different rules apply."

Akitada snapped, "For a loyal servant of His Majesty only His rules apply. How dare you tell me that you work for another master?"

Nakahara cried, "You misunderstood. I would never serve anyone but His Majesty. I only meant that things work differently here. This is not the capital, and I have no resources to fight crime or even to protect confiscated goods. I have nothing. So I must call on the prefect and the governor whenever there's a need for assistance. I have no choice but to work with them."

"That is not at all the same thing as opposing an imperial investigator sent here specifically to check into irregularities because the investigation may prove uncomfortable for Oga and his lapdog Munata. Both officials have gained nothing from their behavior but my suspicion that their hands are dirty. And mind you, that was not what I expected when I first arrived. At that time, I considered all of you innocent. But I found that you, Nakahara, have either been following their orders by choice, or they are holding something over you that allows them to dictate your actions."

"No, oh no! Nothing of the sort." Near tears, Nakahara waved his hands again. "You're wrong about them, about me. It's just . . . a matter of friendship. Of loyalty. Nothing more. We are congenial. My son works in the provincial administration, and Governor Oga has been very kind to him." Nakahara paused, then confided, "His Honor has even mentioned that one of his daughters is coming of age, and that he might not be averse to a connection between the families. That would indeed be a great honor and a blessing for a man of my lowly status. I'm not what you would call a successful man." He paused, then added, "And I'm a father." He heaved a sigh and added in an aggrieved tone, "My poverty is proof enough that I haven't enriched myself in my post."

The situation was a common enough. Provincial lords and court appointees tried to obligate local officials and wealthy landowners by offering favors and forming alliances through marriage. It was a dangerous practice. No one in the central government knew precisely who owed what to whom and what obligations would be called in when a local lord decided to rebel. Nakahara's situation smacked of conspiracy, but it did not constitute criminal behavior.

"What do you propose to do to clear yourself of the suspicion that has fallen on you?"

Nakahara looked at Akitada dumbly and shook his head.

They were wasting time. Akitada rose. "From what I have seen, the paperwork of your office has been careless. Put your clerks to work—both of them—getting documents in order. I shall examine them again before I return to the capital. Now I'm going to call on the governor and the prefect to see what they have to say to the matter. Where exactly is Munata's residence?"

Nakahara looked relieved that nothing worse had happened. "Munata has a manor outside the city. It's on one of the smaller arms of the river. He has rice lands there and also works fields belonging to the governor's family. But the governor is not there any longer. His Honor has returned to the provincial capital."

Akitada muttered, "Inconvenient," and decided to call in at the prefecture. As he rose, Nakahara said. "Oh, this came for you during the night." He held out a letter. "By special courier."

Akitada recognized Tamako's elegant, spidery hand.. He snatched it from Nakahara's hand, muttered a "Thanks," and rushed out. At the door, he almost collided with Tameaki carrying a huge stack of documents.

He tore open the folded letter in the hallway.

It was trouble.

13

The Bawdy Postmaster

Tora had set out even earlier, dressed in his neat blue robe and white trousers. These, along with the black hat and boots and the sword pushed through his black sash, were typical for upper servants in noble houses. He planned to have his morning meal before tackling the post office.

But on his way out, he found the skinny girl crouching just inside the door, looking hungrier and paler than any child should. Her fat lout of a father was nowhere in sight. The sight of the child took his appetite away.

"Hello, there," he said with a smile.

She stared back and said nothing. He wondered for a moment if she was mute but then remembered hearing her talk to her father.

"I'm just on my way to have a bite to eat," he said. "Have you had your morning gruel?"

She shook her head. The tip of her tongue appeared briefly and she swallowed. The sight twisted Tora's heart. "Don't they feed you, then?"

No answer, just that hungry, hopeless look.

He said, "Don't go away. I'll bring you something."

He hurried from the hostel and almost immediately came across a man who was selling hot stuffed dumplings from a steaming kettle. Tora bought a generous helping and carried it back, wrapped in oiled paper.

The girl had moved to the door and watched him as he came running back.

"Here," he said, out of breath. "They smell good. Eat!"

She hesitated, glancing over her shoulder, then held out her hands.

"Careful. They're hot."

She took the food, flinching a little, bowed her head in a nod, and dashed inside.

Tora looked after her, a silly smile on his face. Poor little one, running off to eat in some corner so no one could snatch the precious food away. Then he heard a masculine roar and the sound of a slap.

"Stupid little bitch! Look what you did!"

Tora went in. The fat manager sat at his desk, chewing. The savory dumplings lay before him.

There was a greasy stain on his ledger. The little girl cowered in a corner, holding her cheek.

"What the devil?" roared Tora. "I bought the food for her, not for you, you lazy bastard. Give it back to her!"

The man's mouth dropped open, dribbling bits of dumpling and stuffing down his chest. "Umm," he said and swallowed. "She's my daughter. She's a good girl and gives her father what she gets. That's only proper. Honor your father and mother! What's it to you, if she shares her food?"

"You're not sharing, and you hit her. I heard you."

"Stupid girl made a mess on my ledger," he said, wiping his chin with his sleeve and dabbing at the stain on his robe. "She's a bit slow." He touched his head. "I've got to be after her all day long. It's a great trial, raising a backward child. You got to knock some sense into them."

Tora took a large step forward, grabbed the neck of the man's shirt, twisted, and jerked him forward until their faces nearly touched. "If I catch you beating her again," he snarled, "I'll make sure you get a double dose of that medicine. Now give the food back to her. She looks starved."

The manager's face turned red, and he made choking sounds, but he nodded his head. Tora released him.

"Here, Fumiko," the man said to the child. "You should've told me that it was yours. Thank the gentleman and then go into the kitchen and eat it."

The girl slunk forward, bobbed her head at Tora, snatched the food, and ran.

Tora nodded. "Good! And remember what I said about hitting her." Then he walked out of the hostel.

Still very upset, he made for the harbor. He liked harbors. There was always business there, people coming and going, some waiting for boats to arrive, others waiting to leave on far journeys. One could learn things because people liked to chat while they waited. Besides, there was also a sense of excitement in the air. What would the next boat bring? What would the travelers find at their destination?

But it was still early. The gates of the post station were closed. He wandered about for a while, stopping for a bowl of noodles, eyeing the boats, chatting with a porter about loading and unloading goods and with a sailor about his home port and the places he had visited.

Eventually, the gates of the post station opened. The large compound was marked by a fluttering banner and conveniently located between the harbor and on the main road inland. It served as one of the government barriers where travelers had to show permits and pay tolls. An office, stables for post horses, and fields for the horses to graze made up the whole.

The bulletin at the gate listed the services and fees. Apart from renting horses, people could book passage on boats between Naniwa and the capital or the port of Kawajiri on the Inland Sea. In the yard, a groom was saddling a horse as a messenger stood by. Tora also saw armed guards. Post stations took great care not only of the post, but also of their animals and foot messengers. Several of these runners, in loincloths and short jackets, squatted beside the door, waiting for assignments. Tora walked past them into the office.

Two scribes sat bent over low desks, working on papers. Near them, stacks of parcels waited to be posted or delivered locally. Two more men in loin cloths crouched beside the parcels, ready to carry items to their recipients or to one of the boats. There seemed to be no other customers, and one of the clerks sprang to attention with a bow.

Tora looked past him into the next room. A solitary official sat at a desk: the local postmaster. Postmasters were appointed by the central government in the capital and held to strict account, because official messages, news, and orders from the capital passed through their hands and because post stations regulated travel throughout the country.

Tora told the clerk, "I'll have word with your boss," and walked into the postmaster's office.

He was a middle-aged, plain man with thinning hair who pretended to be busy. Tora cleared his throat.

"Yes?" The postmaster raised his eyes to give him an appraising look.

Tora, neatly dressed and with a black cap on his shapely head, smiled. "Good morning, sir. May I have a word, if you're not too busy?"

The postmaster smiled back. "I'm always happy to be of assistance. My name is Toyoda."

"That's very good of you, Toyoda." Tora approached. "I'm Tora, from the capital and a stranger here. You're the first person to show me a friendly face."

Toyoda positively twinkled with friendliness. "I'm sorry you've had a hard time of it. We must try to do better. What can I do for you?"

"Well, it's a complicated story. I work for an important official in the capital. He sent one of his clerks down here to deliver a payment. The young man seems to have disappeared without a trace and never made the delivery. I'm here to ask if anyone remembers him."

Looking concerned, the postmaster pushed aside the ledger he had pretended to work on and said, "You suspect him of a crime? That's shocking. Hmm. Here's a puzzle to solve." Gesturing to a reed cushion in front of his desk, he said, "Please sit down. I'll do my best to help you. Can you give me some particulars? Like what he looks like and when he was here? We take pride in the service at Naniwa station, and visitors from the capital are particularly noted."

Tora took this as a wish to impress his superiors in the capital in case this visitor reported to his master. "He arrived in Naniwa six days ago," he said. "On the fifteenth day of the month. The master thought he would make the delivery later that day or the next. Either he's run off with the gold or something happened to him before then."

"Ah. He may have rented a horse or a boat. What is the clerk's name?"

"Miyoshi. First name Sadenari."

The postmaster jotted this down. "And the name of the person or place he was visiting?"

Tora hesitated. He had not thought his tale through very far. "As I said, this is a delicate matter." He put a finger to his lips and winked.

The other man sighed. "Yes. Quite so, but it makes it harder." He called one of the clerks, who went to the shelves of document boxes and brought two to his master. The postmaster riffled through the contents and took a list from each. "Ah, I see," he muttered, frowning as he compared them. "Yes, a person called Miyoshi called in on the sixteenth day of the month to post a letter. As for renting a horse or boat . . ." He switched to the second list. "Ah, yes. Here he is again. He took a boat to Kawajiri." He looked very pleased with himself. "Does that solve your problem?"

It did not. Tora did not have to pretend chagrin. "Looks like the master has been cheated. I don't suppose you remember any details?"

The postmaster chuckled. "Maybe. Seeing the list brought it back to me. A young fellow, handsome and well dressed, a little like you, in fact, except he wore no boots and had no sword? He didn't look at all like a crook. More like a student. You know, good class, well educated, naive. And he was poor. He asked about the cheapest rates and then he counted his coppers very carefully. That's what made me pay attention. I remember thinking how strange it was that someone of his background should have to be so frugal."

It had almost certainly been the clerk. "Hmm. Was he alone?" Tora asked.

"Well, he came in alone, but I got the impression someone was waiting for him outside."

"Did you see who was waiting?"

"No. But he kept looking over his shoulder and seemed in a big hurry."

"Ah. That's not much to go on."

The postmaster's face fell. "I'm sorry. I hope you find him."

Tora was about to take his leave, when the man's face brightened. "Wait! I seem to remember he posted two letters, the one to the capital and a local one." He reached into the first box and brought out the list again. "Yes, here it is. Addressed to the Foreign Trade Office, in care of Senior Secretary Nakahara. That sounds very respectable."

Tora's jaw sagged. He went around the desk to look at the list. It was true. Why would Sadenari write to Nakahara? Straightening, he said darkly, "I wouldn't be too sure about that. There's corruption in the highest places these day. Well, I'd better go there and ask some questions. I wish I could repay you with a cup of wine, but it's early and you're at work."

The postmaster laughed. "A man in my position can leave at any time. But you needn't, you know. As I said, we pride ourselves on our service." He paused. "Still, perhaps just a short one."

Tora regretted his generosity, but said, "A pleasure, postmaster."

"Call me Toyoda." The man was up in an instant and led Tora to his favorite wine shop. There the "short one" turned into several long ones. Since Tora had led him to believe that he served a high-ranking courtier, Toyoda questioned him minutely about the sexual habits of those who "lived above the clouds", forcing Tora to resort to outright lies to satisfy his curiosity.

He had just told a lurid tale about a princeling who had seduced his half-sister, when Toyoda said, "I heard of a good story myself. There's a great palace on the Yodo River, just outside Eguchi. It belongs to an imperial princess. I think she's the aunt of the present emperor, an elderly lady." He chuckled. "She has a taste for young men, and her servants scour the countryside for well-built youngsters. People say she's very hard to satisfy. If the young men don't perform to her taste, she gets rid of them. But if she likes them, they live like the blessed souls in paradise."

Tora was familiar with such tales and did not believe a word, but the mention of a palace on the Yodo River made him curious. "Where exactly is that place?"

Toyoda guffawed. "Are you thinking of applying?"

Tora did not think that funny. "Don't be silly. I wondered because my boat passed a very elegant pavilion just before we reached Eguchi."

Not surprisingly, Toyoda did not know the precise place where the princess entertained her young lovers. But the topic had reminded Tora of the professor's tale.

"I expect you know the local pleasure towns quite well," he said. "Are there any very young Korean girls working there?"

The postmaster cocked his head. "Korean? Not that I know, and I do know my way around the better houses in all of those towns." He chuckled and preened himself a little. Seeing Tora's raised brows, he confided, "My own old lady is the very opposite of the princess. Cold as a fish! If it weren't for some of the beauties in our river towns, I don't know what I'd do." He winked. "I could introduce you to some very charming flowers, if you're interested. You like them young, did you say? I know where there are some as young as twelve, if that's what you like. How about it? A man must do what he can to take care of his health, you know, and they do say the young ones have more of the long-life essence in them."

Tora disliked the postmaster very much by now. He thought of the dead girl, and shook his head. "Thanks, not for me. My wife's enough for me. And children don't appeal to me that way. It's unnatural. Like sleeping with your own children. I just overheard some talk on the boat coming down. Umm, it's getting late."

But Toyoda did not give up easily. He described a variety of bed partners and their amazing skills to Tora and told him about a barbarian woman from the far north who had some enticing peculiarities.

In desperation, Tora reminded Toyoda that he had to get back to work, even if postmasters lived more leisurely lives. He paid the large bill, and they walked back to the post station, the postmaster singing a bawdy song, and Tora nursing a headache.

At the post station, Tora questioned the porters and the two clerks about Sadenari.

They had no information. Apart from Sadenari's sending a letter to Nakahara, he had extracted nothing useful in his morning's work, while his funds had shrunk considerably.

He was walking glumly from the post station, when his master hailed him. Startled, Tora stopped. The look on his master's face told him that he had bad news.

14

Karma

The journey was rapid and allowed little time for conversation. In Naniwa, as they waited for horses to be saddled, Akitada had read Tora his wife's letter. They reached home after dark.

Tora pounded on the gates and called out. A fully armed Genba threw them wide. He knelt, knocking his head on the gravel of the courtyard. "Forgive me, sir," he cried.

Akitada said, "Get up, Genba. This was not your fault."

He and Tora dismounted, leaving the horses to Genba, and ran straight to the main house. Monks chanted in the reception room. Tamako came to meet them, bowed to her husband, and said in a low voice, "He's very weak. Oh, Akitada, I'm so afraid."

It was not a proper greeting, and Tamako was always proper. Akitada took her hand and drew her close as Tora looked away. "Are you and Ya-suko well?" Akitada asked, his cheek against her hair. Her familiar scent moved him deeply. All that was precious to him was contained in his home.

She nodded against his chest. "Genba blames himself."

"Why?" demanded Tora suspiciously.

Tamako gently moved from Akitada's arms. "He was not here, Tora. Cook had sent him to the market. He thinks if he'd hurried more, he could have stopped them. It's nonsense, of course."

"Yes," said Akitada heavily. "Come, I want to see Seimei now."

He lay in his room, stretched out on his bedding, pretty screens set around, incense wafting from a small brazier, and costly wax candles lighting his pale and rigid face. He was very still; only his breath rattled softly.

Akitada knew the signs. Death was near. He sank down on his knees beside the old man and whispered, "Seimei?"

Seimei's lids flicked open. "S-sir?" It was no more than a breath. Then, with an effort, "I t-tried to stop them."

"I know, old friend. Don't exert yourself. Tora and I came as soon as we heard. How are you feeling?"

The lips quirked into a smile. "You're home," he whispered. And after a pause for a breath, "In time." Then he sighed and fainted.

Tora plopped down on Seimei's other side. "Seimei," he cried, "Seimei, it's me, Tora. Speak to me? Don't die, old man. Not yet. Not without a word to me."

"Sssh." Akitada put his finger to the old man's neck. "He isn't gone yet, Tora," he said softly and got to his feet. "He's just resting, I think." He glanced at Tamako. "How bad is it?"

"He took a blow to the back of the head and lost a lot of blood. At his age . . ." Her voice trailed away, and she wrung her hands. "I'm afraid, Akitada."

"Yes," Akitada said heavily. He looked down at the frail body, the waxen face with its sharp hollows, already like those on a lifeless skull, the hands with fingers that were bones held barely in place by transparent skin. "Yes," he said again. "Let's go to my study. Tora, will you stay and call us if he wakes?"

In his study, he took Tamako into his arms again. "I'm so glad you and my daughter were not hurt," he said. "That thought was too terrible to contemplate."

She clung to him for a moment. "It was you I was worried about."

He released her reluctantly. They went to sit on the veranda, and looked at the dark garden where fireflies danced above the moss and over the *koi* pond. "What exactly happened?" he asked.

"They came just before midday. Two armed men wearing half armor. Genba had left for the market because cook wanted a sea bream. Seimei opened the gate to their pounding. He thought they'd lost their way and greeted them politely, but they stormed in, flinging him aside.

Trouble rushed out, barking, and snapped at their legs. One of them struck him with his halberd and nearly killed him. He's lame and still very weak. Seimei ran after them and tried to bar their way into the house. That's when they swung the halberd at his head. A glancing blow, but . . ." She bit her lip. "Cook and Hanae came out of the kitchen and saw it all. When they started screaming, the villains drove them into the kitchen building and locked them in. Then they came to find me." Tamako gulped and took a deep breath.

Akitada reached for her hand. She squeezed it and went on. "Yuki and Yasuko were with me in my room. They came in with their weapons ready, and Yuki attacked the first one. I screamed. I was so afraid they'd kill the child, kill us all. But they pushed Yuki at me and only delivered a message. 'Tell your husband to come home and look after his own, or we'll be back and you will die.' Then they walked out quite calmly."

Akitada felt a deep anger. "Did they say who they worked for? Who sent the message?"

"No. I think it has something to do with your work in Naniwa."

"Yes. Probably." Akitada was no closer to knowing what was going on, while the person behind the pirate attacks had evidently felt he was getting much too close. "Come," he said, "Let me take a peek at Yasuko. Then I'll go back to Seimei."

Yasuko woke. He held the little girl tightly, so tightly that she squirmed while she told him about the bad men and what they did to Seimei and poor Trouble.

"What's the matter with Trouble?" Akitada asked his wife.

"He's lame. And he doesn't bark and rarely goes into the courtyard anymore."

"Not much of a guard dog, then," said Akitada, putting his daughter down.

"Don't say that. He nearly died defending us."

Akitada nodded. "You're right. It's only . . . I wish Seimei had been spared."

In Seimei's room he found Tora weeping like a baby and went to touch Seimei's hands, half afraid he was too late. The hands were cold as ice, but at his touch the old man's eyelids twitched. He said quite distinctly, "I'm a little cold." Akitada found another quilt, put it over Seimei, and then sat down to warm his hands between his own. Seimei opened his eyes. "Is it snowing?"

"No. It's a beautiful autumn night."

"Autumn chill turns to winter cold. I'm a little cold, but isn't snow beautiful?"

Akitada shuddered, and Tora sniffed audibly, then shuffled closer. "Seimei? Can you hear me? It's Tora."

"Tora? You must try harder with your brush. Then your father will be pleased. Your father loves you."

They exchanged a glance across the old man's figure. "He has us confused," Akitada said softly.

Seimei smiled suddenly. "The gods have been good to me. Two such sons! What more could a man want?" His eyes looked from Tora to Akitada, and he grasped a hand of each. Then the smile faded, a distant look passed over his face, and he lost consciousness again. After a while, his breath resumed its horrible rattling.

They sent for the doctor, but stayed at the old man's bedside. Seimei did not wake again. The doctor arrived in time to pronounce death.

Early the next morning, Superintendent Kobe arrived. He was startled and dismayed to find the Sugawara household in mourning. After paying his respects to the dead Seimei, he met with Akitada in his study.

"I'm very sorry," he said simply. "I liked him and envied you such loyalty."

Akitada, who had sat up all night with the body, nodded wearily and tried to gather his thoughts. "Thank you for coming. The two men who killed him need to be found and arrested. My wife tells me that she has reported their descriptions."

"Yes, to the warden. The matter just reached me this morning. Apparently, these men were no ordinary criminals. Robbers in our capital do not carry swords and halberds. They use cheap knives that can be concealed easily. Neither do they wear half armor over figured silk. From their clothes and particularly their weapons, I would say they're trained warriors attached to some nobleman's household. That makes the situation serious and difficult."

"They may belong to someone in Naniwa. I think they didn't intend to kill anyone, but rather to warn me away from my assignment in Naniwa.

More than likely they are attached to either Governor Oga or his prefect, Munata."

Kobe frowned. "Then I doubt I can be of use. Perhaps you'd better report to His Excellency, the minister, and let him handle it."

Akitada sighed. "I will, but first I must take care of Seimei's funeral."

Kobe left some of his men to guard Akitada's residence and departed.

Akitada returned to the reception hall where Seimei's body, wrapped in white hemp, rested amidst tall candelabra. The candles cast weird shadows of the seated monks on the walls, and the draft from the open door stirred the shadows into a ghostly dance, as if the spirits of the underworld had also gathered to welcome Seimei's soul.

He closed the door and went to kneel beside the old man. Death had not been kind. The flesh seemed to have shrunken from his face, leaving only yellowed skin stretched taut over the skull. Already, he was a stranger. Akitada suppressed a shudder and reached for Seimei's hand. Bowing his head, he let his thoughts go back to his childhood. Seimei, who could not have reached fifty yet, had seemed old even then. Akitada recalled kindness rather than embraces. Seimei's hand on his head or shoulder, or holding his own small hand as they walked through the garden, were the most vivid memories of their closeness.

Seimei's hand had guided him into young adulthood. On the day the young Akitada had rebelled against his father's harshness and left his home, there had been tears in Seimei's eyes, and his hands had clutched Akitada's shoulders almost desperately.

Later, Seimei had fitted himself into Akitada's young family, being ever present and caring. He had kept the accounts, served as Akitada's secretary when the young official could not afford to hire one, treated the family's wounds and illnesses with his homegrown herbs and medicines, taught his young master's son, and stood by Akitada when the boy had died.

What would they do now? Who would he turn to for advice?

Who would fill the awful void that twisted and sickened his belly?

The candles flickered, and the chanting stumbled briefly. A touch on his shoulder.

He looked up and saw his wife's face, her eyes swollen and red from weeping. He rose and together they walked out into the corridor. The monks continued their chanting, and Tamako slipped into his arms and sobbed against his chest. "I'm sorry," she said. "I wish I could take away your pain, but I have too much of my own. I loved him as I did my father."

"Yes, I know," he said, grief thick in his throat. "I know." He had not loved his father. Seimei had taken that place.

She detached herself. Taking his hand, she led him to Seimei's room. An oil lamp flickered on the floor and cast its light on Seimei's books and boxes. "I've been sitting here, thinking about all he has done for us. And . . . and about how little we've done for him. I'm so ashamed, Akitada. He had so little in his life."

Akitada looked around at the simple shelves holding Seimei's treasured books on Kung Fu Tse and his herbals; at his small jars of medicines with the neat lettering on them; at the plain and worn roll of bedding and the plain and threadbare robe that hung over a stand; at a picture young Yori had drawn and another, a mere daub that was likely Yasuko's work. "No," he said almost angrily, "don't say that. He loved us and we loved him. He was happy. We were his family."

She sniffled and nodded her head. "Yes. It's just that I wish I'd told him how we felt."

"Our worst fears and doubts make us look for blame. Tora is angry with Genba. I blame myself for having caused this with my work."

"Genba is blameless, and so are you," Tamako said firmly and turned to leave the room. "No one is to blame. It happened. It was karma."

Akitada would have none of it. "It happened because of my investigation in Naniwa. Someone wanted to make sure I abandoned it."

Tamako stopped in the corridor and looked back at him. "Are you meddling in something very dangerous?"

He did not like that "meddling" but said only, "Perhaps. It has to do with the pirates on the Inland Sea. They may have abducted Sadenari, sent thugs after me in Naniwa, and now they have struck at my family. This time they succeeded."

She drew in her breath sharply. "I don't suppose you can get out of it?"

"Not unless the Minister of the Right drops the investigation or replaces me."

"You must be careful of yourself, promise me."

Akitada promised and they parted, she to see to household matters, and he to work on his report. He would have to use a messenger. Because of Seimei's death, they were ritually unclean and could go out only for emergencies, and then only while wearing a tablet to warn people in case they had been preparing for Shinto worship and would have to begin their elaborate purification rites all over again. Members of the court were particularly likely to be involved in Shinto ceremonies.

He had just sent off the messenger, when Tora brought Superintendent Kobe into his study.

"I'm back." Kobe gave Akitada a sharp look. "You look terrible."

Akitada brushed a weary hand over his face. "Is there any news?"

Kobe sat down. They had been close friends for years now and dispensed with formalities. "It seems your attackers were strangers in the capital. We checked all the retainers of the local families. As you suspect, they must serve some provincial lord."

Seimei would have arrived by now with wine and refreshments. For a moment, Akitada felt utterly bereft; then he got to his feet. "Excuse me. There must be some wine." He looked about, at a loss.

Kobe said, "It doesn't matter."

"No, no. I'll be only a moment."

In the kitchen, Akitada found wine, cups, and some nuts. He carried these back to his room.

Kobe served himself and then filled Akitada's cup. "We're now checking the hostels and temples that provide lodging. Something may turn up there. They enjoyed a certain degree of status. Good quality clothing and arms. If they arrived on horses, they would have stabled them someplace, and the innkeepers or monasteries can tell us more."

Akitada sighed. "I'm sure these men have been sent from Naniwa or Kawajiri. Someone protects not only a lucrative business but also a position of considerable power. It's possible that piracy is only a small part of a larger conspiracy directed against the emperor himself. I don't like this at all."

Kobe raised his brows. "You're thinking there is another Sumitomo uprising brewing?"

"Perhaps. The government has been notoriously lax about controlling provincial governors and local families. That proved dangerous in the past. They contained the Sumitomo and Masakada rebellions with a loss of many lives and at great expense — and the expense matters more to them. This time they may not be so lucky. Our man may think that they'll be unwilling to interfere on this occasion."

"But who is behind it?" Kobe refilled his cup.

"I have no idea. I have not only failed in my assignment, but brought about tragic calamities. No doubt, I shall soon hear from the Ministry of the Right. Perhaps they'll send me back. Or they'll reprimand me and send someone else in my place. If they send me back, my family will be in great danger."

Kobe cleared his throat. "You know, Akitada, you have a very bad habit of always looking at the worst outcome. And you certainly lack confidence in your abilities. You should be a little more like Tora. He thinks he can do anything."

Stung, Akitada said, "Even Tora makes mistakes. And I cannot afford to make mistakes."

Kobe raised his hands. "Forgive me. That was a thoughtless remark, especially under the circumstances. If they send you back to Naniwa, I'll do my best to keep your family safe."

"Thank you. I'm deeply grateful. Unsolved cases make me peevish." Akitada emptied his cup. He trusted Kobe, but at the moment he could imagine all sorts of circumstances that could arise and leave his home unprotected. He forced a smile. "No doubt, this one will unravel in time. Let me tell you what I've learned so far."

Kobe listened attentively to Akitada's account. "It seems to me," he said finally, "that the matter is in Sanesuke's hands. There's little sense in proceeding until you know what the great man and his brothers wish to do. They may be protecting private interests on the Inland Sea."

Akitada agreed glumly. Since Fujiwara Michinaga's retirement, the government had been in the hands of three of his sons, Yorimichi, Kinsue, and Sanesuke. They occasionally changed places, but one of them usually occupied the chancellor's seat, while the other two served as the two ministers of state. At the moment, Sanesuke was Minister of the Right.

They sat quietly for a while, considering the political difficulties. Eventually, Akitada abandoned the subject and mentioned the drowned girl and Professor Otomo's strange idea that young Korean girls were being abducted and prostituted in Eguchi. Kobe was intrigued and chuckled. "You're insatiable. Not satisfied with a case of high treason and piracy, you find a drowning victim and suspect multiple murders of child prostitutes. But this case at least is a good deal more promising and less dangerous. Let us pray that Sanesuke drops his investigation, and you can solve a simple murder instead."

For a while it seemed as if this was precisely what would happen. Akitada's report to Sanesuke's staff received no more than an acknowledgment. The Ministry of Justice was another matter. His immediate superior, Fujiwara Kaneie, a distant relative of the ruling Fujiwaras, was nominally in charge of all that pertained to import taxes and the laws governing foreign goods and merchants. He responded by letter, expressing considerable anxiety and shock at the attack on Akitada's family. Kaneie was a decent man and begged Akitada to take the time to bury his faithful friend before reporting to the ministry.

Akitada made funeral arrangements and had several talks with Genba and Tora. Genba said little, but his eyes were bleak, and Tamako told Akitada that he had lost his usual appetite and barely touched his food. It was Genba who took care of the injured Trouble. Trouble was Tora's dog, and Genba's care of the poor dog eventually touched Tora. This, more than any words from Akitada, healed the rift between them.

The funeral was quiet, but Akitada saw to it that it was done properly and with the care for detail that Seimei would have approved of. Seimei's idol, Master Kung, had liked ritual. After the funeral, Akitada and Tora took Seimei's ashes to his ancestral temple, where another service was performed.

When they returned home and Akitada walked into his house, he felt Seimei's presence almost physically. For forty-nine days, a man's soul lingered in the place where he had died, but Akitada thought Seimei would be with them much longer. This had been his home, this house and the Sugawara family. He could not leave them. Rather he would be a benevolent spirit watching over them.

He thought this rather guiltily and would not have shared such sentimental beliefs with anyone. Instead he put on a calm face and directed his family's affairs with the utmost attention. He played with his little daughter and chatted with Tamako about Eguchi and Naniwa, subjects she seemed to find enormously interesting. The distraction was a welcome thing. She thought the disappearance of Sadenari most likely a matter of youthful hijinks and a lack of responsibility on the part of the youngster, but she was quite upset about the young drowning victim in Eguchi.

"The way very young girls are forced into that profession breaks my heart." Tamako got up to pace around the room. She paused before Akitada. "Can you imagine how they must feel? They are children who are suddenly in a different, harsher world where men are allowed to abuse them for money. Accustomed to the love of their family, they are abandoned to pain and despair. It's no wonder they drown themselves." She was flushed with anger and quite beautiful.

Akitada wanted to argue that in a poor family such love was probably not very deep since it was the family who sold them, and that life as a pampered courtesan had its consolations, but he knew better and only said, "Hmm."

In the evenings Akitada withdrew to his study, ostensibly to work or to read, but really to remember Seimei. Akitada wept in private.

Two days after Seimei's funeral, Akitada steeled himself to pay the overdue visit to Sadenari's parents. Kaneie had suggested that the news would come better from him. He had been right.

Dressed soberly, he made his way to the modest neighborhood where Sadenari's father, a low level official in the bureau of palace repairs, lived with his family. As he walked, he prepared the sort of speech that would apprise the parents of their son's disappearance without throwing them into a panic that he had been murdered.

When he found the house and heard the cheerful voices of children, he felt worse. He should have informed himself better about Sadenari's background. In retrospect, the youngster now seemed naïve and innocent rather than disobedient and willful. He knocked at the gate.

Excited voices burst into shouts: "Someone's at the gate!" "Tell Dad!" "Maybe it's a letter from Sadenari." The gate flew open, and five youngsters, boys and girls of assorted ages, stared at him. Their faces fell simultaneously. The big-gest, a boy, said, "This is the Miyoshi house, sir. Did you want to speak to our father?"

"Yes. Thank you. My name is Sugawara. Would you please announce me?"

It was not necessary. A middle-aged man al-ready hurried down the steps of the house, blue robe fluttering and a pair of incongruous straw sandals flapping on his bare feet.

He clapped his hands. "Children, run along now! Don't detain the gentleman." He followed this up with a deep bow to Akitada. "Welcome, sir, welcome! Please come in. I apologize. My home is very humble, and my family large and uncouth. We don't see visitors often."

Akitada smiled. "You're blessed with a large family, Miyoshi. Most men would envy you. I'm Sugawara. Your oldest son works for me as a junior clerk at the ministry."

"Oh, indeed. Yes, that is so." Miyoshi's round face broadened into an even wider smile. "What an honor, sir!" he cried, bowing several times quite deeply. "Sadenari has spoken much about you, my Lord. He'll be so pleased to hear that you have called on his family." He caught sight of Akitada's taboo tag. "Oh, my condolences. Not a close family member, I hope."

This was not the sort of thing that made Akitada's errand easier. He cleared his throat. "Thank you. A trusted family retainer. Perhaps we could go inside?"

"Oh. What was I thinking? Leaving you here standing in the open while I babble on. Please come into the house." He made a move toward the stairs, then decided that the honored guest should go first. But how would he find the way? He stopped again in a small panic.

"Perhaps you would be kind enough to lead the way?" Akitada said mildly.

"Yes, thank you! This way then."

He bustled ahead, muttering apologies for the lack of comforts. The house was, in fact, small, plain, and so filled with people that the one room that should have been reserved for guests had been turned into family living space. It was cluttered with shabby trunks, piled higgledy-piggedly on top of each other, and enough rolled-up bedding for a small military contingent. In addition, abandoned robes, books, arm rests, small desks, braziers, cosmetic boxes, bird cages with birds, and the toys of small children had gathered in its four corners and along the walls.

Miyoshi rummaged and found two cushions under some bedding. These he placed on the floor in the center of the room, inviting Akitada to sit. From several doorways peered the faces of children, only to be withdrawn when Akitada glanced their way.

This would be difficult.

Looking at his beaming host, Akitada said, "You know, of course, that Sadenari just recently accompanied me to Naniwa."

Miyoshi nodded eagerly, beaming more widely. "Oh, yes. He was so excited, so honored. He's such an admirer of Lord Sugawara's brilliant work that it was a stroke of the greatest luck to him. He told me he hoped to learn from you so that maybe someday he also might become an investigator. And here he was, selected to assist in such a very serious matter! It was an honor, a great honor. The greatest! We are very indebted to your generous regard for our boy, sir."

"Hmm, er, thank you. Sadenari is indeed a very eager young man. I returned because of a death in my family and had to leave him behind."

His host was nodding his head with apparent satisfaction. "I understand," he said. "He wrote to me about his assignment."

"He wrote to you?" Akitada wondered what Sadenari had told his father about being left behind in Eguchi and having to walk all the way to Naniwa.

"Oh, yes. The letter got here a few days ago. He's very excited about being given a special assignment. Says it's of the highest national importance. And he writes that he has already made excellent progress and hopes he'll soon justify your faith in his abilities. Isn't that wonderful? I said to his mother only this morning that my eldest son will bring great honor to the family. We're very proud of him."

Akitada digested this with surprised dismay. "He wrote a few days ago?" It sounded as if Sadenari had written his father after he had disappeared. "Where exactly was he, er, making this great progress?"

"He didn't say. Would you like to see the letter, sir?"

"I would indeed. I haven't had a report from him myself." And that thought brought back anger. Perhaps all his worry had been for nothing. The rascal was gallivanting about again without a thought to his duties. No telling what damage he had been doing. Or perhaps Akitada knew well enough: there had been the two soldiers and Seimei's death.

Miyoshi returned with a much creased sheet of cheap paper. "Here it is. I could wish Sadenari would take more care with his brushwork, but he was clearly pressed for time, and the note was just to his old dad." He chuckled.

Sadenari's brushwork had given Akitada some concern in the past, and this sample was distinctly worse than what he produced at work.

"Honored Father," Sadenari scrawled. "You'll wonder how I'm doing here. Be assured that your son has finally gained his lordship's complete confidence. He has given me an assignment of the greatest national importance. I've already made excellent progress, but the secrecy involved doesn't allow me to write about it. Suffice it to say I'm on the trail of a villain who plots against our Divine Sovereign himself. I'm filled with an energy that could move mountains. Give my best love to my mother and to my brothers and sisters. Tell them to expect their big brother to return covered in triumph."

Sadenari was not precisely modest, thought Akitada sourly. The letter was dated after his disappearance. Akitada turned the sheet over, looking for some clue to where it had been posted. There was nothing but the superscription and some grease stains that might have been put there by the grubby fingers of all the little brothers and sisters. He glanced toward the doorway and caught sight of two little girls and an older woman. She must be Sadenari's mother. She was smiling proudly until she met his eyes and ducked away with a small cry. The two rosy-cheeked girls remained, wide-eyed at the visiting courtier who sat in their living room.

Akitada did not know what to think or tell this family. Sadenari might indeed be well, though Akitada doubted he would cover himself in glory or even uncover any clues to the identity of the traitor. Alternatively, he might have encountered trouble shortly after sending this letter and be dead even now.

He returned the letter with a heavy heart and cautioned, "There may be some danger. We must hope he's being careful. He is very young."

Miyoshi chuckled. "Oh, Sadenari is one lucky fellow. It's always been that way with him. His karma is excellent. He'll be fine, sir, don't you worry. Nothing bad ever happens to Sadenari."

15

Return to Naniwa

A week after Akitada had arrived home, Fujiwara Sanesuke decided that Akitada should return to Naniwa and finish his assignment. An official arrived toward nightfall to meet with Akitada. The gentleman outranked Akitada and threw the household into consternation as his retinue waited in the courtyard and no one knew whether they should be shown inside and offered refreshments.

Akitada paid no attention to the nervous whispers in the corridor. He had bigger problems. His career might well hang in the balance.

Lord Takahashi was stiffly formal. He refused an offer of wine, indicating that he was there on business.

"His Excellency has taken note of the death of one of your retainers," he said. "He regrets this. However, no mourning period can be involved since this man was not a close family member.

His Excellency has decided that you will return to your duties immediately."

This sounded a good deal like a reproof for neglect of duty, and Akitada bowed humbly, expressing his apologies and acceptance. When Lord Takahashi merely nodded, he dared a question. "May I ask if the assignment has changed in any way as it regards the local governor, or the prefect and the administrator of the foreign trade office?"

"No. His Excellency has addressed separate instructions to the governor and the man at the trade office. You are to deliver these and finish your investigation. Weekly reports are expected, but surely it will not take that long."

More pressure: Finish this quickly or we will consider the delays another instance of dereliction of duty!

Akitada hated begging for protection. It made him sound like a coward. He murmured, "I must urge the danger faced by any official who ventures into this hornet's nest of piracy and profiteering."

Lord Takahashi gave him a cold look. "You surprise me. I had heard that you faced much greater odds on that convict island. Surely you can handle a simple information leak without requiring body guards?"

Akitada mentioned humbly that on Sado Island he had carried secret orders that had gained him the support of the local governor. On this occasion, the local authorities not only did not offer protection but seemed aligned against him.

"Enough!" Lord Takahashi drew a rolled up sheaf of papers from the voluminous sleeve of his black court robe. "Here are your instructions and official letters to the governor and the others. It will be up to you to decide whom to trust. You may collect funds and travel tokens at your ministry and are expected to start out early tomorrow."

And so Akitada and Tora departed after a night that had allowed them little rest. Akitada's visit to his ministry to pick up travel funds had been time-consuming as it involved a lengthy and convivial visit with Fujiwara Kaneie, who congratulated him on the trust the Minister of the Right placed in him and proceeded immediately to a discussion of his own problems. A number of questions of a legal nature had cropped up during Akitada's absence, and besides two pending cases might prove tricky. He desired input from his senior secretary. Their working session was accompanied by many cups of wine, and Akitada did not get home until nearly dawn. He still had to pack, and issue funds to Tamako and instructions to Genba.

The loss of Seimei weighed more heavily than ever on him. The old man had been the heart of the household, making sure all ran smoothly. Eventually, Akitada said farewell to Tamako and peeked in on his little daughter Yasuko, still fast asleep with a doll clutched to her chest.

Except for the fact that he was with Tora instead of Sadenari, the trip resembled the previous one. They went by boat down the Yodo River, the time of day was the same, and the passengers were again pilgrims and men on business. The boat master was different, but he, too, was accompanied by two helpers.

Autumn had progressed in even the short span of time since the last journey. Here and there, brighter splashes of gold and crimson showed among the sober green of the wooded banks of the river. The thought of autumn had made Akitada think of old age and death and had proved sadly premonitory. The loss of Seimei would pain him for a long time to come.

The river carried him toward the unknown. He leaned over the side of the boat and peered into the water. Dark shadows moved below the surface. Already they were close to Eguchi. He found himself watching for the place where they had found the dead girl.

The charming pavilion overhanging the river hove into view first, and he recalled his longing for such a retreat, or for something like the professor's house, a modest place where he could wander down to the water and feed his ducks.

Oh, to be free of the obligations and fears his work placed upon him!

The finely wrought railings, brilliantly red in the sunlight, were nearly level with their boat when a thought struck him. He called out to the boatman, "Can you take us closer to shore, to that pavilion there?"

The boatman was eager to please a nobleman, and immediately ordered his assistants to pole the boat toward the pavilion. They entered a cove normally hidden from view. The other passengers craned their necks, wondering what the court official found so interesting.

Tora came to sit beside Akitada. "Is that the place?" he asked in a low voice.

Akitada nodded and pointed. "We found her over there, where the river makes the bend. She could have gone into the water from this pavilion. She had not been in the water long, and it's much more likely than that she should have drifted upstream from Eguchi. I don't trust that Eguchi warden."

Tora looked dubious. "She could have fallen or been tossed from a boat."

"Yes. It was just an idea." Akitada eyed the pavilion. For all its glowing beauty, the place struck him as somehow menacing now. It seemed just the sort of place where a beautiful girl-child might meet her death.

"It's a grand place," said Tora, looking up at elegant rooflines and red lacquered columns. "The emperor himself might live in a place like that."

It was indeed palatial. As they had come closer, they could see other buildings raising their blue-tiled gables over the tree tops beyond the pavilion. Akitada called to the boat's master again, "Do you know what this place is?"

"We just call it the River Mansion, sir," the man replied. "The pavilion marks the place where we start the turn for the Eguchi landing stage."

"Who does it belong to?"

"It's a summer place for some great nobleman from capital. Sometimes they play music up there over the river, and fine gentlemen and ladies in silk of many colors walk around." He shook his head in wonder. "The good people live every day of their lives in the Western Paradise."

Yes, the elegant buildings in their beautiful setting looked like those in painted scrolls depicting the Western Paradise. To ordinary people, the lives of the rich and powerful were the most accurate image of ultimate bliss. As they gradually moved downriver and away from the site, Akitada got a vivid impression of music floating out over the water while celestial figures moved about under the trees or leaned over the red railings of the pavilion to watch the river traffic. It was a far cry from the rustic hermitage he had imagined as the perfect haven for his old age. Perhaps the reward for a good life was exactly the sort place one had dreamed of during his lifetime. He wondered what abode Seimei would find waiting for him.

Tora snorted. "'Good people'? Hardly good. They may live in paradise, but their crimes send them to hell after they die," he said, shocking the boat's master and his assistants, but getting some nods and grins from passengers.

Like Tora, Akitada knew well enough that the lives of the powerful were far from perfect or desirable. He was tempted to stop over in Eguchi to find out who owned the River Mansion. He could ask Harima, the former *choja*. The thought of the two old people brought a smile to his face.

Tora must have read his thoughts. "Shall we spend the night and ask a few questions?" he asked eagerly. "We can go on to Naniwa the next morning."

That was what Akitada had done last time, and it had led to nothing but trouble. Besides, while Tora doted on his pretty wife Hanae and had turned into a good family man since his marriage, his past had been spent among the women who earned their living on their backs. Tora might be tempted to take advantage of his temporary freedom from domesticity to return to his old ways. He said, "No, Tora. Have you forgotten Seimei's death? As long as the villain who sent his men to my home is alive and free, your family and mine are in danger."

Tora's face fell. He nodded. "You're right. I shouldn't have been so stupid."

They fell silent. Akitada wondered if Kobe could guard his family adequately if more armed men showed up at his house.

Tora said, "That postmaster's story about the old princess and her young men sort of fits, don't you think?"

"What?"

"What the boat master said about parties at the River Mansion. What if that's where the princess lives?"

"I doubt it very much. It's just a salacious tale told by a lecher." But it struck Akitada that a nobleman might well use such a remote place to enjoy forbidden pleasures the court would frown upon or a highborn first wife might object to. Those pleasures, in the close proximity of a town that catered to all sorts of sexual perversions could involve the abuse of poor young girls, abuse that would lead them to commit suicide rather than face more of the same. It might even result in murder.

He thought of Otomo and his insistence that Korean girls were being abducted and put to work in Eguchi. There was something very odd about the way Otomo had pursued him with his suspicions. But the professor had never mentioned the word murder.

They stayed on board while the boat docked at Eguchi and watched passengers disembark and new passengers take their place. The short distance to Naniwa was uneventful. The skies were still blue, the broad expanse of the river glistened in the sun, and a fresh breeze brought the tang of the open sea.

In Naniwa, they walked to the government hostel. The fat man sat in his usual place. There was no sign of the little girl. The manager eyed them glumly.

"You had a visitor," he told Akitada. "Right after you left. Ugliest bastard I ever saw. He left this." With a smirk, he produced a badly wrapped package that seemed to contain a scroll. "I told him you'd gone and I didn't know if you'd be back, but he said to keep it and he'd be back to pick it up if you didn't show. Only he never came back."

Akitada stared at the package and then at the fat man. It was clear that someone had opened and then rewrapped the package clumsily. He took it and said coldly, "Thank you. We'll share a room. Bring our saddlebags."

The fat manager got to his feet with difficulty, grabbed a saddlebag in each fist and lumbered down the corridor. He took them to the same room Akitada had occupied before and collected his tip.

"Where's your daughter?" asked Tora.

"With her mother," the fat man said and lumbered out.

"I wonder how the child is." Tora looked after him with a frown.

"Let's hope her mother is looking after her better than her father was." Akitada was unwrapping the package. It turned out to be no more than a piece of bamboo pipe of the sort used in gardens to direct water into a basin. It should be hollow, but he could not see through it. He shook it and heard a soft sound inside. He looked about the room, then stepped out into the small yard where he saw a dry stick and used that to probe inside the tube. Some brown fibers fell out. He poked harder, and more fibers emerged, and then a small, heavy object wrapped in a piece of paper fell into his hand. When he unfolded the paper, he saw the Korean amulet. The ugly man had returned it.

"What is it?" asked Tora.

"It's an amulet I bought and lost. Apparently, someone found it for me." Akitada tucked the coin away in his sash. No sense in further stirring Tora's interest in the dead girl from Eguchi. "Let's have an early night. I plan to see the prefect in the morning. Nakahara is useless, but he did inform me that Munata is a close associate of the governor's. If one of the two is a villain, then the other is also, and Munata is less likely to slip away to the capital. What about you?"

Tora stepped out on the veranda and sniffed the air. "I'll go to Kawajiri. To that hostel."

Akitada nodded. "The Hostel of the Flying Cranes." He looked at Tora's neat blue robe, his black hat, and good boots. "But not in those clothes, I hope."

"No, of course, not. I'll change into some rags, but I'll take my sword. It's short, and an old jacket will cover it. I may be gone for a couple of days. Will you be all right?"

"Yes. It's you who is going into the tiger's lair. Be careful."

16

Family Ties

The next morning, Akitada walked to the district prefecture, ruminating about the return of the Korean amulet.

Why had the ugly man returned it? If he had taken it in the first place, what had made him change his mind? If he had not taken it, how had he found it? Hiding it inside the bamboo pipe made more sense. He had clearly taken the measure of the fat man. But the rest of his impressive feats still bordered on the unreal.

Before setting out, Akitada had looked at the amulet again. Otomo was right. It was too finely made to have belonged to a mere courtesan. If he had the time, he would return to Eguchi with the amulet and get to the bottom of this mystery.

Having got this far, Akitada saw the prefecture looming ahead and forced his mind back to the piracy case. What, for example, should he make of the close ties between Governor Oga, a court noble assigned to the province for the customary four years, and Prefect Munata, a local landowner?

Professor Otomo also claimed acquaintance with the governor. He had taught his son, but was that a sufficient reason for Nakahara to have invited him to his party? He was a poor academic, quite clearly a different species from the others. The governor and the prefect, two powerful men, had not treated him precisely as an equal, but they had accepted his presence. Yes, Otomo's role in all this was another puzzle.

He was received politely at the prefecture, but Munata's assistant told him that the prefect was still at his residence outside the city and not expected until later that day.

Impatient at the delay, Akitada demanded a horse and a guide, and set out for Munata's home.

Munata clearly owned a substantial property. The compound extended over several acres and had an impressive roofed double gate. This gate stood open, so that Akitada rode all the way across the wide entrance court to the steps of the main house where he dismounted. Servants came running to take his horse. More servants ran down the stairs to receive him. Near a secondary gate, leading perhaps to stables and retainers' quarters, a group of men with bows had gathered near their horses. They were apparently preparing to hunt, but Akitada thought of the armed retainers who had attacked his home.

Self-interest governed allegiance, and Munata would not willingly take actions that conflicted with Oga's interests, but had he gone so far as to dispatch two of his men in order to frighten Akitada into leaving Naniwa?

His arrival had caused initial consternation, but after some running back and forth of agitated servants, Munata himself appeared to welcome Akitada into his reception hall.

He was dressed more elegantly than last time. No plain black robe on this occasion. He wore a red hunting coat of figured brocade and blue silk trousers. Perhaps he had only worn the black robe because he had come from work in the pre-fecture, or because he had not wanted to upstage the governor. Clearly, here he was the master and overlord of his domain.

His reception hall also revealed wealth and hereditary status. A large silk banner with his family crest hung over the dais, and the beams and columns were carved and colored.

Munata invited Akitada to sit and then seated himself with a rustle of his stiff red coat. "We had thought you had left us for good, Lord Sugawara," he said with a smile.

"No such luck. I returned from court with instructions for the governor and thought to find him here."

"Ah, yes." Munata folded his hands. "He does stay here frequently. But he has the affairs of the province to deal with. Hearing court cases and settling land disputes, you know. He's a most conscientious official."

Akitada said coldly. "I know quite well what a governor does, having served in that capacity myself."

Munata lost some of his composure. He bowed. "My apologies. How may I be of service?"

"You will oblige me by sending for him."

"Sending for him? Surely you jest. I cannot send for the governor."

Akitada raised his brows. "I would hope that you do so, for example, in cases of district emergencies. But if you don't feel empowered to ask him to return, I will. Call in a clerk, and I'll dictate a letter."

Munata flushed and obeyed. An elderly man appeared, carrying a small desk and writing tools. He bowed to Akitada, sat, and immediately began to rub ink and ready his brush.

Akitada dictated, "To Governor Oga Maro: You are hereby requested to return to the Naniwa prefecture immediately to receive the instructions of His Most Honored Excellency, Fujiwara Sanesuke, Grand Minister of the Right. Signed, Sugawara Akitada, Imperial Investigator."

The title of "imperial investigator" was one that Sanesuke (or his senior secretary, since the great man did not necessarily dictate letters) had used in Akitada's own instructions. It proved to be useful on this occasion, since imperial investigators could subsume powers not necessarily available to a mere senior secretary in the Ministry of Justice. When the clerk was done, Akitada read the letter, corrected one character, and then impressed his seal to it. "Very well," he said to Munata, who had been sitting speechless, nervously twisting his hands. "Have a messenger deliver this immediately. I expect the governor to-morrow."

Munata took the letter and dismissed the clerk. "I shall see to it, sir . . . er . . . if that's all?"

Akitada glowered at him. "No. I have some business with you."

The prefect paled. With a muttered apology, he rose and rushed from the room, bearing the letter with him. Akitada heard him speak to someone outside, then he returned. He slipped back to his seat and said, "I regret extremely that our last meeting was unpleasant. I hope you will believe, sir, that I had to follow the governor's wishes."

So the little weasel was trying to blame his disobedience on Oga. Akitada looked at him with disgust. He disliked this man more than any of the others who had been present at Nakahara's that night. There was, in truth, something very weasel like and predatory about his smallness, his sharp features, and his quick movements.

"His Majesty's laws pertain to all men equally," he pointed out coldly. "I asked for the assistance you had been told to give, and you refused it."

Munata bowed several times. "My apologies if I have offended. It was never my intention . . . and I carried out your instructions if you'll recall."

"Not quite. You informed Oga, and then you and he met with Nakahara to plan your strategy. When I returned to the trade office, the three of you refused me any further assistance. The gov-ernor—speaking for all of you, I take it—told me to leave Naniwa."

The prefect squirmed. "The governor makes his own decisions. It isn't up to me, or Nakahara, to correct a man of his standing."

There was no point in arguing about it. Akitada snapped, "What has been done to find my clerk?"

"If he's on Watamaro's ship, he's out of our jurisdiction. Messages could be sent to all the provinces and harbors where the ship calls. I take it that Watamaro has done so."

"In other words, you have done nothing to investigate what happened. Have you made any progress in finding out who is passing information about shipments to the pirates?"

Munata swallowed and glanced around the room as if the answer lurked somewhere in a corner. "Umm, we had nothing to go on. I, umm, believe with the governor that the informant must be in Kyushu."

Akitada said angrily, "Nothing again!" and got to his feet. "I want you back in Naniwa instructing the local police to give me assistance as I need it. Nakahara will investigate his own staff, and you will prepare for me information about anyone in your district who has known ties to current or former pirates. That includes men who do business with the captains and fishermen who ply the Inland Sea."

"But . . ." started Munata when the door opened abruptly and a tall young man burst in. "Uncle Koretoki —" He stopped, blinked, and muttered, "Oh, forgive me. I didn't know you have a guest." Her made a jerky movement toward the door, then stopped and stood at a loss.

Munata looked frustrated but controlled himself. "Lord Sugawara, allow me to present Oga Yoshiyo."

Akitada's eyebrows rose. The young man turned, made a quick bow, and stared at Akitada blankly. He looked unnaturally pale, and Akitada wondered if he was ill.

"Oga?" he asked. "Any relation to the governor?"

"Alas, I'm his son," said the young man. "And I wish I'd never been born."

"Please, Yoshiyo," cried the prefect. "Not here and now."

Taken aback, Akitada looked at the young man more closely. The bond between Munata and the governor evidently involved their families. Oga Yoshiyo was handsome for all his pallor and listlessness. He guessed the youngster was eighteen or nineteen years old. "Are you related to the prefect also?" he asked, trying to find out just how close the relationship was between governor and prefect.

The youth blinked and said, "Oh, no!" so emphatically that Akitada's brows shot up again.

Munata flushed and explained. "I've known His Excellency's children since they were small. They are frequent guests here and do me the honor of calling me 'uncle'."

The governor's son did not smile. He seemed irritated with the delay and said, "I came to inform you that I'm leaving. You may tell my father whatever you wish."

Munata started to his feet. "Wait, Yoshiyo. Just wait another day. I promised your father —"

"No! We've said all there is to say." Yoshiyo turned on his heel and stormed out.

Munata stood for a moment, then he murmured, "Forgive me. I must stop the young fool," and rushed after him.

As he listened to Munata's shouts until they receded, Akitada thought of Sadenari, who was about the same age as the governor's son. The young were often rash and foolish. But the Miyoshis did not have the money and connections of the Ogas, and Sadenari's foolishness could not be curbed like young Oga's. The poor paid with their lives for mistakes. He shivered and felt the familiar anger at those who enriched themselves illegally at the cost of the throne and the rest of the country. In the larger scheme of things, he, too, would perish if he made a "foolish" mistake in this investigation. Men of power, like the ruling Fujiwara clan, or like Oga and Munata, yes, even such men as the wealthy merchant Watamaro, would crush him if he threatened their positions.

And yet he kept risking his life, his career, and now also his family. Was that courage and a desire for justice? Or was it mere stubbornness, a selfish wish to satisfy his own desires? What about Tamako and his little daughter? Would they want him to play the hero at all costs?

What would Seimei have advised?

Munata returned, looking agitated. He echoed some of Akitada's thoughts. "I beg your pardon, but the young man is very upset, and I feel responsible for his actions while he's here. When a young man is disappointed in love, he loses all common sense and may do himself or someone else harm." He sat down, then jumped up again. "I must send people after him. The heavens know where he's off to. His father will be angry." He gave Akitada a pleading look.

It was not clear whether such anger would be directed at Munata or the young man, but Akitada decided that the governor's family affairs were none of his business. Getting to his feet, he reminded Munata of his instructions and took his leave.

It was well past the hour of the midday rice when he reached the city, and he was very hungry. He had not been offered a meal by Munata, proof of how distracted the man had been. It had not been Akitada's visit that had upset him most, but rather the governor's son. And that proved that orders from the Fujiwara minister counted for less than the power of the governor of Settsu.

17

The Evils of Gambling

As Tora walked to the Naniwa waterfront, he got the peculiar feeling that he was being followed. A sudden turn to scan the street revealed nothing but harmless activity. No one paid any attention to him, and yet he felt it again a little later when he bought boat passage to Kawajiri—that sense that someone's eyes were drilling holes into his back. He swung around and thought this time he saw a man's back disappearing into an alley. Tora ran to check the alley, but only a scarecrow of a beggar was rifling through garbage for something to eat. He put it from his mind as a case of nerves.

The regular passenger boat took him swiftly and uneventfully to Kawajiri. Like Akitada, Tora was greatly impressed with the large ships docking and the sight of more ships at anchor in the bay. Unlike his master, he postponed sightseeing. He chose a narrow street leading to a district of small shops and poor shacks. It thronged with sailors and laborers. Cheap prostitutes leaned from windows even at this early hour.

Tora discovered what he was looking for within a block of the harbor. Squeezed between two larger buildings was a tiny shop that sold used clothing. He ducked in under the low lintel and found himself in a sort of cave where the walls and ceiling were made of clothing draped over beams, ropes, and racks. In the tiny open space sat a tiny woman sewing. She had a wrinkled face and her hair cut short like a nun's. Peering up at him, she asked, "What will it be, handsome?"

The light was dim. Tora let his eyes adjust a little. Recalling what his master had said about the poor needing to make a living, he smiled at her. She smiled back.

"Can you keep a secret?" he asked.

Her eyes twinkled. "What did you steal? Let me see it."

"What? Do I look like a thief?"

"Maybe not, but you'd be surprised what people walk in here with stolen goods. Gamblers will stop at nothing." She added glumly, "There ought to be a special hell for them,"

He crouched down. "This is legitimate business, auntie. I'm being followed and I need to throw them off my trail. For that I need to change clothes. I'll pay you for the outfit, but I want you to keep my own clothes for me until I pick them up. Will you do that and not tell anyone?"

She stuck her needle into the woman's robe she had been mending. "How exciting! Who's been following you? Some girl who's fallen for your looks? Or maybe her husband or brother?"

He laughed. "No, nothing so romantic. Find me some clothes that a man would wear who's down on his luck."

She cocked her head. "Plenty of those around," she said, getting to her feet. She felt Tora's robe. "Nice. I could get some money for this. The boots, too. And the sword. You sure you don't want to sell?"

"I'm sure, and I'll keep the sword. Where can I change?"

She pushed aside a curtain of clothing and revealed a narrow space between it and another line of robes, coats, and trousers. "As private as you could wish," she said. "Is your business dangerous? Is that why you carry the sword?"

"Too many questions. Let me see what you have."

She disappeared among her curtains of clothing. Tora sniffed stale air mixed with the smell of dirt and garbage.

When she reemerged, she carried an armful of clothing. This she dumped on the floor. "Take your pick."

Tora rummaged through the pile and came up with a pair of full knee-length cotton trousers that once had a black and white check pattern but now were mottled gray. He combined these with a torn shirt that was almost white, and a full jacket of a rust brown color with a large number of stains.

"I can sew up that tear," said the woman.

"No, it's perfect like that. What about shoes?"

She studied his feet. "No boots, but plenty of sandals."

Tora made a face but nodded reluctantly.

She scooped up the rejected merchandise, disappeared among the swaying, odoriferous lines of clothing. This time, she brought forth five pairs of sandals and one pair of leather shoes. The leather shoes had once been boots, but a previous owner had cut off the tops for some other purpose. Tora slipped them on. They looked ridiculous but fitted like gloves and would last longer than sandals. He nodded.

He changed behind a wall of clothing. Then he untied his hair and let it hang loose. He had not been shaved since they arrived in Naniwa. The stubble added to his derelict appearance. He handed over his own clothes and paid for the rags. The price was high but Tora counted the overcharges as a fee for safe-guarding his property.

She tucked the money away, looked him over by walking all around him, and brought out a square of red and white fabric. "Here," she said, "No extra charge. Twist it and tie your hair up with this. Anyone can see that you used to wear a topknot."

Tora gave her one of his big smiles, twisted the square of fabric and tied it around his head. She came and stood on tiptoes to disarrange his hair, tucking parts under, so that it looked uneven. "Now you look fine," she said.

Tora made her an exaggerated bow. "You've been blessed with superior intelligence as well as an eye for fashion, madam. Many thanks," he said, and pushed his sword into the belt, making sure that the jacket covered it. Then he headed for the door.

"What do I do with your stuff if you don't come back?" she called after him.

"If I'm not back in a week, you can sell it."

As he walked away, he realized that she did not expect him to be back and thought about what lay ahead. If all went well, he should be done in a day, perhaps two. He carried very little money, but even this could spoil his plan. He stepped behind a shed and secreted the two silver pieces between the leather and lining of his shoes. When he reemerged into the street, he collided with a man who was hurrying past. Tora called an apology after him, but the man neither turned nor acknowledged it. He disappeared around the next corner. Tora shook his head and walked on. There had been something familiar about that thin, angular back in its non-descript gray jacket and pants. Still, half of the inhabitants of the poorer quarters of any city were scrawny and dressed in old clothes. He looked down at his own outfit with some complacency. It marked him as a poor man but it was colorful and gave him a certain presence. Plus, he was tall and muscular. All quite useful for this adventure.

After a while, he stopped to ask a small boy the way to the Hostel of the Flying Cranes. The grimy child pointed to a side street up ahead. Tora approached the hostel from the front. When he passed an old woman enthroned on an up-turned basket beside her front door, it occurred to him she must be the one who had seen Sadenari leaving with the sailors from the Black Dragon. He gave her a smile and a nod.

"Stop a moment to talk to a lonely granny," she cried. "What's your rush? Come give Granny a kiss, you handsome dog!"

Tora laughed and did as she asked. With the speed of a striking adder, her hand darted to his groin, and he jumped back several feet. She cackled. "As skittish as a virgin! With such fine jewels, you needn't be shy, handsome. I've a good mind to take you to bed."

Tora flushed with the shock. "Where's your modesty, old woman?" he demanded from a safe distance.

She shook with laughter. "Lost that more years ago than you've been alive. Come back here," she wheedled. "How about just a little fondling? A little tongue?" She stuck it out.

Tora decided the incident was funny. "Sorry, Granny, you're too much woman for me," he said with a laugh. "I hear you've got your eye on all the sailors from the hostel." Shaking his head, he walked on. First the postmaster's tale of the aged princess with her young lovers and now this. What was the matter with old women here? Something in the water maybe.

Her cackling laughter pursued him all the way to the hostel.

He liked the looks of it. This was the very sort of place that attracted men who lived outside the law. When he reached the door, he heard angry shouting and squeals. He walked in and followed the sounds to the back of the place.

They had been gambling again. Dice lay on the scuffed floor, and a large man with a tattoo of a writhing dragon on his bare thigh had a smaller, older man by the neck and was shaking him like a rat. The smaller man did the squealing, while the big brute shouted. Coins dropped from the smaller man's clothes. Three other men, also middle-aged, cowered in a corner.

The shouting involved words like "thieving bastards" and "I'll make you eat your dice." Tora grinned. No doubt, fleecing customers was a regular pastime here, but this time the customer had caught on.

The customer with the dragon tattoo was a brute, easily twice the bulk of the little fellow he was throttling. Tora decided to take the side of the underdog, regardless of the underdog's offense. He waded into the fray with a roar, seized the brute's topknot and jerked him back sharply.

The man howled, let go of his victim, and swung around. What followed was one of the uglier battles Tora had engaged in.

Dragon Tattoo twisted out of Tora's grasp, leaving a handful of hair behind, and rammed a fist into Tora's stomach with such force that Tora flew back and hit a pillar, doubling up. The pillar saved him from falling flat on his back. He pushed away and butted his head into the other man's middle as he came again with fists flying. There was a grunt, and then the brute vomited up an evil-smelling flood. Tora waited for the vomiting to stop, and when the other man's head came up, he smashed his fist into his face. Blood spurted, and suddenly a knife appeared in the man's hand.

Tora stepped back and drew his sword.

For a moment, the action froze. Then the brute cursed long and volubly. He snarled, "This isn't over, you bastards! I'll be back and get you both." Raising the knife, he made a slashing motion across his throat. Then he turned and lumbered from the room.

Tora put away his sword. His stomach was on fire, and he felt a sudden nausea rising. Moving away from the stench of the vomit, he asked, "Who was that?"

His audience exchanged glances and then stared at him. The huddle in the corner dissolved as the three men crept forward. The one who had been throttled, coughed and bent to pick up the coins and dice. "One of the sailors," he rasped.

"He's a pirate," offered one of the others. "Said he's coming back. What will you do, Kunimitsu?"

So the man he had saved was the manager of the hostel. Tora considered briefly that it might have been wiser to befriend the pirate than him. "You run this place?" he asked.

Kunimitsu massaged his throat. "What do you want?" he asked sourly.

"What? Not a word of thanks?" Tora raised his brows in mock horror. "Shall I run after the guy and tell him to go ahead with what he'd planned for you and offer to help him? I take it, you've been cheating him at dice?"

"That's a lie," blustered Kunimitsu. "And you made things worse."

The others burst into assorted dire predictions.

Tora sighed and sat down. "I have a few coppers," he said, "but I'm out of work and need a place to stay. I'll play you for it." He tried not to think of the promise he had made his wife, Hanae. But this was not for pleasure. This was part of the job.

Kunimitsu looked him over. "How many coppers do you have?"

Tora fished ten from his jacket and laid them down tenderly in two rows of five.

Kunimitsu snorted. "That's all? What about your sword?"

"No. I might need it when that bastard comes to slit your throat."

Silence.

The one who had spoken earlier said, "You're a greedy cunt, Kunimitsu. He tried to help you."

Kunimitsu frowned. "Shut up, Yoshi. You talk too much." But he leaned forward and pushed the coppers toward Tora. "You can stay."

Tora grinned and scooped up the coins. "For free?"

"For free."

The chatty fellow clapped his hands. "Let's drink on it."

Kunimitsu got up and shuffled to an old barrel. He fumbled around in its depths and brought out an earthenware bottle. Sitting down again, he removed a rag that served as stopper, drank deeply and then passed the bottle to Tora. Tora drank, smacked his lips, and passed the wine on.

The pain in his stomach subsided, replaced by a pleasant burn.

"So, who was he?" Tora asked.

Kunimitsu looked glum. "Gave the name Tojo. I wouldn't take his word for it."

"And he's a pirate?"

Kunimitsu snorted. "Of course not. Yoshi likes to make up stories. He's just a sailor."

"He's got the tattoo," offered Yoshi.

Kunimitsu glared at him. "So what? Anybody can have a tattoo. You're gonna give my place a bad name, Yoshi."

Yoshi muttered, "Sorry."

Tora said, "So he's a sailor. I don't get it."

"It's not important. I don't think he'll be back." Kunimitsu took another gulp of wine. "What's your name and where are you from?"

"I'm Tora." No point in confusing himself with too many aliases.

"So you're a tiger?" They grinned at that. Kunimitsu sneered, "If you're so good, how come you're looking for work?"

"Got into a fight with my overseer in the capital. He messed with my woman. Had to leave kinda quick."

They stared at him. "You killed him?" asked Yoshi, his eyes large.

Tora did not answer. "How about that game?"

Kunimitsu fished out the dice and some of his money. The others brought out their coppers. Tora picked up the dice and inspected them. They seemed all right. They played fast and with total concentration. Though Tora watched carefully, he did not see anyone cheating. He won a little and lost a little, and after some time had passed with grunts and moans from the others, he asked, "Who owns the ships here?"

Kunimitsu counted his money. "Watamaro owns most of them in Kawajiri and Kanzaki, and on some of the islands in the Inland Sea. Why?"

"I need a job. I hear the pay is very good on some ships."

Silence fell. Then Yoshi said, "You're not a sailor. It's dangerous work. People get killed on some ships."

Tora grinned. "Maybe, but if the reward is big enough, I'll risk it."

They stared at him. Then Kunimitsu sighed and put the dice away. "It's getting late." he said. "You can stay the night because I promised, but if you want to stay alive, don't meddle in other people's business."

The party broke up quickly after that. When the others had left, Kunimitsu looked at Tora. "Who told you about pirates?"

"Oh, come on. All a man has to do is to watch and listen. Someone said this was the place to get in touch with them."

Kunimitsu shook his head. "You must be mad. Let me show you where you can sleep."

Carrying an oil lamp, he led the way to a room on the ground level. Unlike the open areas of the hostel, this had wooden walls and a wooden door out to the back of the building. Tora was flattered. "Thanks, Kunimitsu. This is nice."

Kunimitsu dragged in a roll of bedding. "Well, get some rest. If you haven't changed your mind in the morning, I'll ask around."

Tora slapped his shoulder. "Thanks, brother."

It had been a long day, and Tora was tired. He checked the two doors and found that he could bar them. Then he unrolled the bedding, kicked off his shoes and lay down. He kept his clothes on and his hand around the grip of his sword and was asleep in an instant.

Sometime in the night, he became aware of a scratching noise. Rats, he thought, but there was something too persistent about it. He stayed very still and listened. The scratching was accompanied by hissing and seemed to come from the door to the outside. Getting up silently, Tora tip-toed to the door and put his ear against it. Yes, someone was outside, scratching and whispering. He considered, gripping his sword. Then he eased the bar back slowly. The scratching continued, and Tora opened the door a crack.

It was dark, but there was a full moon. Outside his door crouched a creature. Pushing the sword through the opening, Tora asked, "What do you want?"

The creature popped up, and in the moonlight, Tora saw the horrible head of a demon. He slammed the door shut, rammed the bar across, and recited the spell against evil spirits.

After a while, he heard steps receding and crept back to his bedding. It was a long time before he dozed off again, and then he dreamed. He was a pirate and they were attacking a ship. On the ship was a beautiful lady. She screamed when she saw him, but he did not care. He was

about to kill her, when he saw that she was
Hanae and lowered his sword.

18

Melons and Courtesans

Akitada's worries increased during the day. There had been no progress. Tora was in Kawajiri looking for pirates. Neither of them had a full understanding how these men operated. They were the highway robbers of the sea and said to be far more cruel and murderous. And he had already lost Sadenari. He reminded himself that Tora was not Sadenari. Tora knew how to fight and he was shrewd about the underworld.

In the afternoon, he returned to the prefecture. Munata was there, but the governor was still absent.

Munata still looked very distraught and nervous. "I've done everything I could," he assured Akitada, "but His Excellency is a proud man. Besides, I had to inform him of his son's departure. I don't think he will come to Naniwa until Yoshiyo is found. Surely you can understand a father's feelings?"

"No. Enlighten me," snapped Akitada. "I would have thought that an imperial order takes precedence over the vagaries of adult sons."

Munata twisted his hands. "An only son. Allow me to explain, sir. His Excellency has had many tragedies in his life. He lost four sons in their childhood. Only Yoshiyo, his heir, survived. If I may explain: the boy was always a dreamer, but he did well at the university, and his father had high hopes for him in government service. Alas, Yoshiyo wished to become a monk. His Excellency was aghast, as you may imagine, and called him home. Since then, they've had a great quarrel. Yoshiyo made some wild threats. His Excellency was afraid of pushing his son too far and let him come to stay with me. Now Yoshiyo has run away, and we don't know where he is. You can see how worried we all are."

Akitada frowned. It seemed that every time he tried to force compliance from the men involved in the piracy matter, they came up with some convincing excuse why they could not obey. He said, "I am required to report to the Minister of the Right, and I suggest you remind the governor of this. He must learn to handle his family problems without ignoring his duty."

"I regret, sir, that the governor has departed to look for his son. I have no way of contacting him."

Akitada just looked at the prefect.

Munata swallowed and added, "My clerks are gathering information about pirate activity and possible local connections, and I have informed the local police to give you every assistance. Besides, I can offer you my own men, in case you should meet with armed resistance. The prefectural guard numbers twenty-five trained men, and I have personal retainers who can raise another two-hundred soldiers. They are at your command."

The offer was unexpected and extremely generous. Akitada was mollified. Two-hundred armed men was a small army. "Thank you. I shall avail myself of your offer if the need arises, but on the whole I'd like to avoid bloodshed. It always falls heaviest on the innocent."

The prefect bowed.

"Send a clerk with the paperwork to the government hostel. I'm staying there."

Munata bowed again.

Akitada had to be satisfied with partial success and decided to speak to the professor again. He was still puzzled by the man's interest in the dead courtesan.

The professor's wife, looking pale and worn and dispensing with any effort to hide behind a fan, told him that her husband was down by the river.

A breeze had sprung up, and as Akitada strode down toward the little inlet of the ducks, it seized a crimson maple and scattered its leaves before him like a shower of blood. He shuddered, and an irrational fear gripped him. Surely, his strange moods were due to his recent loss. Seimei gone, leaving a great void, and before him his small son Yori. And Tora was even now walking into the same danger that had swallowed the unfortunate youth Sadenari. Some days he felt that they were all being tossed about as helplessly as the leaves.

He found Otomo in an odd posture of despair. He sat on the ground, hunched over, his elbows propped on his knees and his face in his hands. When Akitada cleared his throat, he came upright and then rose awkwardly to his feet. "Your Excellency," he said, his voice thick. "I didn't know you had returned."

There were tears on the old man's face. Embarrassed, Akitada said, "I didn't mean to intrude. We can talk later."

The professor shook his head with a sad smile. "No, no. I'm glad you came. It's too beautiful here to have sad thoughts. They say, you cannot stop the birds of sorrow, but you can prevent them from building nests in your hair." He chuckled weakly.

Akitada looked away from Otomo's reddened eyes and at the river, gilded by the setting sun. The ducks bobbed on the water of the cove, and pines grew close and dipped their branches into the stream. On the opposite shore, the trees wore their autumn colors: shades of green and gold, copper and flame against the fading blue of the sky, more exquisite than the many-layered sleeves of court ladies at an imperial progress. He wondered what troubled Otomo but dared not probe his grief.

He said instead, "You're to be envied for this place. It is indeed like a small corner of paradise. But since you don't mind, I do have a question.

When I called on the prefect, I met the governor's son. I think you mentioned that he was your pupil at one time?"

Otomo nodded. "Toshiyo? Yes, I taught him. A very bright boy, and a nice one. I had no need to lie to his father. I hear he did very well at the university."

"I'm sure he's a credit to you, but Munata seems to think the young man is about to do harm to himself or to someone else. What do you think? Is he the type?"

Otomo stared at him. His lips worked, but he said nothing for a moment. Then he shook his head. "Oh, dear! That doesn't sound at all like Toshiyo. What can have happened? He was always a happy boy when I knew him. Perhaps Munata exaggerates?"

"Perhaps. I hoped you could throw some light on it."

Otomo turned away to look out over the water. His voice sounded strained. "I wish I could. I'm fond of him. It's true that Yoshiyo was always a very sensitive child. Sometimes I think he has too soft a heart for someone of his birth. Young people are so easily hurt." He sighed deeply, and murmured, "And we are helpless to protect them."

"So you think the young man has committed some offense?"

Otomo's head came up. "Oh, no, I don't believe that. I was speaking in general terms only."

His comments had lacked the detachment of someone speaking in general terms, and he seemed near tears again. Akitada decided to let it go and changed the subject. They chatted about the ducks and fishermen, about the tastiest fish found locally and how to prepare them, but the professor's mind seemed to be on something else.

On an impulse, Akitada said, "I find I have a little time on my hands, and it occurs to me that I might spend it looking into your mystery of the Korean girls. If you like, we could go to Eguchi tomorrow and ask a few questions. I've been feeling guilty about that poor young girl with the amulet."

Otomo gasped, then he shook his head violently. "Oh, no. No, that isn't at all necessary. It was a mere whim of mine. I shouldn't have troubled you. You were quite right. It was all my imagination. I would not dream of troubling you."

"Nonsense," said Akitada, astonished by this sudden about-face. "I may pick up some information about piracy while we're there."

Otomo became more agitated. Wringing his hands, he said, "Better not, sir. You never know what trouble may ensue. Please do not pursue this matter."

"Why not? What has happened to change your mind?" Akitada was becoming irritated.

"Nothing. Nothing at all. I'm just . . . this is all becoming too much . . . please excuse me." He turned away, his shoulders shaking.

Akitada said nothing for a while. When Otomo did not seem to gain control again, he spoke more gently. "Well, never mind. We can talk about it tomorrow. I'm a little tired and will say 'Good night' for now."

Back at the hostel, he lay awake for a long time wondering about the puzzling behavior of the people he had dealt with that day. The most perplexing had been the professor. Something must have happened to change his mind and upset him to such a degree. He had decided not to give him the amulet just yet.

And what had the governor's son done to send the father after him in such a rush? Or was the son merely a pretext, and Oga was in the capital, busily causing trouble for Akitada?

He finally fell asleep and slept well.

When he returned to the Otomos the next morning, dressed for the trip to Eguchi, the professor's wife received him. Her eyes were reddened and her hands shook as she apologized for Otomo's absence, saying, "My husband is distressed that he cannot see you today. He became quite ill last night and keeps to his bed."

"I'm sorry to hear it," said Akitada. "Is it serious? Should I go for a doctor? Please tell me how I can be useful."

She bowed. "You're very kind, sir, but it is merely some trouble with his belly. Something he ate, he says. He took a laxative." She blushed. "I hope Your Excellency is not inconvenienced?"

Akitada looked at her. She seemed more upset than her words suggested. "Not at all. I trust your husband will soon be better. Please tell him that my business will take me out of town, but I should be back tonight or tomorrow."

Akitada did not believe that the professor suffered from an upset stomach. Most likely, he wanted to avoid going to Eguchi with him. This sudden change of mind was extremely irritating, and Akitada thought he deserved a dose of laxatives.

He returned to the harbor and purchased passage on one of the regular boats between the river towns. The weather was still clear, but there was a new chill in the air, and the cries of flying geese overhead told of the coming cold season. Akitada was glad that the oppressive heat of the last weeks had gone. The cool air seemed to give him new energy.

Even at this relatively early hour, Eguchi's main street was already busy. Akitada tried in vain to suppress his distaste for this particular crowd. Slatternly older women swept before the doors of the brothels, while the younger inhabitants emerged to trip off to the temple up the street. The religious fervor of females in this profession was legendary. They were superstitious, worshipped phallic gods, prayed to the Buddha to cleanse them of their sins and send them wealthy patrons, and lived forever in the hope of miracles. The wine shops were mostly still closed, but a few drunks still lay around in doorways, snoring or eyeing the day blearily. Food vendors did a good business, shouting out their dumplings and noodles and greeting the passing harlots with obscene comments.

Somehow all this did not match up with his image of the young, beautiful, and very dead girl. Shaking his head, he turned his steps toward the bamboo grove and the shack of Furuda and Harima.

He heard the clucking of chickens before he got to it, and when he emerged from the bamboo thicket, he saw that there were many more fowl than last time. The garden, too, had doubled in size. A new section was freshly dug, and already some young plants were growing in rows.

"Harima," he called out, and she came to the door of the shack. Her face broke into a smile, quickly hidden behind a hand as she came to greet him. He admired again that inimitably graceful, swaying walk of the great courtesan. "I came for a little visit," he greeted her.

She bowed deeply. "Welcome, my Lord. Oh, how I wish Furuda were here! He's delivering melons and vegetables in town. Oh, sir, you were so right. We are doing a lot of business with our garden. Did you see the new garden with the little cabbages and radishes and turnips? Please come sit under the tree. I'll fetch a cushion, and if you'll stay a little while, Furuda may return."

Akitada laughed. His heart warmed to this old couple all over again. "I'm very happy to hear you're both well. By chance, might there be a melon left?"

"For you, of course. Oh, sir, we owe it all to you." Her eyes shone and she forgot to cover her mouth as she smiled at him. "A moment, sir." Hurrying back to the shack, she returned with a cushion for him and went to cut a melon.

Akitada sat under the tree, watched the chickens scurry out of her way, noted that the shack had a new roof and a door, brushed aside a late bee, and felt cheerful.

The melon was as sweet as last time. He asked her to share it with him, but she shook her head. "It would not be seemly. May I offer you something else? We have no wine here, I'm afraid. Furuda has sworn off it. But I could run to town and be back very shortly."

He could not imagine making someone of her age run such an errand for him. She was in her seventies, surely, and while she was still slender and moved with great grace, she also moved slowly. He thought of Seimei and how painful had been his final years because of the many chores he had insisted on performing to the end. Tears rose to his eyes. "Thank you," he said, "but I don't drink wine this early and I don't want you to deprive me of your charming company."

She smiled at him with her eyes and acknowledged the compliment with a little bow, still so practiced that he felt subtly flattered. by her attention. She had moved close to him to serve him bites of melon. It was ridiculous to feel attracted to a woman old enough to be his mother, or even grandmother, but so it was.

Putting his mind firmly to the purpose of his visit, he said, "You're very kind, Harima. That's why I came to ask you a favor."

"If it is in my power, sir, I shall do it."

"I need some information. Your past life has given you knowledge about the way the local brothels are run."

She flushed and turned her head away. "It has been a very long time since I was a part of that, but please ask your questions," she said.

Inwardly cursing his blunt language, he said, "The day before I came here the first time, a young girl had drowned in the river. Do you remember?"

She nodded, her face sad. "Yes. She was very young. It can be a difficult life for the young ones. I grieved to hear of it."

She seemed calm, but he noticed her hands, folded now, pressing against her waist. Even work-roughened and twisted by age, they were still graceful and expressive. The gesture suggested grief, pain, and pity for the dead girl.

"I was told that she was not Japanese, that she had been brought here from Koryo," he said.

"That must be a false rumor, sir. There are no foreign girls in Eguchi. Unless . . ." She paused, frowning.

"Unless what?"

"We have many sailors here. One of them may have brought a woman from that far place, but I never heard about it."

"The rumor also maintained that not just the one, but a number of young women— mere children—had been taken from Koryo and sold into the trade here because there was a special demand for them."

Now her eyes widened in alarm. "Oh, no. That would be a very cruel thing to do."

"Yes. But you must know that there are men who find children, both boys and girls, attractive in that way. The dead girl I saw looked as young as thirteen."

She shook her head. "I have known of such men, but not recently. This particular girl was young, but not quite so young. And she was one of our people."

This was news! Akitada took the amulet from his sash. "She was wearing this around her neck when she was found. It's Korean workmanship."

She looked at it and shook her head. "I don't know where she got this, but she was not from Koryo."

"Then you knew her? Or knew of her?"

She said simply, "I was a *choja* once. Some of the girls still visit me sometimes to ask my advice. They tell me about their hopes and fears and about their hardships and jealousies. She was never here, but several others talked about her." She sighed. "You must understand that women compete with each other, and since they pin all of their hopes on finding a generous client who will buy them out, they often blame each other when they fail."

That raised an interesting point. "Then do you think she was driven to commit suicide, or . . . could she have been murdered by a rival?"

Spreading her expressive hands, she said, "I don't know how she died, and neither do my young friends. There's gossip, of course, but I don't want to spread lies. I've found that you cannot always believe what these young women say." She smiled a little sadly.

"Nevertheless, will you trust me?"

She hesitated, then nodded. "The dead girl was a *shinju*, that is, she was still in training. Her name was Akogi. She lived in the Hananoya, the House of Blossoms. The Hananoya is the biggest of the Eguchi houses." She twisted her hands in her lap. "It's an unhappy house, I think, and yes, there was jealousy there, but I don't think it led to murder. More likely, she found her life too hard. It cannot have been a happy one for her. The others thought she had gone into the river herself."

And that proved once and for all that Professor Otomo, that nice and caring man, had lied to him. Had lied to him repeatedly with his stories about the kidnapped and possibly murdered Korean girls. The only conceivable reason he could have had for such an elaborate fabrication was to send him away from Naniwa and from his investigation into piracy. It made perfect sense. First they had distracted him with the disappearance of Sadenari, then they had tried to send him on a wild goose chase after kidnapped Korean girls, and finally, when all that had not worked, they had attacked his family in the capital.

But there remained the fact of the dead girl. Akitada was puzzled by what Harima had said. It did not add up. He said, "If she was still in training, why were the other girls jealous of her?"

"Sometimes the owner of a house shows favor to a particular girl and allows her privileges others don't enjoy. Akogi was fourteen or fifteen and being groomed for a special presentation."

"A presentation?"

Harima's lips quirked a little at Akitada's puzzlement. "Some man pays a great deal of money to be the first one. There's a kind of celebration with special gowns and musical entertainments."

Akitada shuddered. He was repelled by the whole flesh trade that tempted men with foolish and expensive perversions. And surely the desire to initiate a mere child was a perversion of the sexual act. Fourteen or fifteen! The child had no choice in the matter, and that made it repulsive.

They sat in silence for a while. Chickens clucked, the wind rustled in the bamboo, and the honey-sweet smell of the melon slices lingered in the air. Harima's head was bent, her hands clenched tightly. It occurred to him that she, too, had once been used in the same way. It was his belief that most of the women in the trade became corrupted by it. Their only aim was to enrich themselves and thus triumph over their past servitude. Harima had not followed that path. He respected her for it.

Furuda returned while he was searching for words to express his regard and sympathy to her. Akitada saw her face light up and the joy in Furuda's when their eyes met, and felt a pang of envy. His own marriage was again stable, and he was very fond of Tamako, but neither of them was demonstrative. And neither was so completely absorbed by the other. He had his work, and Tamako had a child and her household to tend. These two people had only each other.

Furuda slipped off the empty willow basket he had carried slung over his shoulders, and came to greet Akitada with the same warmth Harima had shown him.

"What a happy day, Your Honor," he said, bowing several times. "I've been worrying how to let you know that you've given us back our lives. We're doing very well now, Harima and I, and it's all thanks to your lordship." With a wide smile, he gestured to the garden and to his empty willow basket. I get more orders than I can fill. Everything I took this morning is sold and they are begging for more." He dug a handful of coins from his heavy sleeve, showed them to Akitada and then passed them to Harima, who cried out with pleasure.

"Oh, Furuda, that will pay for firewood this winter. How wonderful!" She hurried off with their wealth.

Furuda looked after her fondly and said, "She handles the money. I've got no head for it. I'd waste it on useless things. How smart she is! Firewood, of course. We nearly froze to death last winter." He shook his head in wonder at Harima's management of their affairs.

Akitada's eyes moistened. It took so very little to make these two happy: a bit of simple food and some warmth during the coldest part of the year. He said, "Husband and wife share the labors. It is right that it should be so. You work very hard at growing food and selling it."

Furuda shook his head. "She won't marry me. No wonder. I'm nothing and she is a *choja*. It's truly a miracle she stays with me. I wake up sometimes at night and fear that she is gone. That's a terrible feeling."

Such confidences were beginning to make Akitada uncomfortable. To change the subject, he asked to see the new garden. Furuda led him eagerly to the new section, pointing out the different kinds of cabbage plants striving toward the sun, all looking healthy.

Squinting at the sky, he said happily, "The weather is changing. We're getting rain. I won't have to carry the water up from the river tomorrow."

Akitada had not noticed the change in the light. The sun had withdrawn behind clouds that were moving in rapidly. The breeze had strengthened and turned colder. It would mean an uncomfortable day for him, but he said nothing. Instead, he admired eggplants, deep purple among the leaves, and lengthening cucumbers, and the sweet potatoes and turnips in the mature part of the garden. Their season would soon be over, and Furuda would only have the cabbages left. Perhaps the two old people would manage to get through the winter, but it seemed doubtful. "What will you do, when the snows come?" he asked.

"I'll find another job. If the restaurants don't need me, perhaps one of the great houses could use some help. I'm not proud. I'll clean their privies. It will be good for my garden." He stopped and looked abashed. "I beg your pardon for mentioning such a dirty thing."

Akitada laughed. "I suppose even great houses use their privies. Speaking of great houses, do you happen to know anything about the River Mansion?"

"Oh, yes. That's the very large house on the river." He pointed toward the east. "Not a chance there for me. The majordomo doesn't like local help. They bring all their servants from the capital."

"Oh? Who owns it?"

"I'm not sure. They say it belongs to the great chancellor, but he never comes here. He has a splendid palace in Uji."

"Yes, but I'm told someone lives there, a woman perhaps, and that there are parties with many guests."

Furuda nodded. "Sometimes there are parties. But the guests come from the capital in boats. One time the place where I worked was asked to send food. I was one of the waiters who carried all the dishes. Grilled sea bream in black sauce, pickled vegetables, grilled eels, pike wrapped in persimmon leaves, even blowfish. A huge feast. That was when I met the majordomo. They took everything from us at the gate and sent us back."

"Very odd. What about the local brothels? Do they send courtesans?"

"Harima would know more, but yes, I think sometimes they send for the *choja* and perhaps others."

Akitada turned to look at the pitiful hut. The vines that covered it still bore a few flowers, but soon they would die. It did not offer much protection against winter storms, yet Harima had found more peace and protection here than she had had in her past life of luxury.

For him there was no peace, at least not yet. He must return to Naniwa and finish his assignment. Now that he knew Otomo was a part of the conspiracy, he would force the truth out of him. It was time he and Tora got home to his family.

He glanced up at the sky. The clouds were still gathering and moving quickly eastward. He should hurry back to Naniwa. Tora would report either today or tomorrow. But he was strangely reluctant to leave Eguchi. Whatever had happened to the girl Akogi, he had come this far, and he would make one more call before putting her from his mind

19

The Pirate Ship

Hanae would not stop screaming, and Tora jerked into partial wakefulness: he lay on strange and uncomfortable bedding and the screaming continued.

Opening his eyes on darkness, he made out the chinks of a door. The smell and touch of his rough bedding registered. He was in the Hostel of the Flying Cranes, and there was a real woman screaming outside his door.

He cursed and scrambled up. At the door, he remembered the demon and hesitated with his hand on the bar, but another blood-curdling scream overcame his fear. He lifted the bar, flung the door open, and looked out at the moonlit night.

The screams came from the shack near the back fence. He could just make out a shadowy figure struggling with a smaller one. The smaller one was a woman. Some brute trying to rape her? With a shout Tora rushed to the rescue.

The man was big. He let go of the female, who scurried away, and turned to Tora with a welcoming smile. The smile was unexpected, and Tora almost stopped, but it was already too late. Dark figures rose up beside him, behind him, surrounding him as if they had sprung from the earth. His last thought was that he had walked into a whole gathering of demons. A short, sharp pain to the back of his head wiped out any other reflections.

He came half-awake to swaying and bobbing motions. He was wet, and there were strange noises, scraping of wood, splashing of water, rhythmic breathing. The back of his head hurt abominably, and he turned it a little. Nausea rose. He retched, then vomited and vomited again. This woke him completely. Still retching, he tried to sit up and failed because he was trussed up tightly, his feet tied together and his arms caught under loops of rope that passed around his chest. Above him was a dark and hazy sky. It was dawn or dusk— he did not know which— and when he moved his sore head a little, he made out the backs of four men rowing. They were in a boat, and all around was gray mist and black water.

It made no sense.

The boat hit a larger wave, rose up and plunged back down, and Tora's head bounced against the bottom of the boat with such force that he passed out again.

He came round next because he was being manhandled into an upright position. He heard grunts and curses and felt rough hands on his body. Someone above him shouted, "Hurry up, you lazy bastards."

He was still tied up but instinctively kicked out against the men who had hold of him. There were more curses and a ringing slap to his head that made him see stars where there should not have been any, and then the bonds tightened around his chest, the hands fell away, and he rose up into the air, pulled by a rope attached to his back. It was daylight. As he swung, he saw first the side of a ship and then the open water and men in a boat below. And when he looked up, there were, against the pale sky, the outlines of dark heads peering down at him. Like a pendulum, he swung and rose, sometimes out over the angry waves below him, sometimes painfully against the rough timbers of the ship's bow.

They dragged him over the side and let him drop. He vomited again and was kicked in the chest. Some time passed in a haze of misery. His face was raw from scraping against the ship, his head hurt like blazes, and he was dizzy. The kick to his chest might have broken a rib, he thought. There was an excruciating stab of pain whenever the ship rolled or he took a deep breath.

Closing his eyes, he concentrated on taking shallow breaths and waited, feeling wretched. And always, there was the question: Why was he here? What did they want with him?

Ship's noises. Men running about, shouting. Things like "Pull hard," "Make fast," "Heave". Bare legs and feet scampered past his bleary eyes. He heard rattling, creaking, heavy breath-

ing, curses, and a wet flapping sound. The
wooden boards he lay on shifted, rose, and fell,
and the rolling of the ship made him sick again.

After several more bouts of vomiting, he found
that the rushing about had stopped. He turned
his head to look. He was lying amidships near
the railing. Across from him was a roofed cabin,
and above two huge dark sails rose into the blue
sky. Ropes fastened these to the front, back, and
sides of the ship. The flapping sound came from
these sails. Up ahead, four men stood in line,
pushing long oars. As he looked at them, one
began a rhythmic chant, hai, hai, hai, hai, with
every stroke of the long oar. The others joined in
one by one. The ship moved less sluggishly and
with more purpose.

They were on their way. The ship was taking
him away from land, from help, from any chance
of being rescued or escaping. Already, the huge
sails were filling as they caught a breeze.

He struggled into a more upright position and
twisted his body to look back. A fierce pain in his
side made him gasp and close his eyes. When
the pain ebbed a little, he peered through the railing. He was not in a good place for seeing the
land, and he dared not twist any more. As it was,
he saw a sliver of the coast with some houses,
and a ship or two. It was not enough to know
where he was, but he guessed the houses belonged to Kawajiri or a neighboring village.

He had been knocked out and abducted by the
men on this ship. If there was any mercy in his
situation, it was the fact that they were much too
busy to bother with him. But this was a temporary

relief. In the moments of the ship's departure, as the men had been running about on deck, he had seen a writhing dragon tattooed on one of the sturdy thighs.

It seemed a lot of trouble to go to for revenge.

Tora was reasonably sure he was on board a pirate ship. Dragon Tattoo would see to it that he could not talk himself out of his present dilemma by offering to become a pirate. He searched his mind for the man's name. Toji? No, Tojo. At least that was the name the bastard had given at the hostel.

Tora scooted his bound body slowly and painfully against the side of the ship and leaned against the boards.

Nausea returned and dizziness joined it. Not seasickness, he thought, but the knock on his head. The back of his skull hurt badly enough to signal a crack. And there was blood, too. He could smell it. It had soaked into the back of shirt and jacket and stiffened. The rest of him was wet. They must have dragged him through water to get him into the boat.

They had taken his sword. No surprise there, but he had liked that weapon. It was short, but it had fit his hand perfectly, and its weight had been light enough for some clever wrist work. He mourned his sword for a while, breathed carefully, and watched the sailors at their work. Most seemed his own age, with some youngsters mixed in. Altogether, he counted eighteen men and boys, plus the helmsman. There might be more in the cabin and below deck, but he doubted it. The ship was quite large and had two masts with huge square sails. The helmsman at the rudder, issuing orders was probably the captain.

They were leaving the port of Kawajiri and heading out into the Bay of Naniwa—he assumed that was where they were—and this appeared to be tricky work. Where were they headed? The farther they got from the coast, the less likely it was that he could escape. He strained against his bonds. In vain. It was already too late. If and when they made landfall and he escaped, it would take him many days to return to Naniwa.

What would his master do? Would he worry and put himself in danger to find him? Of course, he would.

Bitter recriminations occupied him next: How could he have been so careless? That screaming female had been a decoy to lure him out of his room, and he had fallen for it like a mere novice. But why all this effort? It did not make sense that Dragon Tattoo would carry his revenge this far and get his shipmates to help him. Why not just beat him up or kill him behind the hostel?

He found no answer and turned his mind to how they had worked it. Kunimitsu must have sold him out. Maybe Kunimitsu had offered him up to Dragon Tattoo as an apology for having cheated him at dice. They had all been scared enough of the bastard. And most likely they had been scared because they had known that Dragon Tattoo was one of the pirates, and his companions would return with him to take care of Kunimitsu and his buddies. Add that they could not call on the police to protect them because of the gambling. It was likely that Kunimitsu had had dealings with pirates before.

At this point Tora dozed off.

He woke to a sudden, sharp pain to his injured chest and roared. Dragon Tattoo loomed above him, his foot still in the air. He grinned malevolently. The bastard had kicked him. Tora sucked in his breath and steeled himself for more. The pirate's grin was spoiled by a fresh gap in his front teeth. Tora took some satisfaction from that.

But no other blows fell.

"What the hell did you do to me?" Tora croaked.

"It's not what I did, scum. It's what I'm going do," said Dragon Tattoo, baring his missing teeth again. "You'll be talking to my chief, and when he's done with you, you die."

"Why? What's going on? And where are we going?"

"None of your business." Dragon Tattoo spat in Tora's face and walked away.

Rubbing the spittle off on his shoulder, Tora considered. The chief was not the captain and did not appear to be on the ship. So he was being taken to some pirate stronghold or hideout. Perhaps there was still some hope of talking himself out of this fix. Dragon Tattoo's threat he put from his mind. There was time to deal with him later. He closed his eyes again.

He woke with a terrible thirst. This time, he had lost all sense of time. The sun was high, and he was baking like a fish on a griddle. At the corner of the cabin, four pirates were throwing dice.

Evidently, gambling was their main occupation when they weren't asleep or working.

He croaked, "How about some water?"

They turned their heads and stared at him. One of them muttered something. They guffawed and went back to their game.

"Oh, come on! Just a drink of water. I'm burning up here."

One of them got up, walked over to the side of the ship and dropped a pail on a rope into the sea. Bringing it back up, he carried it to Tora and flung the contents over him. "Wet enough for you, spy?" he asked.

The others guffawed some more.

The water cooled Tora's burning skin for a moment, but the little that got into his parched mouth made his thirst worse, and his skin began to itch.

Spy?

Where did they get the idea he was a spy? He thought back and could not remember saying or doing anything that would have given his purpose away.

Nothing much happened the rest of the day. They ignored him. His thoughts went to Seimei and he grieved. Seimei would be disappointed in him, but he would tell him, "Don't be afraid to mend your faults." How did you mend this fault?

He tried to beg for water one more time when a different sailor walked past and got another kick for his troubles. In the afternoon, clouds moved in, and a sharp wind sprang up. It got cold very quickly. The big sails flapped and the masts creaked. Tora shivered.

Within an hour or so, the sky had turned dark, lightning tore across it, and the wind buffeted the sails, and caused turbulent waves. The ship plunged and rose, plunged and rose. Thunder rolled.

The pirates did not seem too concerned, and Tora decided that they knew what they were doing. He thought about rain. Surely there would be rain. Blessed rain. He was utterly parched and miserable. But the rain held off, and the wind grew stronger. The day turned into a long night.

When the rolling of the ship increased, Tora pushed himself against the railing and held on with the fingers of one hand. The movement and strain hurt his damaged rib, so he tried to find a more comfortable position by moving his arms to ease the pressure of the rope. This proved in vain on his right side, but on the left, a knot allowed his wrist and hand enough room to twist a little. Encouraged, he continued to work at stretching and shifting the loops around his chest. It occurred to him that he might push the rope lower, toward his waist, and gain some extra room. He looked around and saw a large metal ring attached to the deck. It probably served to fasten something or other but was not in use and only a couple of feet away. Lying down, he used his legs to slide his back on top of the ring. When the ring caught against the rope that passed around his back and chest, he started pushing hard.

The heart of the storm came up fast, and all hell broke loose on the ship. The pirates rushed about; sails flapped as men moved the great horizontal beams that held the canvas spread out to lessen and deflect the force of the wind against them. It took three men to hold and move the rudder, and the ship tossed about, rolled, and rose to unimaginable heights, only to drop into precipitous depths over and over again.

Tora's work became immeasurably harder. He kept sliding and had no way of controlling this. Besides, his struggles at pushing the rope down were extremely painful, and he seemed to be making things worse. He was sweating, yet he shivered in the cold wind. Spray came over the sides. He was afraid the rope would tighten further when it got wet, and so he tried to push harder and faster. All the while, he kept an eye on the sailors and made himself as small as he could, afraid that they would stop him.

But there was little chance of that. They were busy reefing the sails and tying things down. Feet stepped on him, stumbled over him, kicked him here and there, but they paid him no other attention.

It got dark very quickly—a good thing, because they could not see what he was doing—but the darkness added to his fear. If the ship went down, he would not be able to save himself.

The rain finally came in great gusts. He let it fall into his open mouth, tried to soak it up with his skin. Blessed rain. And he finally felt the rope begin to give a little. His rib cage protested briefly and very painfully, but then the strain shifted lower, to his flat belly, and he had a little room to twist and turn his left arm.

This was still a far cry from being able to extricate it, but further painful maneuvers, including rolling back and forth on the wet deck, loosened the rope loops some more, and he freed first his upper arm and then, with a final excruciating effort, his elbow. The rest was easy, but he was by then utterly worn out from pain and effort. He lay exhausted, flexing his free hand.

The storm did not rest. Lines snapped, a sail came loose and tore, the roof of the cabin came off, piece by life-threatening piece hurling about the deck and overboard. Then one of the masts cracked and slowly leaned, tilting the ship.

Tora slid hard against the railing and held on with his free hand. The sea washed over him, and he pulled himself up to catch a breath, muttering a prayer under his breath. Only a short while ago, he would have been lost, bound hand and foot and washed over the side.

Suddenly he was not alone. One of the pirates had slid down, hit the rail beside him, and started to go over the side. Instinctively, Tora let go and grabbed the man. For a moment, their lives hung in the balance. The next roll of the ship would toss them both overboard.

But the sailor, having both arms free, caught himself and clasped the railing, then pulled them both back from the brink. They stood, staring at each other, and Tora released him. They would come now and tie him up again, he thought. All that effort and pain for nothing and he would still drown in the end.

The sailor suddenly pulled a knife, and Tora jerked away and fell. Never mind drowning, he thought, lying on the wet deck, the knife will be quicker. But the man bent to his feet, and Tora felt those bonds parting. Then he cut the rope that still held his right arm. When he was done and Tora was free, he turned away and plunged back into the driving rain where the others were using axes to cut loose the broken mast.

Tora sat against the side and held on. The storm was still fully upon them and water came from all sides. It was impossible to tell what was rain and what sea. Waves washed across the deck, and once, as the ship pitched hard, he almost tumbled over the side again.

While lightning flashed and thunder rolled, and ever larger seas swamped the ship, Tora thought of his family, and how he loved his sweet, dainty wife Hanae with every fiber of his being. She had been the one to make sacrifices to be with him and she had given him his son Yuki. He felt a fierce pride that Yuki had attacked the armed intruders. The love and the courage of that act! If he died in this storm, he would lie lost and unburied among the shells and fishes. They would mourn him for years, hoping in vain that he might return some day. He wept at the pity of this, and then he prayed to the Buddha and clutched the railing with icy fingers.

But the storm abated at last, and dawn came, and with its silver light, a shout from one of the pirates. Tora turned his head and looked around blearily. He saw an island, a mere dark silhouette against the gray of the sea and the paling sky. Beyond, vague shadows might be other islands. A gull circled overhead and gave a shrill cry, and the pirates burst into shouts and happy laughter. They had reached home.

Tora sighed. He doubted he had much to be happy about.

20

The Lady of the River Mansion

Having made up his mind to make one more attempt at solving the mystery of the girl with the amulet, Akitada walked to the Eguchi post station where he rented a horse and got directions to the River Mansion. On an impulse, he said to the groom, "Do you know anything about the lady who resides there?"

The groom eyed Akitada with an impudent grin. "The lady's choosy, but it may be your lucky day, sir."

Akitada flushed with anger but decided to let it pass. He was in a den of iniquity, and one could hardly expect either good morals or good manners from the local people. Still, whoever lived in the River Mansion clearly had a reputation.

The ride was short and pleasant, in spite of the increasing clouds. His mood improved, and he soon found himself at an elaborate blue-tiled gate decorated with golden dragons. Beyond rose trees and more blue-tiled roofs. Birds sang, and through the trees beside the road he could see the green Yodo River.

What sort of person lived in this near-paradisal state? Was it really a lustful princess who scoured the countryside for handsome young men to take into her bed? Akitada smiled. The ludicrous tale was typical of Tora. When it came to sexual exploits or scandalous behavior of the nobility, Tora was very gullible, and this story had both.

He called out, and one wing of the great gate swung open. He rode in under its elaborate roof trimmed with gilded fretwork and found himself in a large courtyard covered with white gravel. Before him stood a lovely building, a smaller version of Chancellor Michinaga's great Phoenix Hall, though it was by no means so very small, being more than twice the size of the Sugawara residence.

A servant took his horse. Another servant asked his name.

"Sugawara," said Akitada. "Special investigator for the Minister of the Right. I would like to speak to the majordomo." He would soon have some answers, he thought. A senior servant could tell him the owner's name and who was in residence, and he would also know about visits from young women belonging to the Eguchi brothels.

"We have a *betto*, sir," the servant said. "*Betto* Kakuan."

A monk?   How very proper!   "Very well, Kakuan, then."

The servant took him up the wide stairs and into an extraordinary room. The first impression was of color, movement, and ornament. The carved columns and the ceiling were painted and decorated with carvings. The dais had a backdrop of water scenes painted on sliding doors, and deep blue and green brocade cushions lay on its mirror-smooth floor. The other walls, lying in the shadows, displayed paintings on hanging scrolls. It was a noble, even a princely abode. Tora's imperial princess came to his mind again.

As he waited, he walked around, looking in astonishment at the carvings on the columns and ceiling.   These were of water creatures: fish, crabs, cranes, ducks, and gulls, while the paintings on the paper-covered doors depicted scaly fish jumping in waves, a pair of ducks swimming among reeds, *koi* splashing in a small pond, a pair of cranes grooming their feathers on the shore, and—on the center panel—a gorgeous dragon rising from a stormy sea, all serpentine contortions and writhing scales, grasping talons and snapping jaws. The paintings had been done with consummate artistry, and no doubt had cost a great deal of money. He turned to examine the hanging scrolls, when a woman's voice asked, "Do you like my little hermitage, my Lord?"

He swung around. A figure materialized from the shadows, a lady, small of stature and enveloped in stiffened silk gowns of peculiar shades of blues and greens. He took her for an apparition at first, so silently had she entered and so odd was her appearance.

A tinkling laugh acknowledged his stupefaction. She glided closer across the floor, a painted fan held to her face. Her eyes seemed unusually large, but when she stood before him, he saw she had outlined them with black paint, and the effect was misleading. He also decided that her movements were ponderous rather than ethereal, and found himself in a quandary.

He had disbelieved Tora's tale of the aging imperial princess and had doubted some of the other stories. Now he did not know how to address this female. Formalities had not been on his mind. He had come to ask questions of a majordomo or some other senior retainer and not of the owner of the mansion. More disturbing perhaps, she was alone with him. Where were her attendants?

He covered his embarrassment by making her a deep bow. "My name is Sugawara, my Lady. We are not acquainted, I'm afraid. I hope I have not intruded rudely on your seclusion?"

Again that disconcerting tinkling laugh. He thought resentfully that she was too old for it, and wondered again at the colors of her gowns, combinations never seen at court or elsewhere. Those light blues were more commonly worn by men, and here they were combined with greens. All the women he had seen had preferred to use green with rosy reds, or the deeper reds of autumn maples, or—if they were more mature ladies—browns. Then he realized that the diaphanous silks were meant to resemble water.

Of course: the River Mansion. The paintings and carvings, and even the appearance of its owner symbolized the watery realm.

She waved a hand toward the dais and its cushions. "Please, let us sit and converse. Company is welcome in my solitude."

He followed her up to the dais where she extended a hand so he could help her lower herself onto a cushion. Her hand was warm, soft, and rather fleshy and hung on to his heavily as she sat down. He realized that she must be fat under all those stiff gowns. He seated himself on the cushion next to hers and searched for a way to learn her name.

She giggled again. The eyes above the fan twinkled with amusement. "How old are you, my Lord?"

Taken aback, he said, "I'm in my thirty-fifth year, my Lady."

"Hmm. Not so young any longer. And certainly no longer brimming with vigor either."

If she was indeed an imperial princess, he could hardly object to her teasing, no matter how rude. He decided to ignore her flirtatious comments and go to the heart of the matter. "I'm investigating a death in this area, and came to ask some questions of your staff. Your servant must have misunderstood."

The painted moth eyebrows rose. "How dull you are. Here I am, in one of my most fetching costumes, and you ask to speak to my servants. Don't they teach gentlemen manners these days?"

He bowed. "My deepest apologies, my Lady. Your gracious reception has overwhelmed me."

She tittered, switched the fan to her left hand and reached out with her right to touch his eyebrow. He managed barely not to flinch away. A wave of perfume enveloped him.

"Such fierce brows. Such a fierce man," she murmured. "Fierce men have always appealed to the dragon race. Did you know that I have the blood of the dragon kings in me?" The finger traced his cheek and touched his lips.

He could not speak, did not know what to do. The thought flashed across his mind that Tora's tale had been all too true, and that this female had taken it into her mind to seduce him. Worse, if she was in fact an imperial princess, he knew of no way to refuse her without causing an offense that could cost him his career.

"You know the story of the Dragon King's daughter, don't you?" she went on, letting her finger wander down his neck, pulling playfully at his collar and stroking his Adam's apple.

He said hoarsely, "In the Lotus sutra, the Princess Otohime proved that even a woman can attain Buddhahood."

"Ah, yes. A woman may do anything she wishes, even gain Buddhahood. Do you believe that?" Her hand rested on his chest, exerting a slight pressure.

Akitada found it hard to breathe normally. "When I look at your ladyship, I find it easy to believe."

She laughed softly. "Better. But I really meant the tale about the daughter of the dragon king arising from the depths of the sea to find herself a human lover."

The hand had slipped lower, past his sash, and had come to rest on his thigh, near his groin. He knew he was flushing deeply. He was also angrily aware that he could not control his body or avoid the problem any longer. Either he submitted or he offended. He reached for her hand—a shocking liberty with any woman of his class—and raised it to his forehead before placing it back on her skirt. "Fortunate human," he said softly. "But he must have faced a terrible dilemma."

Her eyes narrowed over her fan. "How so?"

"To be offered the love of a divine creature would surely completely unman the average human male."

The frown faded. She giggled. "But her choice was not an average man," she said, leaning close again. "Are you an average man, my Lord?"

"Very average, I'm afraid. A mere lower-level official with a wife and a small daughter."

She withdrew with a little sigh. "Ah!" she said. "That is a great pity." She regarded him silently for a long moment while he cringed inwardly. "What did you want to know?"

The question was unexpected and Akitada gulped before saying, "I came for information about a young woman who drowned in the river two weeks ago. I was on my way to Naniwa on the tenth day of this month when my boat encountered the body below your mansion. The boatmen fished her out and took her to Eguchi. People there said that she was a courtesan who had committed suicide. But she did not look old enough to be in that trade, and her death was not investigated properly. I have not been able to get her out of my mind and came to see if anyone here might know her."

He paused, unable to express the depth of his feelings about the dead girl. In the end, he said only, "She was very young." The grief and anger he felt on her behalf was largely due to her youth and the fact that he was now the father of a girl. The cruel unfairness that a child should have suffered such a fate and encountered death before tasting much of life twisted his heart. He looked at this woman of high rank who sat there in her eccentric finery and resented her. The dead girl had not been privileged and protected; she had been bartered off to be used by men who felt no pity, men who were of his own class and of this woman's.

He had her whole attention now. She was either shocked or frightened and had lowered her fan. Yes, he thought with satisfaction, she is no longer young. The smooth round face with its tiny painted mouth was covered thickly with white paste, but around the jaw line, the flesh sagged in an unattractive way, and two deep lines ran from the nostrils to the corners of her mouth. The contrast between her and the beautiful dead child was poignant.

She saw him staring and raised her fan quickly. "Wh-what did she look like?" she asked.

Akitada felt a small thrill of triumph. So he had been right. Something had happened here, and she was aware of it, perhaps had even known the girl personally. "In Eguchi, they told me her name was Akogi," he said, "and that she was in training in one of the houses but had not started working yet. As I said, she was very young, fifteen years at most. She was tall and already well developed, with very long, thick hair. Her face was exceedingly beautiful." He searched his memory for other words to describe her. "It was oval, but soft like a child's. Enchanting. There was very little make-up, but the water may have washed that off. She wore only a very thin silk undergown." He remembered and took the amulet from his sash. "And this was tied around her neck."

She took the amulet, glanced at it, and gave it back. "Poor child," she murmured, looking away. "Poor child." For a moment every part of her figure seemed to sag.

"You've recognized it? You know this girl?"

Her eyes returned to his. She said angrily, "Surely you joke, sir. I do not know such women. In any case, I have answered your questions. You may leave."

Akitada could only blame himself. Even given his ignorance of her identity, he should have realized that she belonged to a family where matters such as prostitution were never mentioned in the women's quarters. He bowed deeply. "Forgive me. There was a chance that this child was not in the trade. She looked as if she might have belonged to a good family. The amulet suggested as much. I merely mentioned what I was told in town."

Her manner softened somewhat. "She did not belong here," she said. "All of our women are accounted for. You must ask your questions elsewhere."

Akitada bowed again and rose. "Please forgive the intrusion. I have been honored beyond my deserts."

"Well," she said, looking up at him, "if you like, you may return tonight. I am giving a small entertainment for friends from the capital."

It was a gesture of forgiveness that Akitada could not refuse. He bowed again and murmured, "The sun shines on me again. I am a fortunate man."

Halfway to the great doors, he turned to bow again, but the dais was empty. He thought he heard the faint sound of a titter as a door closed somewhere.

Outside, his embarrassment turned to anger. She had toyed with him, and he would not have it.

The servant who had taken him into the reception hall approached eagerly. "Shall I have your horse brought, my Lord?"

"Not yet. I asked to speak to your *betto*. I still wish to do so."

The man's face fell. "But my lady received you herself."

Akitada glared at him. "Do not argue with me. Get him."

The servant bowed and ran. A moment later, he returned accompanied by a tall, handsome man with a shaven head who was dressed a fine green silk robe. He bowed and said, "I am Kakuan. How may I be of service?"

A monk in layman's clothing? Akitada eyed him with interest. Such a one might well serve as a lover. He spoke well and was, no doubt, educated. Taking care with his phrasing, Akitada said, "I confess that I came here in part to see the architecture of this residence. Tell me, is this building not very much in the style of the great chancellor's Phoenix Hall?"

Kakuan smiled. "It is indeed, my Lord. You have a sharp eye. Lord Michinaga had the River Mansion built for my mistress when my lady ended her service at the shrine."

"Beautiful. Which shrine was that?"

"Hakozaki-no-miya. The River Mansion is much larger and more elegant than the shrine, of course. It was a very generous gift."

Hakozaki-no-miya was of minor importance. So the lady was no imperial princess, and probably not even an acknowledged daughter of the great chancellor. Perhaps she was a lesser member of the clan, or even the child of a favorite. In any case, he now knew where he could learn her identity. Perhaps the rest of his questions would be answered tonight.

He thanked the monk-*betto* and took his leave quickly.

21

The Shared Cup

The unwelcome invitation to the River Mansion meant that Akitada had to spend the night in Eguchi. It troubled him because he had arranged to meet with Tora in Naniwa. But there was no getting out of it. The last thing he needed was giving offence to a relative of the great chancellor.

He went again to the small monastery and asked to see the abbot. After begging shelter for the night, he inquired about the mistress of the River Mansion.

The abbot's face lengthened. He shook his head. "Ah, that. I know nothing." His tone and expression were disapproving. "They don't attend our services. I sent a monk with an invitation when the lady first arrived, but he was turned away rudely. Thinking that some mistake had been made, I went myself." He fell silent, shaking his head again.

Akitada waited, but the abbot clearly did not want to talk about the experience. He finally said, "I've been invited to an entertainment there tonight and had to accept. It would help me if I knew more about my hostess. I was told she once served as a shrine virgin at Hakozaki-no-miya."

The abbot regarded him silently a moment longer, then asked, "Is this in any way connected with the poor young woman who drowned? The one both you and your young clerk asked me about?"

Akitada was surprised, though he should not have been. Sadenari was not easily deterred from an interest. He said, "I didn't know Sadenari had spoken to you. In fact, he disappeared not long after we stayed here, but I don't think that had anything to do with the dead child. When did you speak with him?"

The abbot thought. "About a week ago, I think. A few days after you both stayed here. He did not stay. Frankly, I thought he planned to spend the night in town."

Akitada should have been glad to have some word of the tiresome youth, but he was not reassured. He was angry. "You may be right," he said, then asked, "He seemed quite well?"

"Oh, yes."

A brief silence fell, then Akitada suppressed his anger and returned to his main concern. "Perhaps I can learn something about the poor young girl's fate at the River Mansion tonight."

The abbot expressed disapproval. "It is best to let such things go."

Akitada looked at the old man. His shaven skull gleamed slightly in the flickering candle light that also threw deep shadows across his face. Many religious men practiced detachment from human desires and fears all their lives. Another death would mean little to them, perhaps all the less for having been the death of a girl who was a courtesan. He, on the other hand, was deeply shaken by death. Yori's death had nearly destroyed him. And now he had also suffered the loss of Seimei. Little wonder that he was so deeply moved by the death of the beautiful child. And there was danger. "If she was murdered, the murderer may kill again," he pointed out.

The abbot sighed. "The noble lady is related to the former chancellor Fujiwara Michinaga. She came here about three years ago. I have a chronicle somewhere." He got up and rummaged among his books. Selecting one, he brought it back to the light, unrolled it, and ran a finger along the entries. "Shrine virgins. Hmm. Yes. Fujiwara Kazuko, daughter of Fujiwara Tametaka."

Akitada searched his memory. Tametaka was Michinaga's brother's son and was definitely of a rank that made it unwise, if not disastrous, to insult or threaten the mistress of the River Mansion. "Thank you," he said. "It's always good to know what one is up against."

The abbot smiled a little sadly. "You need not go," he said.

Akitada visited the local bathhouse and had himself shaved and his hair arranged. More he could not do because he had brought no clothes. Getting back on his rented horse, he returned to the River Mansion.

It was dusk by then. The air was still and quite warm and humid, but clouds had moved in. Fireflies gleamed now and then among the foliage. At the place where the trees thinned to reveal the broad river, he stopped. A large pleasure boat was anchored in the cove. Lanterns gleamed on board, and the boatmen and servants sat around at their leisure. They had delivered Lady Kazuko's guests.

And now Akitada could hear faint music in the distance. The atmosphere was romantic but seemed also vaguely disturbing. Had someone killed the girl during just such a night of revels?

He assumed the boat had come from the capital, bringing high-ranking nobles for a night of pleasure at the home of a close friend and relative. This made Akitada even more uncomfortable. There would be every opportunity for him to offend men who were not likely to overlook it and had the power to punish him.

The gates, lit by many torches, stood hospitably open, but servants were there to receive or reject arrivals. As before, he rode into the courtyard and gave his name. As before, a servant took away his horse. On this occasion, however, the *betto* himself received him. He wore a splendid robe of green brocade over full trousers of pale blue silk and made Akitada feel utterly shabby in his hunting robe.

Kakuan was courteous, bowed very deeply, and led him past the main building to a roofed gallery from which he could see into the gardens.

They had changed magically. Everywhere, lights were suspended from tree branches. More lights cast colored hues from paper lanterns that hung along the galleries. Torches surrounded a wooden stage draped with colored cloth. An elaborately costumed figure in a large gilded mask gyrated there to the accompaniment of six seated musicians. They played a zither, two lutes, a small drum, and two flutes. Around the stage, guests in fine robes, some twenty of them, both men and women, stood watching. Nearby, cushions were laid out in front of trays, and servants waited to serve food as soon as the entertainment was over.

What struck Akitada most was a sense of unreality. He remembered what the boat's master had said about a scene from paradise. It must have seemed that way to an ordinary working man, but he knew that this also resembled parties he had attended at court or at the homes of wealthy noblemen. Still, there was a subtle difference here. He saw not only the beautiful buildings and the large, well-lit garden, but there was a larger, more mysterious world of forests and river beyond. A sense of being far from the bustle of the ordinary world made this gathering appear celestial rather than human.

Kakuan's voice woke him from his reverie. "Allow me to introduce you to this lady, sir."

Akitada turned, and there stood a lovely woman. She was small and finely made, her costume exquisite, and her bow very graceful. Sparkling eyes peered at him over a painted fan.

Kakuan smiled at his surprise. "Please enjoy yourself tonight, my Lord. I'm sure this lady will see to your every comfort and pleasure."

Kakuan left, perhaps to welcome other guests. Akitada's attention was on this exquisite creature in her rosy silks and flower-embroidered jacket. Was she a lady of rank or a high-class courtesan? Indeed, she could be either with her long, glossy hair, and her bright eyes smiling at him over the pretty fan. Perhaps she was aware of his confusion and enjoyed it.

He sketched a bow. "You're very kind. I'm a stranger here. And you?" He hoped her answer would tell him if she was from the town and brought here to entertain the noble guests, or if she had arrived on the boat and was some nobleman's relative.

It was, of course, very improper for a noblewoman to be here among strange men. No, surely she was a courtesan, and they had done him proud. She was young and very beautiful.

She smiled behind her fan. "I've come here before. The lady of the River Mansion gives the most charming entertainments. Are you fond of music, my Lord?"

He glanced at the stage, where two dancers now twirled and jumped. Some battle between ancient gods, perhaps? Yes, he thought one of them was the god of the sea. The music had taken on a more dramatic and martial sound. "I am very fond of it," he said. "And the dancers are excellent."

"Come." She touched his arm with her fan and allowed him a glimpse of a softly rounded face and full lips, "I know a place where you can see better."

He followed her, the bemusement back because the situation was so odd. He found it easier to go along with it than to object. They skirted the stage and took a path up a tree-covered hillside. She walked very gracefully. From his viewpoint slightly below, he could not help guessing at the youthful body underneath the gown. The jacket fit closely to her back and waist. She was slender but had rounded hips and long, shapely legs under the rose-colored silk of her gown.

The wind had died down, and the night seemed uncomfortably humid. He ran a finger along his collar and looked back over his shoulder. What must people think? The other guests, men with one or two young women beside them, were entranced by the dancers on the platform. None of the women compared to his companion, he thought, though they were pretty enough. He recognized one or two of the men. They outranked him, and his only contact had been mutual attendance at some mandatory court gathering. He hoped they had not noticed him.

She stopped on a small knoll above the garden and gestured at the scene below. "You see? They will soon bring on the *asobi.* Have you seen an *asobi* performance before?"

He knew that they were specially trained entertainers among courtesans, but that was all. "No," he said. "I'm sadly at a loss on occasions like this."

She laughed softly. "You have missed much, my Lord."

Perhaps he had. She was lovely in the half light. The torches below did not reach this far, but they cast a golden glow on her graceful head and that glossy hair. It occurred to him that they were not only alone together, but that the brightly lit scene below them meant that they were hidden from the eyes of others. A man might dare anything. He reached out to brush a wing of her hair aside to see her face better. "Yes," he said with a sigh, "I have missed much, and you are very beautiful." It was neither elegant nor poetic, and he cringed inwardly. A woman like this, experienced in the language of seduction and desire, must think him as awkward as a schoolboy.

But she turned to him and lowered her fan. Her eyes shone, and a smile parted her lips. Her teeth were blackened. He had never liked the custom, but now the darkness beyond those soft, red lips increased his desire powerfully. Mysteries were to be explored. He took a step toward her.

Sudden applause from below distracted him. The music had stopped and the stage was empty. A woman in brilliant red and white stood on it. She wore a man's hat, but her long hair flowed behind her like a mantle, covering the red hunting jacket and the full white silk trousers. A sword was pushed through her sash, and she held a pair of small drums. He had heard of that style and thought it ridiculous and highly improper for a woman to dress in man's clothing, but here the strangeness of her appearance, that unexpected twist on commonly held perceptions of the differences between men and women, was fascinating and part of the magic of this night. The woman below began a slow dance, beating the rhythm on her drums. The musicians joined in, softly and tentatively.

"The *shirabyoshi* Koro," his companion whispered in his ear. She was very close to him; he could feel her breath on his cheek. "She is wonderful and much admired." Her sleeve brushed his and he breathed in her scent.

"She will never be a charming as you," he said gallantly and smiled into her eyes. A part of him wondered what he was about. It was not like him to pursue a courtesan, but on this warm and scented night, with the river plashing softly below them, this extraordinary and licentious gathering had worked a change in him. He suddenly felt that he had become a staid and joyless official long before his time. He was not an old man, but he had not really lived, had never tasted the pleasures that were available here. How could he be fully human without knowing this part of a man's life also? Life was uncertain enough, and death waited at every turning of the road.

"Listen!" she said, her eyes bright with promise.

The *shirabyoshi* sang. She had a full, warm voice that carried on the sudden silence. "No bower of roses for me," she sang. "I'll never be a wife."

He reached for the woman beside him and bent his head to kiss her.

"Oh, love in vain . . ."

Their lips touched. She opened hers and reached up to caress his cheek.

" . . . naked breast pressed to naked breast."

The blatant words of the song both shocked him and stirred his desire. Perversely, he was also moved by the sadness of the courtesan who made love to men who did not care about her.

Naked breast to naked breast.

His companion's scent was in his nostrils, his tongue in her mouth, tasting sweetness. He wanted her desperately. "What are you?" he asked hoarsely into her hair. "Are you . . .?" How to ask this woman if she was available? The difficulties were immense. And how to handle the transaction? The only time he had experienced something similar, the woman had been an ordinary prostitute who had offered herself, and a piece of silver was all she had expected. He had no idea how much he should offer a woman like this one. Or if an offer would be insulting. Would she accept gold, or was he expected to give her gifts?

And where would they make love? Here among the trees, or in the river pavilion, or perhaps in that little boat he had seen tied to it? On cushions in the darkness under low branches overhanging the river while the boat rocked gently . . ." His hands explored her body through the layers of silk.

"Come," said she, slipping from his arms and leaving him bereft. Below the applause died away and the *asobi* left the stage. For a moment, he thought that her mind was also on making love, but she said, "It is time to eat."

Time to eat?

How unromantic an ending to romance!

How banal a response to his lust.

Ashamed of his passion, he followed her down the hillside. When she slipped once, he caught her arm. She laughed softly and leaned against him for a moment. Thoroughly aroused by now, he was glad that he did not have to walk far.

People were taking their seats as servants moved among them to pour wine and offer bowls of fragrant delicacies. His companion knelt close to him, directing the servants to bring him this and that. He looked at her lips and wished he knew her name. Refusing food, he drank thirstily of the wine. She made conversation, and he answered somehow. He was still too much aware of her body near his to know what they said. All the while, he hoped that she would tell him when it was time.

Only once he forced his eyes away from her and looked around. The serving women were pretty enough, and he saw some virile and handsome young men. Tora's tale came to his mind, but why, he wondered, had his hostess invited him when she had so many more appealing males in her service? And why had she provided him with this exquisite companion?

He drank in her beauty and grace. She leaned forward to pour more wine for him. Then, looking into his eyes, she took a sip from his cup and turned it so his lips would touch where hers had been.

A promise.

"Where is our hostess?" he asked nervously, his eyes on the bead of moisture on her lower lip.

"Oh, she may appear later." She let the tip of her tongue catch the trace of wine. "She's probably watching us."

Startled, Akitada looked toward the buildings, but the brightness of torches and lanterns made it impossible to see into rooms and galleries. Perhaps the lady of the River Mansion was like some men who enjoyed to watch others copulate? The thought cooled his ardor, and he gave the cup a slight turn before he drank.

"Did you ever meet a young woman called Akogi here?" he asked when he put down the cup. "I'm told she was still in training."

She stiffened and her eyes narrowed. "Why do you ask about other women? Am I not good enough? Have I offended?" Her lower lip trembled. "You hurt me deeply with your coldness. A little while ago, I thought you liked me. I was happy because I like you very much." To his dismay, her eyes filled with tears, and she gave a small sob.

He was contrite. "Forgive me. I do like you very much. It would be wonderful if you would . . . if we could . . ."

A man's voice cut into this awkward declaration. "Forgive me, but I don't think we've met. We didn't travel down together, did we?"

He turned, flushing with embarrassment. A middle-aged guest, seated near him in a deep red brocade robe over moss-colored trousers, peered at them curiously. He, too, had a very pretty woman beside him. The man was someone he had seen before, in the capital, but he could not place him. He bowed awkwardly. "No, sir. I have come from the town. My name is Sugawara. Her ladyship kindly invited me."

"Ah, our princess," laughed the other. "She's always had an eye for interesting men. You must be the Sugawara who solves murders for our police."

Akitada did not work for the police, but rather with them on occasion, but he did not correct his neighbor. "I had no idea that my occasional activities in that line should make me an attractive guest at a party. I'm sorry, sir. I think we have met, but it must have been at one of the many official functions."

The man grinned. "No doubt. I'm Yorisuke, of the chancellor's clan. Are you enjoying yourself? I see you've won the beauteous Nakagimi as your companion. Lucky man."

So her name was Nakagimi. And she was considered a prize. He had a lot to learn. He gave her a smile—which was received coldly—and said, "I'm the most fortunate of men and hardly able to understand such good fortune yet." He thought her expression softened a little and wished his neighbor would lose interest in him.

He did. After a few remarks about the earlier entertainment, he turned his attention to his companion.

Akitada, who had noticed similar familiar behavior between the guests and their companions, reached for Nakagimi's hand. "I have offended," he said humbly. "Forgive me. I told you that I'm a mere novice at this and hardly know what to say to someone as enchanting as you."

She gave a little laugh and squeezed his fingers. He was forgiven. On an impulse, he raised her hand to his lips and kissed her palm. She gave a little gasp and, becoming bolder, he moved his lips to her wrist and from there to her inner forearm.

"That servant is staring at us," she murmured, withdrawing her arm.

He looked up. One of the male servers had come to a halt a few yards away and positively goggled at them. Akitada's eyes focused.

No, it could not be!

Jumping up, he cried, "Sadenari?"

A broad smile split the young man's face. He pushed the tray he was carrying at another servant and came quickly across. "Why, sir, here you are in person. I've been wondering when I'd finally hear from you. Frankly, I was getting worried. How very fortunate to find you." He glanced at Akitada's companion and said, "And with Nakagimi. My compliments, sir."

"Find me?" said Akitada, his voice trembling with suppressed anger. "What are you doing, playing the servant here?"

Sadenari had the grace to blush. "Shhh, sir. Not so loud."

They had become the focus of interest. The Fujiwara lord and his companion were frankly fascinated. And Nakagimi? She was rising to her feet, gracefully but with every sign of being deeply affronted, and walking away.

Akitada felt a murderous rage.

The Fujiwara lord chuckled. "Now you've done it, Sugawara. She won't come back, you know."

Realizing that he must give some explanation, Akitada said, "I beg your pardon, sir, for the disturbance, but this young man, for whom I bear a responsibility, has been the object of a desperate search for the past two weeks. I did not expect to find him here."

This caused more merriment.

"Ah, these youngsters!" his lordship said. "They cannot resist pretty women. Just a few days ago, Oga, the local governor, stormed in here, looking for his son. Ha, ha, ha. Well, go easy on him. It's part of a man's education after all."

22

The Island

The sun rose brilliantly after the storm, and all around them islands floated on a shimmering sea, some larger and some very small.

The one they approached was pitifully small, apparently consisting of no more than a large picturesque rock formation with a few pines clinging to it and a narrow strip of sandy beach. Tora saw neither buildings nor people.

Under the clearing morning skies, the pirates had got busy setting as much sail as was left. They steered the ship along the small island's coast. Eventually, a promontory blocked the way. They took the vessel close to the land. Tora saw no reason why they would want to land here. The place was desolate and inhospitable. For that matter, the rocks loomed dangerously close. It looked almost as if they planned to ram the ship into them.

When they were almost exactly under the tallest cliff, a shout rang out from it, and the sailors answered with cheers and laughter. A lookout had seen and welcomed them. They were among friends.

They reefed the remaining sail and put men on the oars and the rudders. The ship slowed and made a turn around the promontory, and there was an inlet, a narrow opening between two sheer walls of rock. With the ease of experience, the ship entered and passed the narrows to come to rest in a small bay. Here the land fell more gently toward the water, a few shacks stood on the beach, and fishing boats were drawn up on the sand.

A new worry seized Tora. The secret entrance into this hidden cove, where the pirate ship could lie at anchor without being seen from the open sea, made it the perfect hideaway. If a pirate ship found itself pursued, it could disappear with an almost supernatural suddenness, and the pursuers would be none the wiser. He had witnessed this maneuver, found their hideaway, and could recognize the landmarks. They would not let him leave to reveal their secret to the world.

As they anchored, men and women appeared on the shore to greet them. Tora counted more people than could comfortably live in the few shacks, so there must be a settlement somewhere. He had no time to reflect on this, because the pirates lowered the boat and came for him.

No bonds this time, but neither were they gentle with him. They grunted commands to get in the boat and watched impatiently as he tried to climb down, holding on to a rope. The rope chafed his already raw hands, and he fell the last few feet, getting a kick for his clumsiness. After that, he sat, cradling his sore palms, while they rowed ashore.

There he suffered the curious scrutiny of the women, children, and old men. From their excited babble in a strong dialect, he deduced that he was being introduced as a "spy" and their prisoner. He looked around for a male who might be the chief mentioned by Dragon Tattoo but saw no one who fitted his idea of a pirate chief.

A number of the returned sailors, with Dragon Tattoo in the lead, marched him inland.

The dirt path was well-travelled and showed wheel tracks but no hoof marks. Apparently goods were moved by manpower. Rocky mountain sides, thinly covered with pines and brambles enclosed the track. After about half a mile of steady climbing, Tora saw cave openings, several of them, and it occurred to him that these men lived in caves. Then he smelled smoke. And food cooking. If his mouth had not been so dry, it would have watered. He realized his hunger and thirst were much greater than his fear. Would they feed him before they killed him? He decided he would refuse to speak until he got some food and water.

The path took a few more turns before they reached a plateau. This was surrounded by sheer rock walls pierced by many openings. In front of a large cave entrance was an open fire with a large pot suspended over it. A woman stirred it with a wooden ladle. A short distance from her sat a middle-aged man on a campaign stool of the kind used by generals during a campaign. He had a thick black beard and bushy brows, wore half armor and boots, and had a sword lying beside him. He raised a hand in greeting to Dragon Tattoo before his eyes fell on Tora.

This, then, must be the chief, the man who held his life in his hands. Tora returned the look with equal curiosity.

"Bring him!" The chief's voice boomed and echoed from the mountainside. Tora thought it appropriate for a commander of an army.

Dragon Tattoo grasped Tora's arm, thrusting him forward so that he stumbled and fell to one knee. Catching himself, Tora shook a fist at Dragon Tattoo and then walked the few steps to the pirate chief.

"Hah!" said the chief. "You think you can threaten one of my men?"

"He's a coward and a bastard who likes to hurt people."

Dragon Tattoo ran up with a snarl, his own fist raised.

"No," said the chief. "He's right. You are a coward and I've seen you torturing prisoners. Tell me why you decided to bring a stranger here."

Dragon Tattoo shot Tora a furious glance, but he lowered his fist. "He's a spy, chief. He was asking questions about us."

The chief glowered. "And you thought it was a good idea to show him our island? What am I to do with him?"

Dragon Tattoo's face fell for a moment. Then he said, "You can find out who he works for before I kill him. No harm done." He chortled.

"You're not only a coward, you're an idiot!" the chief roared, getting to his feet so violently that his stool fell over.

Tora saw that the others gathered around the fire where the woman was dishing out helpings of whatever was in the large pot. He was ravenous. "If you don't mind, chief," he said, breaking into the ominous silence before the storm, "I'd very much like something to eat and drink before you go on with this. Your men haven't been exactly hospitable."

The chief's jaw dropped. He looked at Tora speechlessly for a moment, then burst into a laugh. "You're a cool bastard. What if I let Tojo kill you? He wants to badly enough, don't you, Tojo?"

Tojo cringed but nodded his head. "I'll do it, chief. Right here and now. Just say the word."

Tora gave him a pitying look. "He can't do it. Not unless you have me tied up again."

Dragon Tattoo exploded into another attack, fists flying. Tora skipped aside, stuck out a leg to trip him and, when he was down, sat on him. "You see?" he said to the chief with a grin.

The chief grinned back. "Let him go and get something to eat. We'll talk later."

Tora got up. "Thanks, chief. And by the way, the name's Tora."

The food was good and plentiful, fish cooked with rice. The rice was of the best quality, very white and with a rich flavor. It was what the wealthy ate. No doubt, it came from those bales he could see stacked inside the cave. Life was good to pirates.

The chief was now deep in conversation with the man who had been at the rudder of the ship, its captain or master. A small but heavy bag changed hands. The chief peered into it, then shoved it inside his shirt. He said something, and both men turned their heads to look at Tora. Tora quickly raised his bowl to his face. He was nearly done and still hungry. Holding the empty bowl out to the woman who was stirring the pot, he gave her a pleading look. She spat and turned her back on him.

"Fill his bowl!" roared the chief.

She glared at Tora but gave him another helping. He bowed to the chief and thanked her, adding a compliment on her cooking. In vain. She turned away.

Tora sighed. A spy's life was hard.

And dangerous.

Dragon Tattoo came for his own meal and gave Tora a look of such sheer hatred that he choked on his next bite. The chief might be a man of some humanity, but the same did not apply to his people. There was little doubt that Dragon Tattoo would kill him at his first opportunity.

Tora finished his food and felt better. There was nothing to do but to await developments. The fact that no one made a move to unload the ship meant that they had made a delivery in Kawajiri and been paid off. That was why the master had passed a bag of money to the chief.

Perhaps he could find out who had bought the pirated goods.

He glanced around and saw nothing but hardened faces. The chances of getting information were not good. He had better think about getting away and let the government take care of the pirate hideout.

Chances were that on its next departure the ship would resume the hunt for prey. He could not escape that way. And even if he could convince the chief that he was a promising recruit, Tora shuddered at what he would be expected to do. Pirates were ruthless about slaughtering ships' crews.

Was there some other way?

The plateau around the great cave was high above the sea but enclosed by rocky ridges and forest. Only toward the west, he could catch a glimpse of the water. He saw two other islands, fairly close, and knew there were many more. But even so, he could not hope to swim that far.

"You! Tora! Come here."

Tora spun around. The chief was gesturing. He got up, dusted himself off, and strolled over.

"They say you're a spy," the chief growled.

Tora chose a rock and sat down across from the chief. "They're idiots," he said, grinning.

The chief narrowed his eyes. "What were you doing in the hostel?"

"I needed a place to sleep. What else?"

"You'd been asking questions all over town. Don't lie to me."

"I always ask questions. I like to know what's going on and who people are."

I. J. PARKER

"You asked questions about us."

"No. I didn't know anything about you. I asked about pirates."

"Why?"

Tora looked up at the sky. After the storm it was a clear blue again. High above him circled several birds of prey. Below he could hear the cries of gulls. "I was thinking of becoming one," he said, "but now I'm not so sure. Are you going to split that money with your men?"

"What?"

Tora brought his eyes back to the chief's bulging shirt and grinned. "The master of your ship brought you a bag of coins. It looked heavy. Maybe it was gold. Anyway, I guess being a pirate is a dangerous and bloody business. I'd like to think there's quite a lot of gold to be earned. The food was good, but I don't work for food alone."

"You're a cocky bastard all right," said the chief. "Cocky bastards are trouble. Best make short work of them."

"Cocky bastards are what you need more of. Not idiots like Dragon Tattoo. And by the way, he stole my sword. I want it back."

The chief snorted. "He took it off you; you take it back. I'd like to see you try."

"Very well." Tora got to his feet. "It's been a pleasure, chief," he said, made a slight bow, and walked away.

He did not really feel very cocky, but by now and with a full stomach he was very angry. Part of the anger was directed at himself for having been careless. Part was directed at Dragon Tattoo, the man he held responsible for his capture. It had become clear that the bastard had acted out of personal spite rather than because he really thought Tora was a spy and a danger to their enterprise. Sometimes a fool is more dangerous than the slyest villain.

Since they made no effort to restrict his movements, he wandered around, trying to get an idea how to get away. They watched him though, and he knew better than to go off by himself. Instead, he stayed with groups of the pirates, watching their work, asking questions from time to time that received no answers, and surveying as much of the island as he could.

They would not let him explore the cave where they stored their loot, but nobody objected when he joined some men who headed down to the hidden harbor. They got into the boat that had brought them ashore, and rowed out to the ship. Tora sat on the sandy beach and watched them begin repairs.

When the boat returned to pick up some lumber, he got up to meet them. "I can help," he offered. "I'd rather work than sit about doing nothing."

They looked at each other. Tora thought he recognized the man he had stopped from going overboard during the storm. He said, "Let him come. There's no way you can escape."

Tora grinned. "I don't want to escape."

They did not become any friendlier or more talkative after that, but they pointed out the lumber stored in one of the shacks, and sail cloth, and big bundles of hemp rope. These he helped them load into the boat and then joined them for the return trip to the ship.

In the afternoon they rowed back to the shore to drag a large tree trunk to the ship. It would be the new mast, replacing the one the storm had taken away. This was very heavy work, and Tora was drenched in sweat. He had long since stripped to his pants. They had stared at him when he did this. Tora's torso and upper arms bore many scars from fights and battles of the past, and he thought they treated him with more respect afterward.

For his part, he developed equal respect for their ability to make these repairs and for their determination and pride in their work. He was too clumsy for most of the chores, but he knew how to carry, lift, pull, use a hammer, and generally lend a hand.

Dusk came early in the small bay hidden by the tall rocks, and they stopped their labors for their evening rice. Tora could not remember when he had last been so utterly exhausted. He was still bruised from the stormy night, and his head was sore and hurt. But the pirates had taken more punishment during the storm, and he was not about to show them how weak he was. He dragged his weary body from the bay to the plateau above, seriously doubting that he could make the climb.

The sinking sun still left a golden glow in front of the great cave. Once there, he collapsed and emptied his mind, lying on the ground, watching birds circling above in the fading light. When he gathered his wits again and sat up with a groan, he saw that the chief was listening to the report on the repairs. Some of the men he had worked with stood around him, and by their gestures and glances he guessed that they talked about him. He had been unable to glean anything useful about their habits or his chances of escaping, but perhaps he had won himself some goodwill.

Feeling a strange bristling on the back of his neck, he turned his head. Dragon Tattoo was sitting a few yards behind him. He was looking at him, his eyes filled with raw hatred. Only now, Tora thought, there was something new: a hint of triumph and gleeful anticipation.

The attack would come soon.

He was still weighing his options against Dragon Tattoo when the chief called them both over.

He told Tora, "I could put you in chains tonight, but you've made yourself useful, and besides Tojo would just slit your throat. On the other hand, left free, you might try to escape while the camp is asleep. So I've decided that Tojo will watch you while you sleep."

Dragon Tattoo protested. "Chain him up. I want to sleep myself."

Tora said nothing. He eyed his sword at Dragon Tattoo's side and wondered if he could snatch it and cut the bastard's throat. Maybe the chief would overlook it.

The chief growled, "No. It's your punishment for being an idiot and a coward. And if he gets away, or if something happens to him, I'll personally cut off your balls."

23

The Goblin's Tale

It started raining long before the end of the party. Guests scrambled to get inside and preserve their finery. Akitada did not bother to bid his hostess farewell. He was simmering with suppressed fury and did not trust himself to speak to her or, for that matter, to Sadenari.

"We're leaving," he growled at the annoying young man, who was still smiling broadly and fondly at him. "Now!"

"Yes, sir," said Sadenari, looking a little puzzled.

"I have a horse, but you'll walk."

Sadenari gazed at the drizzle but said only, "Yes, sir."

As they were leaving the River Mansion with gusts of wind and rain buffeting them, Sadenari tried to speak again. "I was so glad to see you, sir. I have much to report—"

"Later," snarled Akitada, not at all moved by the rain-wet face turned up to him.

They finished the trip in silence. When they reached his room at the monastery, Akitada wanted to shout at Sadenari but he could not risk waking the monks. He pointed to the bedding. "Get out of your wet clothes and wrap yourself in that." He himself stripped, draping their clothes around the room in hopes that they would dry by morning.

Sadenari, naked and shivering, covered himself with one of the quilts, leaving the other for Akitada. Outside the wind increased. It shook the walls and sent branches crashing down on the roof.

"I think you realize that you no longer have a government career," Akitada said through clenched teeth. "After this escapade and the trouble you caused, I will not have you work for me or anyone else if I can help it."

Sadenari stared. "But—"

"We spent the past two weeks searching for you, afraid that you'd been abducted and might be dead. When I found that your father received a letter from you, it became clear that you'd gone off adventuring on your own, without regard for your responsibilities or word to me. And now I find you, by mere accident, in Eguchi, playing the whore to an old woman."

Sadenari had become pale. In a weak voice, he said, "But I did write."

"Nonsense. Or at least not to me or the ministry." A suspicion crossed Akitada's mind. "Why did you write to Nakahara?"

"I didn't write to him. The letters were to you, under cover to Nakahara. You were staying there. You mean he didn't give them to you?"

Akitada stared at him. "No. There was more than one letter?"

"Oh, yes. I wrote a report every day. Then my money ran out, and I had to look for a job. After that, I wrote several more times but not every day. Working made it hard to do any investigating."

"Working? You should have returned!" Akitada took to pacing, while Sadenari huddled into his cover. The room had become cold, and the storm sounded worse. "That's why I got none of the letters. Nakahara knew," muttered Akitada. "All the time, Nakahara knew. And Otomo was sending me off on wild goose chases. The villains!"

"You think Nakahara is the guilty person?" Sadenari asked.

"Oh, yes. He and the prefect, and probably the governor, too." Akitada recalled himself. It was really too frustrating the way everyone seemed to have perfectly plausible explanations for their dubious behavior. "You're by no means out of the woods yet. Report!" he snapped.

Sadenari paled again. "Yes, sir. I had some good luck at first. I found out that the pirates operated from Kawajiri. I set out for there. That was in my first letter." He paused uncertainly.

"Go on."

"In Kawajiri, I ran into difficulties. The sailors I spoke to didn't want to talk. They claimed there were no pirates in Kawajiri and never had been. I stayed another day in some cheap sailors' hostel, but by then I was running very low on funds. Fortunately, I picked up a rumor of some sailors who had a lot of money and were going to Kaya or Eguchi to spend it on women and wine. I used my last money on a boat to Eguchi. And another letter to you."

Akitada cast up his eyes. "I might have known you'd end up in Eguchi. We tracked you to the Kawajiri hostel, but thought you'd gone on board a ship. Tell me, did your investigation into the girl's death produce better results than the ones into piracy?"

Sadenari fidgeted. "Yes, sir. But I really went to find the pirates."

Akitada grunted his disbelief. "What about the girl?"

"I took a job in Eguchi. In the restaurant where we ate, remember? I thought since they fired the old waiter, I might have a chance, and I needed the money. Besides, pirates might just show up there."

Akitada grimaced. "Get on with it."

"The restaurant delivers food to the River Mansion when there's a party. I'm quite strong, and there was a lot of food to carry. The *betto* Kakuan sent the others away but asked me to stay and help. I was glad, because I thought it was the place where the poor girl had been murdered, but I didn't find out anything that night, and in the end I had to walk back to Eguchi by myself. Only, the next day, Kakuan came to the restaurant and offered me money to work at the mansion. Much more money than that skinflint paid

me. And that's how you came to find me there."
He stopped with a happy smile.

"What is it that you found out about the dead girl?"

"Well, sir, her name was Akogi!" He paused to gauge the effect of this, but Akitada only nodded.

"She was with one of the courtesans who attended a party of noblemen from the capital. They say a guest asked to buy her out, but something happened, and it came to nothing."

"So?"

"That's all I know for sure, but whatever happened was just before we found her. So they must have killed her."

"They?"

"Well, someone objected to the buy-out. That will be easy enough to find out."

"Has it occurred to you that the girl could also have committed suicide out of disappointment?"

Sadenari's face fell, but he looked stubborn. "Well, that's all I could learn before you came."

Akitada snapped, "Surely that's not all. I gather, your duties at the mansion were much more personal than mere household chores."

A flush rose to Sadenari's hairline. "Wh-what do you mean, sir?"

"Apparently the first female you slept with is old enough to be your grandmother."

Sadenari looked shocked, then angry. "What? Oh no, sir. It wasn't like that. Her ladyship was very kind to me, that's all. And besides, I had occasion before . . . I mean, I'm an adult. Begging your pardon, sir, but I don't see where such questions have anything to do with my work at the ministry."

Akitada ran a hand over his face. "Forget it." The infernal youth was right. This was not the time to deal with moral lessons. He would unravel Sadenari's infractions when his head was clearer. He listened. The wind seemed to have died down a little. "Go to sleep," he said. "I'll decide what to do with you tomorrow."

They returned to Naniwa by the first boat. The sky was clear again, but everywhere the storm had left broken limbs, roof tiles, and shutters strewn across roads and waterways.

Sadenari was subdued. Akitada had not mentioned his sexual exploits again. It would have been hypocritical to do so. His own behavior had been questionable, and Sadenari had witnessed it. Besides it was too late to offer the youth guidance in romantic matters, even if he had felt obligated to do so. The relief that the youth was alive overshadowed the frustrations he had caused. He confined himself to a reminder that Sadenari should have known all was not well when he had received no answers to his letters. His continued absence suggested that he had not wanted to lose his freedom to do as he wished.

In Naniwa, they returned to the hostel, Sadenari to get his things and return to the capital, and Akitada to await Tora.

"I will report to the minister by separate post," he told Sadenari when he was ready to leave.

Sadenari looked stricken. He was not being trusted to carry what must be a negative report about his activities. Akitada hardened his heart. He was about to be rid of the troublesome Sadenari, and in a short while he would meet Tora. They would manage the case together, now that he knew Nakahara was at the heart of the conspiracy.

Tora did not return. Akitada spent the rest of the day, writing his various reports and thinking about what he had learned in Eguchi.

Early the next day, he headed for the trade office, phrasing his charges against Nakahara in his mind. He would extract a confession from the man, and the rest should be easy.

But when he approached the gate, a familiar thin and disreputable figure detached itself from one of the pillars and came loping toward him.

The lopsided face seemed more twisted than ever and the bad eye rolled horribly in its socket. He folded his thin frame into a deep bow. "I've been praying to find you, sir."

"Later," said Akitada, side-stepping him. "I'm in a hurry."

But the ugly man followed and caught hold of his sleeve. "Please. It's about Tora."

Akitada stopped. "What about Tora?"

"The pirates got him. Night before last. Just before the storm broke."

An icy hand squeezed Akitada's insides. "They got him? Is he dead?"

The ugly man made a jerky movement. "No. Not dead. At least . . . no, I think they took him away unconscious. I don't think they meant to kill him. But they put him on a ship and left."

Akitada seized the fellow by the shoulders and shook him. "Who? Where?"

"In Kawajiri. Pirates. The ship was at anchor in the outer harbor. It left as soon as Tora was aboard. I've been asking questions, and then came here to look for you."

No point in seeing Nakahara now. Akitada turned back. "Come, you'd better tell me all you know. I'll buy you a cup of wine."

The ugly man's face twisted. "Not wine. A bowl of food would be very welcome. I haven't had time to eat."

A short time later, Akitada watched once more as the ugly man gobbled his food. His own stomach clenched with nausea. He was impatient, but the man deserved to eat. And Tora must still be alive. At least he hoped so. There had been the storm.

Finally, the ugly man put down his bowl. "Thank you. I was getting faint. My stamina isn't what it used to be, and I've been on the move ever since last night, at first finding out what happened, and then trying to find you."

"Start at the beginning."

The ugly man either smiled or grimaced. "When you decided you didn't trust me, I kept an eye on things on my own. Then you left for the capital, and I thought you weren't coming back. When I caught sight of your assistant talking to the postmaster, I followed him." Again that lopsided grin. "A capable man. He nearly caught me twice. In Kawajiri, he disguised himself as a laborer and went to the Hostel of the Flying Cranes. He spent the night there."

Akitada nodded. "He was seeking information about the pirates."

"Ah. Kunimitsu works for them. I decided to sleep in a shed in back of the hostel. That's where I overheard Kunimitsu talking to one of the pirates. A big brute called Tojo. Tojo was up to something and Kunimitsu pointed out where your assistant was sleeping."

Akitada nodded. "I've met Kunimitsu. So he's a rascal?"

"Oh, yes. When they went away, I tried to warn Tora, but he didn't trust me. A few hours later, some men and a woman came. The woman started screaming. Tora ran out and they jumped him and knocked him out. I followed them to the harbor, saw him put on the ship, and the ship set sail."

The tale was concise and disastrous. "Go on. You said you asked questions."

"Yes, in Kawajiri. The pirates have a hideout on a small island. It has no name, but it's past Azukishima. I think they took Tora there."

"That hideout is common knowledge in Kawajiri?"

"No. I have a friend who owes me a favor."

It sounded very dubious, but Akitada could not afford to brush the ugly man off again. "What else did this friend tell you?"

"Very little. He thinks they were making a delivery in Kawajiri but doesn't know or won't say to whom."

Akitada studied the ugly creature across from him. It was human nature to link a repulsive appearance with an evil character. Tora must have taken him for a demon. Yes, that was probably the reason why he had not heeded the warning. It tended to prove that the man was telling the truth. He asked, "What do you want for your information?"

The man looked down at his empty bowl and shook his head. "You owe me nothing," he said. Then he looked up. "Did you get the amulet?"

"Yes. Thank you. Very clever." No point in asking where he got it. Why he had returned it was puzzling, though. "Why are you doing this? Why are you following us around? Nobody goes to this much trouble for nothing."

"Since I have no work, I must hope to earn my food with small services of this kind. Following people and asking questions are the only things I know. And you seemed to require information."

Akitada made up his mind. "Very well. You can work for me until we find Tora. What's your name?"

The smile was a little sad. "It's still Saburo."

"Come along then. We must find a way to get Tora back."

Easier said than done. He had an offer of armed men from the prefect, but Akitada could not go to him. The same was true of the governor, even if he had returned by now. That left Watamaro. Everything depended on the merchant now. He had the ships, and had offered his help before.

After asking questions in the harbor, they found him in one of his warehouses. It dated back to the time when Naniwa had had a bustling harbor. Built high above ground on thick tree trunks to protect it from flooding, it was in good repair, and Watamaro kept an office there, tucked under the eaves of a large, dim, open space filled with stacks of goods ranging from bales of rice to imported woods, jars of medicines, and other, unidentifiable goods stored in the dark recesses. It smelled exotic.

Watamaro was at his desk, working with an abacus over an open ledger. He looked up when he heard their steps and rose immediately.

"What a surprise! Welcome to my workplace, my Lord. Please forgive the poor and rough surroundings. I regret there is no news yet of your assistant."

"Please don't apologize. I came to bring you the news that my clerk has been found in Eguchi." Akitada looked around at shelves filled with more goods, some wrapped, some plain, and at other shelves holding ledgers. A large map hung on the wall behind Watamaro. It showed the lands surrounding the Inland Sea, with harbors marked all the way to Hakata.

Watamaro chuckled. "Enjoying himself, no doubt. A great relief to you and his family, I'm sure. Shall we sit down?"

Akitada accepted and said diffidently, "I'm afraid I have another favor to ask. A bigger one this time. Last night my retainer Tora was taken by pirates in Kawajiri. Saburo here brought me the news." He turned to his companion. "Tell Watamaro what you told me."

Listening to the tale with apparent astonishment, Watamaro exclaimed, "Outrageous! And they anchored in Kawajiri, only a few miles from here? How dare they? You will want a ship to search for them." He paused, frowned. "But they may not have gone far. That storm last night was terrible. A number of ships foundered or lost their cargo in the harbor. I have been adding up the losses for my own fleet."

Akitada bit his lip. "Thank you. I must hope that he is alive." Saying it did nothing to dissolve the heavy lump in his belly that seemed to take his breath away. He must not lose Tora, too.

Watamaro got busy. He issued orders, and servants ran. They waited, and then Watamaro himself accompanied them to the harbor where a flat-bottomed vessel waited.

"It's small," he said apologetically, but it will save time not having to go to Kawajiri first, and the weather is quite calm again. With any luck, we'll find them quickly and be back by nightfall."

24

The Bodhisattva

The chief sent Tora and Dragon Tattoo to one of the small caves some distance from the main one. Apparently he had no fear whatsoever that Dragon Tattoo would doze off and let Tora escape.

The cave was a mere ten feet deep and fifteen high. Grass and weeds grew at its entrance, but inside the surface was dry, hard rock. It was also cold. A very small oil lamp sat on a ledge. Not much chance of sleep, even if either man had been tempted. They settled down against opposite walls, staring at each other suspiciously.

Tora was desperately tired. His body had finally rebelled against the abuses of the previous night and the hard labor of the day. Every muscle hurt, and his headache, which had lessened during the day, grew worse again. Besides, his eyes felt as if they were covered with sand. He doubted that Dragon Tattoo could be this sore and tired.

Would he attack? He had Tora's sword lying next to his right hand.

Time passed slowly. The silence was worst. Neither spoke, and the camp went to sleep after the hard work of the day. Tora thought of home and Seimei. He tried to suppress his grief when he felt tears filling his eyes. Too late. He sniffled, and Dragon Tattoo bent forward to peer at him.

"So," the pirate said with a sneer, "you're nothing but a cry baby after all. Maybe I should make an end of you now. It's a pitiful sight to see a grown man cry." His hand touched the sword.

Tora said nothing, but he wiped the tears from his face. This was not the time to mourn. The old man would have expected better from him. He searched his mind for an appropriate lesson from Seimei's favorite Kung-Fu-tse, and settled on "A man must be wary before a move and gain his end by well-laid plans." Yes, he had got into this trouble by not thinking before he rushed into action. This time, he would think carefully about his next move.

He tried to settle himself more comfortably against the rock, but there was no comfort to be found among all this hardness at his back and the sharp edges of loose stones he sat on. An idea began to form in his mind.

He gauged the distance between them and eyed the flickering oil lamp. Outside, it was dark, but there was a somewhat feeble new moon. Without the oil lamp, the world outside the cave entrance would be much lighter, but here they would be plunged into utter darkness. Good for sleep but not for defending yourself against someone swinging a sword.

It was too soon. Someone in the camp might still be awake. Dragon Tattoo also seemed to be waiting. Tora had no illusions that the bastard would obey the chief. He had read murder in the other man's eyes. The pirate had little to lose and could always claim that his prisoner had attempted to escape. It would be easy. He would kill Tora, and then start shouting for help. Who was to prove him wrong?

On the other hand . . .

"You're a coward," said Tora into the stillness.

The other man's eyes flared and his hand went to the sword again, but then he relaxed. "Why don't you make a run for it and find out?"

"I know already. Back at the hostel, you gutless dog brought your friends to help you. You'll always be a coward. Doesn't matter what happens."

"Shut up," growled the other, "you're a dead man. Dead men don't talk."

Tora grinned. "Want to bet? The chief likes me. He doesn't like you."

"You won't live long enough to find out."

"You're stupid. There's nothing you can do to me. If you try anything, I'll start shouting, and the others will come." Tora laughed. "And then you'll lose your balls. Not that you have any to start with."

Dragon Tattoo grasped the sword and started up. "It'll be worth it, scum," he hissed.

Tora got to his feet also. Inside his sleeves, his fists were filled with small stones. "Come on then, coward!"

Dragon Tattoo hesitated. Perhaps he gauged the distance for a fatal blow.

"Come on, big baby," taunted Tora. "I won't make any noise. Let's see what you can do with a sword against an unarmed man."

Still the other man hesitated, though he trembled with rage.

Tora laughed and sat back down. "I knew it."

With a growl in the back of his throat, Dragon Tattoo came, his sword arm swinging back to cut off his enemy's head.

Tora moved like an uncoiled spring, though his muscles rebelled with stabs of agony at the sudden strain. Avoiding the slashing blade by ducking, he flung himself toward his attacker and hurled the gravel into Dragon Tattoo's face. In the dim light of the cave, the pirate's eyes had been wide open and fixed on his intended target when the sharp stones hit them. He recoiled with a gasp, dropped the sword, and clawed at his eyes.

Tora scooped his sword up with his right hand and seized Dragon Tattoo's topknot with his left. Jerking his head back as hard as he could, he cut the other man's throat. The pirate fell forward, made a horrid gurgling sound, kicked out once and then lay still. Tora wiped the sword on the man's back, and stepped out into the night.

All was still. Behind him, the feeble oil lamp still glimmered. He moved away from the cave entrance and headed toward the edge of the woods as quietly as he could. He needed to reach the cover of the trees. The moonlight was weak, but a man moving across the open space and the rock face would be visible to a watcher.

He remembered the look-out who had hailed the ship. Surely, they posted men at night also. He realized he had not planned as well as he thought. Too late!

As he ducked under the low branches of a pine, a voice rang out, "Who's there?"

Tora froze. He did not know their names, and besides, the watcher would recognize a voice. His heart hammered so violently that he was confused when someone close to him answered the watchman's challenge.

"Masaji. Just having a pee."

Laughter. "Weak bladder or too much wine?"

"Too much wine."

"Come up here and talk to me."

"Sorry, Koshi. Can't keep my eyes open."

Under cover of this shouted exchange, Tora moved away cautiously. He stepped on a few crackling branches and once skidded on a loose stone. But he thought he was clear and had put some distance between himself and the two pirates when a voice right behind him hissed, "Not that way. You'll fall to your death."

He stopped and turned slowly. The man who stood behind him looked familiar. Yes, he was the one he had kept from going overboard during the storm. He had not given the alarm, and Tora did not want to kill him. "What're you going to do?" he asked in a low voice, thinking that, one way or another, his life was probably over. Even if the pirates did not kill him, they would find Dragon Tattoo. He would die for murdering one of their own.

"I'll show you the way," said the other man. "Follow me."

Not having a better option, Tora followed him along a narrow path that descended steeply to the small harbor. They clambered down without speaking. When they reached the last trees, his guide put out a hand to stop Tora.

"Wait here and watch for my signal," he said. "They've a watch posted on the ship. Rokuo was pretty drunk, but you never know."

He strolled out on the sandy strip where the fishing boats lay pulled up. Peering toward the ship from time to time, he busied himself with one of the boats, pushed it into the water, and then jumped in. Taking the oars, he started rowing toward the far end of the harbor, gesturing to Tora to meet him there.

Tora kept as much as possible inside the tree line and clambered over several rocky outcroppings. He wondered what the pirate thought he was doing. The man was clearly helping him to escape, and that was a very dangerous thing to do.

They met near the entrance to the secret harbor. The other man was sitting in the boat, which bobbed slightly in the water, and looked impatient. Tora had taken some unlucky turns and backtracked a few times.

"Sorry," he said, wading out and getting in the boat. "Who are you and why are you helping me?"

"I'm Masaji."

Masaji was small but very muscular, perhaps from the hard life he had led as a sailor. He did not look like a pirate. There was something smooth and friendly about his round face, and the smile he gave Tora was childlike and innocent. "You saved me," he said, giving Tora a look of melting adoration from his brown eyes. "You are my bodhisattva."

Tora had guessed at the first part of that explanation and found even this astonishing in a pirate. The bodhisattva business took his breath away. He sat staring at Masaji, who started rowing vigorously toward the entrance of the harbor and the open sea beyond.

"Take the rudder," said Masaji.

"You're coming with me?"

Masaji nodded.

Tora had no experience with boats, but he did his best to steer. They did not talk for a while. Masaji was pulling hard at the oars, at first to get away from the harbor, and then to contend with the rougher waters of the open sea. Tora had planned to steal one of the boats and escape by himself, but he could see now that his lack of experience and skill would have led to recapture or death on the open water. Boats were not very stable, and he would have overset it, trying to steer and work the oars at the same time. It was another failure in planning. His gratitude to Masaji grew.

Steering was simple enough as soon as the first light appeared on the horizon. Tora's mood lifted. Already the rocky outlines of the pirate isle receded, and the softer contours of a much larger land mass approached. They could do it. He considered what to do about Masaji. The man had saved his life. He could not just abandon him to the vengeance of the pirates or the punishment of civil authorities.

Masaji said, "Steer toward the rising sun now." Tora obeyed, and Masaji rowed, his round face alight with happiness, his lips moving.

"Are you praying?" asked Tora.

Masaji bowed his head to him. "Yes. I'm filled with great joy, Reverent Master. I'm giving thanks to Amida that a humble man like myself has been given such a miracle."

"It's not a miracle, and we're not safe yet." Tora glanced at the approaching land. "And there's no need to call me Reverent Master. My name's Tora."

Masaji rowed and laughed. "There's a halo all around you, Tora. I can see it. If you aren't a bodhisattva, then you must be Bishamon." Pulling in the oars, he knelt and bowed his head until it touched the bottom of the boat.

Halo? The man had gone mad. Tora turned and saw the red orb of the rising sun against a bank of dark clouds, its strange color gaining rapidly in brightness. Turning back, he said, "You've been looking at the sun behind me, that's all. Best pick up those oars again."

Masaji obeyed with a smile. "I saw what I saw, and I know what I know, Master. I'm a changed man. You have saved me from my evil life."

Tora sighed.

25

Treading on the Tiger's Tail

They sailed westwards. Akitada and Watamaro reclined on cushions in the cabin. Watamaro had poured wine and offered refreshments, but Akitada was too impatient and sick with worries to do more than take a sip or two.

Watamaro was cheerful and reassuring. "My men know the area well. We should reach Azukishima by midday, and then we'll simply call at every island in the vicinity until we find them. We may find them sooner, if the storm has damaged the ship."

"Thank you." Akitada frowned. Watamaro seemed very sure. But then the man must be thoroughly familiar with the Inland Sea. "How is it," he asked, "that you have not been able to stop these pirates? A man with your means and knowledge of the sea routes surely is in the best position to do so?"

Watamaro chuckled. "Nobody has asked me to do so, and a man in my business cannot afford to act on his own. People would never forgive me."

Astonished, Akitada asked, "Your people would not forgive you? I don't understand. These pirates are men of no mercy who kill and steal at will. Surely, by capturing them you would win praise and gratitude."

"Ah, but the pirates are our people, my Lord. They are the fathers, brothers, husbands, and sons of people living around the Inland Sea. Most were poor fishermen who turned to piracy when they couldn't earn a living catching fish."

Akitada shook his head. "Thieves are thieves. The ones in the capital may be said to be of the people also, and most are poorer than your fishermen. Our country has been blessed with rivers, lakes, and oceans that provide our food in great abundance. There is no excuse for not reaping the harvest when others starve."

Watamaro nodded. "You're quite right, of course. I was simply explaining the bonds that exist and make it difficult to arrest pirates. They are protected by local people. And on the whole, they do little enough damage. The days when pirates worked for great lords who raised their arms against our divine emperor are over."

"Perhaps, and perhaps not."

Watamaro fidgeted and changed the subject, talking instead of famous places and telling stories about local gods and goddesses. Akitada was reminded of the tale the Fujiwara lady had mentioned. He asked, "Have you heard anything about the lady in the River Mansion outside Eguchi?"

Watamaro threw back his head and laughed. "The daughter of the Dragon King?" He stopped laughing. "Oh, forgive me. That was very rude of me. I don't know her, but I've heard the stories." His eyes twinkled again but he suppressed more mirth. "Why do you ask?"

Akitada made a face. "Apparently she entertains a good deal, inviting friends from the capital to sample what the Eguchi brothels have to offer."

Watamaro cocked his head. "You don't approve?"

"No. Not when children become part of the entertainment."

"Ah. This happens?"

"Yes. One of them died in the river below the mansion. It isn't clear whether she committed suicide or . . ." Akitada let his voice trail off.

Watamaro was no longer laughing. He sounded angry. "A child? The young girl you mentioned at Nakahara's dinner?"

"Yes. She looked no more than fourteen. The brothel was grooming her for a 'presentation'."

Watamaro clenched his fists. "For one of the nobles from the capital, I take it. Our masters take whatever they please, and we must bear it. The lady of the River Mansion is a member of the ruling family. She has very powerful friends and protectors." He shot Akitada a glance. "Sorry, but these things are very upsetting to a man like myself."

"Not at all. I agree with you."

Akitada pondered the similarities between the crimes of the wealthy and those of the poor. Neither could be brought to justice, apparently. Watamaro was a wealthy man, but he was also a commoner. His sympathies were with his people.

Toward noon, they stepped outside, Watamaro to talk to his sailors, and Akitada to check their progress. It seemed to him that they were barely moving. The huge sails flapped weakly. But he saw with pleasure the blueness of the water and the deeper blue of land in the distance. Seagulls circled and shrieked overhead, and the air was brisk and pure.

Saburo appeared beside him. "I'm uneasy, sir," he said in a low voice. "Something doesn't seem right. We are barely moving. The wind is against us. I've spent the morning watching the sailors. They act as if they were on a pleasure cruise. You'd think they'd try to speed up this ship."

"What do you mean?"

"Can you trust Watamaro?"

Akitada gave him a sharp look. He said, "Of course. He has generously offered to help."

"Hmm." Saburo looked around. "I could swear we're on a wild goose chase and everybody but us knows it."

"They can't do anything about the wind. It may be your imagination."

"Maybe. But there's something else. Considering we're going to tangle with pirates, you'd expect soldiers and weapons on board, wouldn't you?"

Akitada considered this. "Watamaro knows a lot about pirates and fishermen. From the way he talked to me, he may plan to make a deal with them, perhaps offer them payment to release Tora." The thought appalled him because he would be honor-bound to repay Watamaro. "If there's no bloodshed, all the better," he added.

Saburo nodded. "It's possible." But he looked dissatisfied.

Akitada studied the coastline and looked at the sun. The islands should be to the west. This coastline lay to the north. He suddenly had a hollow feeling in his belly. If Saburo was right and Watamaro could not be trusted, they not only would not rescue Tora but would end up in deep trouble themselves. And he had no one to blame but himself.

An hour later, one of the sailors sighted a ship. It was on the opposite course and, with the wind in its sails, approached quickly.

Akitada joined Watamaro. "What ship is it?"

"A merchant. Probably bound for Kawajiri. There. They're hailing us. They may want to sell something or ask for news."

As the ships drew closer, Akitada could make out the faces of the sailors on the larger ship. They shouted from one ship to the other in a local dialect Akitada did not understand. Watamaro apparently spoke the language and looked excited.

"They say they have two castaways on board," he told Akitada. "One of them says his name is Tora and he is from Naniwa."

Akitada's heart started pounding. "Can you take me across?"

"No. We'll bring them over here. The ship is bound for Kawajiri, and they're glad to get rid of them." He left to give orders.

A short time later, Akitada was leaning over the side to peer down into the boat as it returned. Two men lay on its floor between the legs of the rowers.

Saburo pointed. "That one looks like your man, sir."

"Yes. Yes, I think it's Tora. Are they unconscious? I hope Tora isn't badly hurt. Is that blood on him?"

When they hoisted the two limp figures aboard, Tora was so filthy and ragged, his clothes covered with dried blood, his hair and beard tangled and his face red and swollen that he was hardly recognizable. His companion was not in much better shape.

But Tora's eyes were open, and he managed a weak smile. "Thank God, it's you, sir," he mumbled.

Akitada felt limp with a mixture relief and concern. He turned to Watamaro. "It's Tora. He must have escaped." He knelt beside Tora. "You're covered with blood. Where are you wounded?"

A weak chuckle. "Not mine. Had to kill a man who wouldn't give up my sword. But my head hurts like blazes." He sighed and closed his eyes.

Akitada felt Tora's scalp and found a large swelling. Getting to his feet, he told Watamaro,

"He has a head injury. Tora is very dear to me." He looked down at the exhausted men. "I think it will be best if we make all speed back to Naniwa. He'll need medical care."

Tora protested. Watamaro hesitated a moment, then nodded. "Fate had a hand in this," he said, "and so, no doubt, did your friend's resourcefulness. We should be home by nightfall. There's a very good physician who lives near my warehouse."

Akitada had hoped for better, but he accepted the offer. Tora looked very weak.

Several of Watamaro's sailors helped the two men into the cabin, where they were made comfortable on the floor. Tora opened his eyes again, and muttered, "He's Masaji." Akitada glanced at the other patient.

"Masaji's my disciple," Tora said with a grin. "I'm trying to live up to his good opinion."

Akitada thought Masaji looked like a terrified rabbit and wondered for a moment if Tora was hallucinating. "He must be mad," Akitada said, smiling.

Tora chuckled. "You never had great faith in me. He's a simple man and does."

Saburo came up and leaned over Akitada's shoulder.

"Aiiih!" Tora came upright, his eyes wide with terror. "The demon!"

Akitada pushed him back gently. "No. This is Saburo. He's had a very hard life, but he is a good man. He's helped me find you."

Tora blinked, then asked Saburo, "Who the devil did that to you, man?"

Saburo raised a hand to his face. "Human devils. But that's in the past. It's the present I'm worried about, sir."

"Why?" asked Akitada.

"What if Watamaro is working with the pirates? Who is that man with you, Tora?"

"Masaji. He's one of the pirates, but you can trust him. He helped me escape."

"He knows. Look at him. If I'm right, they'll kill him and all of us."

They all looked at the terrified Masaji, who looked back and nodded. Akitada blamed himself. He should have suspected Watamaro. Who, after all, was more likely to be involved in piracy? And the man's sympathies clearly lay with the pirates.

He glanced outside, where Watamaro was busy directing his sailors. Trying to stay calm, Akitada said, "You may be wrong, but it's as well to be cautious." He added to Tora, "I think you and Masaji, had better pretend ignorance."

Tora sighed and closed his eyes again.

Akitada went to speak to Watamaro. The merchant was pacing the deck like a cat walking on hot coals. Akitada suppressed a surge of panic. All of them, including the renegade pirate Masaji, were in Watamaro's power. On the high seas, they would not have a chance if Watamaro decided to do away with them. Their chances were minimally better back in Naniwa.

He said, "I'm very concerned about Tora's head injury. He rambles, claims he's Bishamon and the other man is his disciple. He doesn't seem to know what happened to him. Can we make more speed?"

Watamaro was solicitous. They would do their utmost to get back to Naniwa. The wind was with them now and was freshening. In a couple of hours perhaps. Akitada thanked him.

The heavens alone knew what awaited them on land.

26

A Sword in his Belly

They reached Naniwa at dusk. Watamaro's manner had changed. He was still moderately courteous but cool. As they walked to his warehouse, Tora leaning on Akitada while Saburo and Masaji tottered behind, Watamaro's men surrounded them on all sides. Escape was impossible.

They were prisoners.

At the warehouse, Watamaro took them to his office and gave orders to his men to stand watch. Then he closed the door and turned. "Please sit down." They all sat. Watamaro's eyes rested thoughtfully on Tora and Masaji. "It seems we have a problem, my Lord."

For a moment, Akitada was tempted to continue the pretense of ignorance, but then he nodded. "You mean, you have a problem. Perhaps you'd better tell me about your relationship with the pirates."

"Ah, I see you guessed. Very clever of you to make me think Tora had lost his memory. The man with him works for me. He knows he's a dead man."

Masaji prostrated himself with a wail. Tora glared at Watamaro. "He saved my life. I won't let you touch him."

"Your words do you honor, Tora, but he belongs to me." Watamaro turned back to Akitada. "I think two reasonable men can find a solution to this unfortunate situation. I've come to have the greatest regard for you, not because of your birth and rank, but because I found you care about common people. You will agree that's a very rare commodity among the nobility. Your feelings for the poor young girl who died in Eguchi impressed me."

Akitada said coldly, "I hope my respect for life extends to all beings, both great and small. Pirates and their masters have little respect for lives or property."

Watamaro sighed. "There's nothing to be gained by anger. I know this well enough because I've been angry most of my life. The young girl you found could have been my sister. We were poor, and she was very pretty. Alas, the pretty daughters of the poor are unlucky."

"Good or bad fortune may come to all people," Akitada said. "I'm sorry about your sister, but that doesn't excuse your present activities. You've become a very rich ship-owner through using both poor fishermen and the local authorities.

When you got greedy and enriched yourself further by engaging in piracy in addition to ordinary shipping, you lost the right to take this moral tone."

Watamaro nodded. "Fair enough, though I've brought prosperity to many poor people. But let me make you a proposition. I'm far richer and more powerful than either Lord Oga or the prefect. You, on the other hand, have nothing but a house in the capital and a poorly paid position in the lower ranks of the administration. Oh, yes. I informed myself about you the moment I met you and realized why you had come. I found you to be a capable and decent man. I can use someone like you, and I'll be far more generous than your current masters. If you agree to help me, you would continue your present life but receive monthly retainers from me. I would only contact you when I needed legal advice in righting an injustice. I would not expect you to do anything illegal. What do you say?"

Akitada flushed with anger. "I'm not for sale. It was you who sent two armed men to my home, wasn't it? They took the life of a man who had been like a father to me."

Watamaro raised his hands. "They didn't intend harm. It was an unfortunate accident. I sent them, yes, but only to make you give up your investigation, nothing else."

Silence fell.

Watamaro looked down at his folded hands. When he looked up again, his eyes went over all of them and came to rest on Masaji. "A pity," he said heavily. He looked suddenly old and sad. "I hate shedding blood."

Masaji scooted forward on his knees to clutch Tora. Tora growled. "You're not touching him."

Watamaro stood. "You've recovered very quickly, Tora. Perhaps it would be best if you gave me your sword." He held out his hand.

"The last man who took my sword is dead."

Watamaro turned to Akitada. "Tell him it's hopeless."

Akitada rose also. "It's hopeless for you, Watamaro. Your threats will make no difference. I'm an imperial official with special powers. If you lay a hand on me and my people, His Majesty will send an army to eradicate you and all your followers. Their blood will be on your hands. It will be much better for you to give yourself up now."

Watamaro snorted. "In the end, you spoiled aristocrats are all the same. You think no one can touch you. We'll see about teaching you a lesson." He walked out of the room, slamming the door behind him. They heard the sound of a metal lock falling into place.

Tora muttered, "Honey in his mouth, but a sword in his belly." He got up, walked over to a bamboo stand, and swept the document boxes and papers from its shelves. With his sword, he cut the vines which held it together. The shelves clattered to the floor, and Tora hefted two of the bamboo supports in his hand. With a nod, he tossed one to Masaji. "They're a bit short, but strong and heavy. Are you good at stick-fighting, Masaji?"

Masaji grinned. "We fought with boat poles."

Tora passed his sword to Akitada. "You really ought to carry yours more, sir."

Akitada nodded. "I'm sorry I got you into this. I counted ten men who brought us here. There could be another ten already in the warehouse."

Tora nodded at the door. "We could break it down and rush them."

"Much the best way," agreed Saburo. "I think I saw weapons among the goods stored outside."

They looked at Akitada. He nodded.

Saburo produced a pair of metal wires from his sleeve. He inserted these into the locking mechanism, then looked over his shoulder at the others. "Ready?" When they joined him, he pushed and twisted. The lock clicked. Tora flung himself against the door. It sprang open, and they fell upon two startled guards outside.

It had been a long time since Akitada had killed a man, and even then it had felt unnatural. He raised Tora's sword, the guard froze, and Tora growled, "Kill him!" Akitada locked eyes with the man.

The other guard, who tried to escape from Tora and Masaji with their bamboo staves, shouted, "They're escaping."

They heard steps and the clatter of arms outside.

Akitada's guard lashed out with his own sword. Akitada parried and shoved his blade into the man's belly. When he withdrew it, the man collapsed with a scream and rolled on the floor in agony. Bile rose to Akitada's mouth, but there was no time to be sick or to think about what he had done.

The large double doors to the outside flew open, and Watamaro's men poured in. The other way, stacks and mountains of stored goods rose nearly to the rafters. Saburo was already climbing the nearest pile like a cat, shouting, "This way." They scrambled after him over crates, bundles, sacks, stacks of lumber, boxes, and *sake* barrels, up high to the dim reaches under the roof. Loosely stacked goods shifted under their feet. Akitada sent an avalanche of rice bags rolling toward their pursuers, barely catching himself with a jump to a stack of lumber.

The warehouse filled with armed men looking up at them. Watamaro came and shouted, "Come down. You're trapped. You'll never fight your way out of this."

They ignored him. Saburo had found a hoard of weapons, enough to outfit a small army, it seemed. He cut the ropes that tied them into bundles—the man seemed to have all sorts of tools on him—and tossed long swords to Akitada and Tora. Masaji exchanged his piece of bamboo for a halberd.

Some of Watamaro's men below started climbing. Let them come, Akitada thought and realized that he was no longer sickened by having killed. He had found his fighting spirit after all.

At that moment, the first arrow hit the beam above his head and stuck there, humming softly.

"Take cover," yelled Akitada, diving behind a box. Something gave under his feet, and he felt himself falling, sliding down with chests, bundles, and assorted sharp objects that seemed to have come alive. Ten, fifteen feet below him, crashes and cries of pain. He scrambled wildly, reaching out with his free hand, when a fist grabbed the back of his robe and held on.

Tora.

"Thanks," he gasped, found a foothold, and climbed away. The "thwack-thwack" of arrows resumed. There was another cry. Watamaro's archers were not very good marksmen, but there were many of them and the distance short. Akitada and Tora found temporary safety behind a beam and surveyed the field.

Watamaro's people had brought in more torches. The floor of the warehouse was well lit. Fortunately, the light did not reach the upper parts of the warehouse. Akitada counted some twenty men below, all armed in some way, but none wearing armor. Watamaro had not alerted the police, but he might have sent for the prefect. They would be lost, if troops arrived before they got away.

"What now?" asked Tora. "It's a stand-off."

"Not for long." Akitada heard the bitterness in his voice. "They are between us and the doors. We'll have to come down and charge through."

Tora grunted.

Below, the men gathered around Watamaro for a conference. Akitada looked for Saburo and Masaji. Masaji huddled on a pile of lumber some twenty feet away. He saw no sign of Saburo and worried for a moment, then remembered the man's talents and looked up into the rafters. Yes, there he crouched, peering down at them and raising a hand.

Tora moved impatiently. "What good is waiting? You don't expect help from anyone, do you?"

"No." For a moment, Akitada saw the dilemma with supernatural clarity. The four of them against twenty, fighting in unfamiliar surroundings. He was badly out of shape after years of government work sitting behind desks or in assemblies. Tora and his companion had spent a night and a day of rowing a small boat in a large sea, and Saburo might be clever and good at throwing odd items through the air, but he could not hold his own in hand-to-hand combat. This was most likely where they would lose their lives. For a brief moment, the pain of never seeing Tamako and his little daughter again twisted his heart.

"All right. Let's go!" he shouted, gesturing their intention to the other two. He grasped the sword firmly and took the shortest route down, jumping, slipping, sliding— hearing Tora following behind. His feet touched solid ground. Though he knew he was facing death, he felt good.

Watamaro's men fell back until Watamaro shouted orders. Then they came. Two, three men at a time. Even if Watamaro had wanted to deal with an imperial official more gently, the matter was now out of his hands. This battle was to the death. In the press of knives and swords coming at him, Akitada was oblivious to anything but the need to fight his way past them.

The long sword gave him reach over the weapons of the sailors and warehouse clerks, and he made bloody work of it. An arrow whizzed past his ear and struck someone behind him. He ignored the scream, slashed, cut, parried, twisted aside to avoid the slashing and cutting blades of the enemy. A bowman loomed, the arrow pointed at his belly, the string pulled back, the man's teeth already gleaming with the joy of hitting his target. He lunged, seized the bow with his left hand, pulling the man forward onto his sword. Something struck him from behind. He staggered into the bowman, pushed him away, freeing his sword as the man fell, and then he was past and saw the way clear to the great doors.

Watamaro, sword in hand, stepped in front of the doors. He looked past Akitada, and shouted an order. Akitada swung around, sword raised. Six or seven of the enemy came running. He crouched, but they rushed past him, the last one staggering as he ran. They were pursued by Tora, teeth bared and clothes soaked in blood. Tora stopped.

The warehouse doors slammed behind the enemy.

In the sudden silence, Tora kicked a body to see if the man was dead. Masaji sat slumped on a rice sack. He was badly wounded. And Saburo? Yes, there he was, grimacing as he pulled an arrow from his forearm.

The floor of the warehouse was covered with dead and wounded men and slippery with blood. Akitada's sword dripped. In only a few moments, this carnage had happened. Suddenly he felt very tired.

"Saburo?" he asked. "How bad is it? And you, Masaji?"

"It's nothing." Saburo ripped a strip of fabric from his jacket and, using one hand and his teeth, made a bandage for his arm.

Masaji said nothing.

Tora killed one of the wounded. The man twitched and lay still. This was not like Tora, this slaughter of the wounded. The good feeling left Akitada. He felt dizzy and nauseated. Wiping his sword with the edge of his robe, he went to sit on a box.

"We need to get out," Tora said.

This was obvious. Akitada did not bother to reply. Tora went to check on Masaji.

Akitada glanced at the great doors. Surely they had locked them. And if not, they were waiting outside. He wondered what time it was. If they could attract attention, perhaps . . . but no, it was late and the warehouse was on the water-side which was deserted at night.

He sniffed, smelling smoke. Someone cooking? Perhaps there were ordinary townspeople nearby after all.

Tora appeared at his side. "Masaji's going to die," he said softly.

Akitada took in the blood on Tora's clothes. "Are you wounded?"

"No. But you are." Tora looked at Akitada's back. "Take off that robe and let me see."

"What? No. I can't be. It's someone else's blood. I was in the thick of it at some point." But as Tora's fingers probed, he did feel a sharp pain on his upper back. And he did feel unusually tired.

Tora said, "It's been bleeding quite a lot. I can't tell if it's just a cut, or if it went deep. You'd best lie down." He sniffed. "Where's that smoke coming from?"

Between them and the doors, tendrils of smoke curled up through the floorboards.

"Amida," breathed Tora, "they're trying to smoke us out."

"No. They intend to burn us alive and claim the fire was accidental." Akitada struggled to his feet, but Tora and the warehouse started spinning, and he slumped back down.

27

Even Monkeys Fall from Trees

Akitada was tired. Perhaps if he closed his eyes for just a moment . . .

Tora pulled him up and told him to walk—in a tone of such urgency that he obeyed. Then he was sitting again. Someone shoved fabric under his robe. After that he was alone.

Resting.

This time he had misjudged matters fatally.

And others would die for it.

Something was burning.

He opened his eyes and staggered to his feet. Wisps of smoke floated between him and the distant light. Behind him, someone was hammering and splitting wood. At his feet, lay Masaji, curled up like a small child. His eyes were wide open, and he smiled.

"We'll be reborn," he whispered.

Akitada said dully, "I hope so," and went to look for Tora and Saburo in the dim back reaches of the stored goods.

He found them using halberds and swords to hack at the back wall. The wood was old and tough, the boards thick. The air was slightly better here, but even so, both coughed and glistened with sweat. He had lost his sword, but he picked up an iron bar and joined them.

Tora looked at him from red-rimmed eyes. "Sit down, sir. You'll open that wound again."

Akitada shook his head. "I have to do something." He shoved the point of the bar between two boards and pried. Nothing. He tried again, this time using both hands. A board popped loose with a satisfying crack. The smoke was growing thicker. Akitada suppressed a cough.

The silence suddenly seemed ominous. Where were Watamaro and his people? "Do you think they can hear us?" he asked hoarsely.

"I hope not." Tora shoved a halberd under the board Akitada had loosened, and between them they forced two more boards out. Fresh air blew in, but the opening was still too narrow. Behind them, the fire crackled. Something fell with a crash, then a thick cloud of smoke engulfed them, and when they turned, the whole front of the warehouse was a fiery hell.

They worked feverishly. Saburo found a coil of rope. He tied it to the nearest beam, tested the knot, and then fed it through the opening.

Akitada put his head out and looked down. It was so dark and smoky; he could not see the ground. He doubted he could hold on to the rope and make his way down. His back was already sticky again with fresh blood, and he could barely lift the iron bar. From what he recalled, it was too far to jump without risking two broken legs. The Naniwa warehouses had been built high above the ground to withstand tsunami.

Tora went back into the smoke and fire that roared behind them. Akitada felt the searing heat and croaked Tora's name in a panic.

"Coming." Tora reappeared, dragging Masaji and coughing. He dropped Masaji next to the hole and peered out. "You go first, sir." He tossed some weapons out.

Akitada hesitated. A voice outside bellowed, "Hey! They're getting out."

Tora cursed. He pushed Akitada toward the opening. "Now, sir. Go!"

Akitada seized the rope and stepped into emptiness.

For a moment he hung suspended. He tried to catch the rope with his feet and go down hand over hand, but his grip slipped immediately and he began to slide. The hemp burned and tore his palms, but he managed to end up on his feet, jarred by the impact. His hands were on fire.

It was dark and smoky under the warehouse. Watamaro's man stood only a few feet away, staring. When he lunged, Akitada barely managed to snatch up a sword.

The sword grip slipped in his raw and burning palm, but he was lucky. The other man tripped over something and fell. Akitada put a foot on his back, and stabbed downward. Agonizing pain shot up his wrist. It was too dark to see if he had struck a vital organ, but he heard a choking cry and felt a weak movement under his foot. Withdrawing the sword, he stabbed down again and again.

Then Tora was beside him. "He's done for, sir," he gasped. "Get ready for the others." Above them the fire cracked and roared, and sparks showered the darkness.

Akitada looked up. The night sky was red, and the rope whipped about in circles. Smoke billowed from the opening, and then Saburo slid down and joined them. He pointed past Akitada. Dark shadows moved under the warehouse in the lurid smoke rent by flames and showers of burning debris.

Akitada still held the sword, but his hand was nearly useless. Trying to get a grip hurt as if his palm had been scorched by the flames. "It's no use, Tora," he called out. "We must get away. There are too many. We cannot fight them all."

Tora shook his head. "Not without Masaji, sir. You go."

Saburo came to stand beside them with his halberd.

Put to shame, Akitada made up his mind to fight. Above them the fire raged. Debris had accumulated under the warehouse and around it. In front of them, their attackers came out of the smoke, their weapons swinging. How many? It did not matter. They would stand and fight until they could fight no more.

A tall man with a long sword was the first to reach them. "Give up," he shouted, breathing hard, "and you'll live." He looked nervous and held his sword as if he were unused to it.

Akitada charged. The man jumped back quickly, looking over his shoulder. The others came and metal rang as Tora and Saburo moved nearby, swinging, grunting, slashing. Akitada went for the tall man again and sent him running. He turned to meet two others—more experienced fighters—who forced him back. One of them fought with a staff, the other had a long sword. Akitada lunged at the swordsman, twisting away just before the staff hit him. But he stumbled over something, barely caught his balance, and knew his strength was ebbing. He could not parry or deflect another attack.

Tora appeared beside him, ducking past the man with the staff, to gore the swordsman in the side. Akitada slashed at the arm of the second man. The staff fell, and the man ran, clutching his arm. He disappeared into a cloud of smoke and fire as the front of the warehouse collapsed. Suddenly they were alone.

Saburo threw down his halberd and loped over. "How are you, sir?"

Akitada felt little beyond relief that he could let go of the sword. He said, "All right," and looked at his palms.

Saburo checked his back. "The bleeding stopped, I think."

A scream. "No, Masaji!"

They jumped. Tora stood looking up at the hole in the side of the warehouse. In the opening stood Masaji, smoke and flames outlining his swaying figure.

Tora ran for the rope, slipped, fell, and scrambled up again, while Masaji swayed above, a smile flashing wide in his sooty face. "I'm coming, Bishamon," he croaked and tumbled forward. His body struck Tora a glancing blow and landed with a sickening thud on the ground.

Akitada and Saburo ran to them. Tora struggled up, rubbing his shoulder. Masaji lay still.

"Damn you, Masaji!" Tora groaned. "Why couldn't you wait? I was coming." He knelt, taking Masaji's hand and touching the still smiling face.

Saburo checked the pirate. "He's dead, Tora," He lifted Masaji's blood-soaked tunic and revealed a big wound in his belly. "He was dying before he fell."

Tora hung his head. "I owe him my life."

Guilt washed over Akitada. This, too, was his fault. None of the past horrors would have happened if it had not been for his foolish mistake of trusting Watamaro.

"I'm sorry," he said awkwardly. "I'm sorry I caused all of this. I hope you'll forgive me."

Tora only shook his head.

Saburo produced his horrible grin. "Never mind, sir. Even monkeys fall out of trees." Then he raised his head. "I hear horses."

It was too late to run. Torches appeared. Metal and leather clanked. Hooves clattered across the hard ground, and the prefect's military guard surrounded them.

28

Reckoning

The prefect's soldiers raised their bows and placed their arrows in unison. Then they pulled back. Twenty-six arrows pointed at three tired and wounded men.

"Well-trained," Tora muttered.

Akitada straightened up slowly. He felt incredibly weary. There was little point in this, but he must make the effort. He took a step toward their commander and said, "You're a little late, but I thank you for coming at all. I'm Sugawara Akitada, special investigator from the capital. These are my people. We will need horses and transport for the dead man. Take us to the prefecture."

The commander shoved his helmet back a little and stared at him. He next looked at Tora, then Saburo with a grimace of disgust, and finally at the body of Masaji. He said coldly, "You're under arrest for fighting and setting fires. Setting fires is a capital offense." He turned to his men. "Tie them up."

"Wait," cried Akitada. "You're making a mistake. You should be arresting Watamaro. He attacked us and set the fire."

The officer gave him a contemptuous look. "Don't be stupid. Why would he burn down his own warehouse? Besides he's a respected man in this province."

Four of his constables had dismounted and now approached with the thin chains used to tie up dangerous criminals. Tora got up and stepped in their way. "I'd rather die than have you put those on my master," he growled.

The soldier closest to him swung the thin chain viciously. It struck the side of Tora's face and wrapped around his head. Tora choked down a cry and clawed at the chain. Blood trickled down his face.

"You'll pay for this," Akitada snapped, but it did no good. The chain came off Tora's head, leaving him bleeding and dazed, and all three had their hands tied. The soldiers attached the chains to three of the horses.

Akitada had seen this sort of thing before and knew what was coming. They would be taken to jail, and if they could not keep up with the horses, they would be dragged along the streets. "Look, Officer," he said, trying to sound reasonable, would you at least notify the prefect before you do this? He won't thank you when the central government in the capital punishes him for mistreating an imperial emissary."

The man laughed. "It's the middle of the night. And you don't look like an imperial emissary to me."

They were covered with blood and soot. Akitada's silk robe was filthy and torn. He had lost his hat, and his topknot had come loose. No doubt he looked like a hoodlum, though he was not quite as ragged as his companions. He felt his sash for some sort of identification but found nothing. Even his silver was gone.

"At least put us on horses and tie us there. We're tired and wounded."

"Serves you right," snapped the officer and raised his hand. "Let's go."

A nightmarish journey took them up the long thoroughfare Akitada had walked many times. They were forced to trot alongside the horses. Akitada stumbled once, and only caught himself by grasping the horse's tail. His hands hurt badly, and he barely escaped a kick. When they reached the prefecture, the gates slammed shut behind them and the horses stopped. Akitada collapsed on the gravel and tried to steady his breathing. He heard the officer call out, "They claim to be imperial emissaries, sir. Thought you might get a good laugh out of that. No question about it, they're dangerous criminals. The warehouse burned to the ground, and we counted at least ten bodies."

Akitada raised his head. Munata was coming down the steps. Perhaps the warehouse fire had roused him early. Behind him, dawn was just breaking. A new day.

Perhaps their last.

He struggled to his feet. "Tell your man who I am," he said. His voice sounded gravelly and incredibly tired.

Munata paused, then came closer. Akitada saw his eyes widen.

"Dear heaven, what happened?" he asked, then bowed. "My deepest apologies, my Lord. Ihara, untie His Excellency immediately."

The officer's face fell comically, but Akitada was too miserable to enjoy the moment or to complain. After a scramble and some agitated muttering, the chain fell from Akitada's wrists. He cradled his sore hands against his chest. "Untie my men, too. Then have the merchant Watamaro arrested along with all those involved in the battle at the warehouse. We need medical attention, baths, and clean clothes. The dead man needs a funeral." He ran out of breath. Perhaps Munata would avoid open defiance of the court and instead try, by whatever means, to clear his name.

Munata looked deeply shocked. His eyes went from Akitada to his companions and the corpse of Masaji on one of the horses, then back again. "Watamaro did this?" Akitada said nothing. He was past speech. "Never mind, sir. My house is at your disposal. But you cannot walk. Perhaps by *kago*? Shall we send for chairmen?"

An offer of a litter and luxurious accommodations?

Akitada looked at his companions and took a deep breath. "No, thank you. We're only going across the street to the official lodging house. You will be here the rest of the day?"

"Yes, Excellency, but allow me to arrange for more comfortable quarters. And my personal physician is at your service."

"Send the physician by all means. I shall speak to you later, after we have rested."

Akitada nodded to his companions, and together they walked out of the prefecture. Akitada forced himself to walk with a straight back and a firm step until they were out of Munata's sight. Then he slumped and heaved a sigh of utter exhaustion.

"I thought they'd put us in irons," Tora remarked, taking his arm. "Are you in pain, sir?"

"No," Akitada lied. "Just exhausted. How's your face?"

Tora touched his cheek. "Stings a bit."

"And you, Saburo?"

"Fine, sir." Saburo grimaced. Akitada was beginning to distinguish between his scowls and smiles. Saburo was smiling.

"You're a good fighter, Saburo," Tora said, "but never wake a man again from a sound sleep by sticking that face of yours at him."

Saburo nodded meekly. "Sorry. I wasn't thinking."

The lodging house seemed almost like home after what they had been through. The same fat man received them, looking both wary and disgusted by their appearance. "What happened to you?" he asked rudely.

"None of your business," snapped Tora. "Where's your daughter? If that's what she is."

The man scowled. "The wife left me and took her. Good riddance. And it's none of your business."

Akitada interrupted and ordered baths to be prepared. A skinny youth showed them to a room and then brought Akitada's and Tora's bags from the storage room where they had left them. They looked forward to taking off their blood-soaked clothes. Saburo had nothing to wear, but they managed to find him a pair of trousers and a shirt.

The prefect's physician arrived right after their baths. He seemed capable, cleaned their wounds, and bandaged them. Akitada needed a plaster on the cut on his back, but he refused to have his hands bandaged. Tora's face had only cuts, but Saburo's arrow wound worried the doctor. The arrow had gone through the fleshy part of Saburo's lower arm, and he had trouble moving his hand.

Afterward, they slept. Akitada was in no hurry to face Munata.

When Akitada woke, it was afternoon and Tora was gone. Saburo meditated in the lotus position again.

Akitada sat up gingerly, and found that the wound on his back felt better. His palms, though, were stiff and sore. He got up.

Saburo opened his eyes. "How are you?"

"I feel better. And you?"

Saburo grimaced a smile. "I've had much worse."

"Yes. Where's Tora?"

"He said he'd check on the little girl and would be back soon."

Akitada nodded. He put on his best robe and trousers. "I'm going to the prefecture and won't need either of you for some hours. Here." He gave Saburo several pieces of silver. "Buy yourself a decent robe and trousers like those Tora normally wears. And a small black cap. A shave and haircut would also be nice. If you're working for me, you'll have to look the part."

Saburo bowed. "I'm sorry to point out, sir, that new clothes and a shave and haircut will not make me as handsome as Tora. Are you sure you want to be seen with me?"

"I'm sure."

This time, the guards and attendants at the prefecture greeted Akitada with nervous respect. Clothes, especially when they bore court rank insignia, had this effect. Munata met him in the reception hall of the prefecture. He had not bothered to change into better clothes, looked pale and distraught, and bowed deeply. He led Akitada with great courtesy to a set of cushions on the raised dais.

When Akitada refused an offer of wine and refreshments, Munata did not persist.

"What about Watamaro and his men," Akitada demanded.

The prefect looked at him dully. "Alas, the merchant has disappeared. His ship has gone, too. And my men are still interviewing people to see who was involved in the disturbance last night."

"Disturbance?" Akitada glared. "It was an assassination attempt that cost one man his life and wounded two of us. Watamaro intended to burn us to death. I shall report the matter as an attack on an imperial official."

"Yes, my Lord."

Akitada took the imperial orders from his sleeve. "As I told you, I have authority to investigate the illegal activities in this province, and more precisely, in your prefecture. Normally, I would present these documents to the governor, but he also seems to have disappeared." He extended the papers.

Munata touched his head to the floor, then received them with both hands, raising them briefly to his forehead. He unrolled the documents, read quickly, and returned them with another bow. "I'm completely at your service, Excellency. As for the governor . . . I imagine you haven't heard. He is in seclusion in the capital. He mourns the death of his only son."

Astonishment and dismay washed over Akitada. "What?"

"You met Yoshiyo at my house. It was a terrible shock and grief to me to hear of his death. I loved that boy. Everyone loved him." Munata looked away and raised a sleeve to his eyes. "Forgive me. I'm not myself."

The man did look terrible. Was he to be foiled again from prosecuting charges against the governor, Munata, and perhaps Otomo? The professor, too, had claimed affection for his pupil.

"What happened?"

"Yoshiyo was deeply upset because his father had forbidden him to buy out a courtesan he had met. He made up his mind to defy his father, but the girl killed herself. Alas, when he found out, he decided to follow her on that dark path." Munata sighed deeply. "Even in the midst of their robust lives, the young are close to death."

Yes, so it had been with his own small son, Yori. Akitada did not know what to say. A deep sadness seized him, and with it pity for those who had loved the two young people. Then he gave himself a mental shake. There had been no one to love Akogi except that unfortunate boy who had brought her death. It strengthened Akitada's conviction that she had been murdered, and his heart hardened against the governor.

What to do about Munata and the other culprits was another matter. On one hand, Munata had finally acknowledged imperial authority and was cooperating. On the other, it was likely that he had allowed Watamaro to escape. Of this, however, there was no proof.

"What do you know about Nakahara's and Otomo's involvement in the piracy matter?" Akitada asked him.

Munata straightened and made an effort to attend to his own problems. "Nothing, Excellency. I swear by Amida. I realize that the burden of guilt rests most heavily on me because I should have known what was going on in my prefecture. Nakahara is my friend and an honest man, if perhaps not a very efficient administrator. Professor Otomo I don't know as well, but he's respected and trusted by the governor. I should think that piracy is not really his area of interest. He's a scholar."

"He's a descendant of Korean immigrants. And the recent piracies involve goods shipped through Korean merchants."

Munata sighed. "Even so, I don't know of anything that would link either man to the pirates, Excellency."

Akitada pondered this. If Nakahara was innocent, the most obvious suspects were his clerks. "You mentioned Nakahara's carelessness in his duties. He has two clerks. Both were in a position to gain information and pass it to Watamaro."

"Yes, that could be the answer. Those two!" Munata paused and thought. "Nariyuki comes from the capital. Nakahara brought him along when he first came here. I think he's a nephew or cousin. Nakahara's much too lenient with him. I rarely see that young man do anything but have a good time in town. That kind of life costs money and brings him in contact with undesirable elements."

Akitada raised his brows. "If you suspected him, you should have mentioned it to me from the start."

"I had no proof. Still don't. How can I accuse a man of a heinous crime without more than a vague suspicion? Or disapproval of his life style."

"Hmm. What about Tameaki?"

"He's the opposite of Nariyuki. Tameaki works hard even though Nakahara doesn't like him and treats him badly. He belongs to a local family. His father was a clerk, too. They were poor but saved and scraped to send him to good schools.

It was I who recommended him to Nakahara."
Munata shook his head. "I may not have done either a favor. Tameaki is very ambitious. Given that and the poor treatment he has received, one has to wonder why he stayed."

"Yes, precisely." Akitada's opinion of Munata rose. The man was a shrewd observer of human nature. Tameaki's efficiency and his subservient manner had indeed been unnatural. "You say his family used to be poor? What has changed?"

"They have come into some land recently. If you like, I'll have the police check on both young men."

"Please."

A brief silence fell. Then Munata asked, "What about me, Excellency?"

"I must report what has happened. If you are in fact guiltless, I doubt you'll receive more than an official reprimand for not having reported irregularities."

Munata breathed a relieved, "Thank you, Excellency."

Akitada went from the prefecture directly to Nakahara's office. He wanted to confront the guilty party now rather than wait for the painstaking investigation by the police.

Nakahara was at work. Perhaps his fear of punishment had had a good influence on his work habits. Both clerks attended him, their brushes busy copying documents.

When he saw Akitada, Nakahara paled and stumbled through a greeting. He made an awkward comment on the Watamaro incident, murmuring, "What a shocking thing!"

Akitada cut him off. What have you done with the letters my clerk sent to me?"

"What letters? There have been no letters except for one. You got that."

"Sadenari sent me regular progress reports." Akitada let his eyes move over the clerks. "Someone in this office has intercepted them. One of you has been working for Watamaro."

They stared at him. Nakahara gasped, "What do you mean?"

Nariyuki cried, "Working for Watamaro? Whatever for?" He turned to Tameaki. "Is that why you were forever carrying papers to his place? I didn't know you were working for him, too. You're a regular glutton for work."

A shocked silence fell. Nariyuki was clearly not very bright. Nakahara understood, though. He flushed and looked at Tameaki.

The thin, pale Tameaki had grown several shades paler. "I wasn't working for Watamaro," he cried. His voice was shrill. "I was told to take those papers to him."

Nakahara rose in outrage. "That's a lie, Tameaki. How dare you accuse me, you repulsive little worm? I never liked you, but you seemed grateful and you worked hard. I see now it was all pretense so you could sell Watamaro information about orders and shipping details." He shook a finger at the clerk. "It was you all the time! You won't get away with this. I'll have you arrested."

Tameaki jumped up, looked about him like a cornered rat, then made a move toward the door.

"Running won't do you any good, Tameaki," Akitada said. "You'll be found and it will all come out. The police are already investigating you."

The clerk turned on Nariyuki. "You brainless, good-for-nothing idiot!"

Nariyuki grinned.

With a shout of fury and balled fists, Tameaki rushed him. The taller, stronger Nariyuki rose with surprising speed, caught him, flung him to the floor, and sat on him.

It had all come apart quite easily.

Tora knocked on the door of a shabby house in the poorest quarter of Naniwa. He had asked people living near the official hostel for directions. The door opened, and an old crone came at him with a long knife in her hand. Tora backed away.

"Careful, granny," he said. "You might hurt someone."

She lowered the knife. "I'd like to hurt the fat bastard that married my daughter. I thought you were him. What do you want?"

"Would that be the fat bastard who runs the official hostel?"

"Runs? The good-for-nothing bum sleeps there to rest up from beating his wife and child."

"That's the one. I'm Tora. I came to see the little girl."

Her face wrinkled up. She wailed, "Oh, the poor child. What he did to her! Ako, come here."

A younger female crept up behind the old one and peered timidly over her shoulder. She had greasy hair, two black eyes, a swollen nose, and a split lip.

"My daughter," said the old one and added, "He says he's Tora."

The woman nodded and gave him a tiny smile that revealed broken front teeth.

The old woman held the door open. "Come in then and see what he's done, the devil."

Tora stepped into the dry stench of abject poverty. They lived in one room and probably did their cooking outside—when they had food. In a dark corner, a bundle of dirty clothes lay on the dirt floor. The old crone gestured to them, and Tora went closer. At first he did not know what he was looking at, then he saw a pair of eyes gleaming like two black beads. Her face was as gray as the rags she lay on, but the feverish eyes were fixed on him.

She whispered, "Tora?"

"Yes, it's me, little one." His heart contracted. "What's wrong?" he asked the women. They did not answer. He knelt beside the child. "What's wrong, Fumiko? Are you in pain?"

A small, dirty hand emerged from the folds of fabric and crept toward him.

The grandmother said harshly, "The devil broke her arm and hurt her back so she can't stand. He beat her with a piece of lumber. They brought her to her mother on a board." She turned to her daughter. "You stupid slut, you should've come to me long ago, but you had to stay with your man and master. Even after he near killed Fumiko."

The younger woman wailed, "I begged him to get a doctor."

"As if that bastard cares what happens to either of you. So he beat you up, too. Serves you right." She spat. Her daughter started to weep noisily.

The little girl watched them all without blinking. Tora peeled back the blanket and saw that her right arm was badly swollen and lay at an unnatural angle." Reaching into his sash, he drew out some money. "Here," he said to the old woman. "Get the best doctor you can find, and have him bring something for her pain."

The grandmother bobbed her head and hurried out. Tora and the little girl's mother waited. After a while, the mother sat down on the child's other side. They did not speak. There was nothing to be said.

Akitada returned to a scene of violence outside the hostel. Screams reached his ears long before he saw the people gathered around its entrance. Still shaken from the night before, he started to run. Then he saw Tora. He was swinging a rope at the bloody back of the fat man who hung, tied by his arms to one of the rafters and with his toes barely touching the veranda floor. With every smacking impact of the rope, he convulsed violently and uttered a high-pitched scream. The onlookers encouraged Tora with shouts, and the rope returned with another whack. The fat man swung and screamed, the rope withdrew, returned to coil across his back, and he swung and howled again.

Akitada roared, "Tora!"

Tora did not turn, but he lowered his arm. The bloody rope curled in the dirt beside his boots.

The fat man went on screaming.

29

Akogi

"Y^{ou} should've seen what that brute did to her. To them," said Tora defensively.

"When I got there, the two women were in fear for their lives. And the poor kid was . . . more dead than alive." He shook his head and looked at Akitada with deeply troubled eyes. "How can a man hurt a little child like that?" He looked at his hands as if they had suddenly turned into the claws of a wild beast. "You saw her, sir. She's so little and weak. He's starved her and beaten her and made her young life a hell. What sort of punishment would you give a man for that?"

"I don't know, Tora, but you cannot take the law into your own hands in such a public manner. It reflects poorly on us and encourages people to do the same without justification."

Saburo snorted. Akitada shot him a repressive glance. "And you stood by and let it happen. I had hoped for better sense from you." The comment about monkeys falling from trees still rankled.

Both of them looked offended now.

Saburo said, "Lecturing a man like that fat slob is like reading a sutra to a horse. Tora taught him a lesson he understands."

"And how will you protect the mother and child after we leave here?"

They were silent.

Akitada relented a little. "Oh, well. I suppose the crowd outside was sympathetic. I'll mention the situation to the prefect."

Tora asked, "How did your visit go, sir?"

"Munata has decided to cooperate."

Tora whistled. "Thank heaven. I thought we'd fallen among all the devils in hell. What about Watamaro?"

"He seems to have taken flight. I'll report to the court, but the matter is out of my hands."

"And the local officials?"

"They, too, will have to face charges. At the very least, negligence in carrying out their duties; at worst malfeasance. I doubt if anyone can prove plans for an insurrection."

"Lots of weapons in that warehouse," Saburo pointed out. "Why collect them if not to outfit an army?"

"True, but the warehouse burned."

Silence fell again.

After a while, Tora brightened a little. "So, shall we go home?"

"Not quite yet. There is still Akogi. We have to go back to Eguchi."

The following day, Akitada rode again through the gates of the River Mansion. He was more elegantly attired than last time. The fine blue silk robe and white silk trousers were the only clothes he still owned and had been intended for the few official occasions when formal clothing was required. Tora and Saburo, both neatly dressed in blue cloth robes, dark trousers, and small black caps, rode side by side behind him. They, in turn, were followed by ten armed soldiers from the prefectural guard.

The lady's servants rushed to help Akitada down and take his horse. *Betto* Kakuan hurried down the steps of the main building. He led him to a small reception room close to the river.

The sounds of water traffic and shouts from passing boats drifted in through the open doors and should have cheered him. But the day was distinctly chilly, the sky overcast. A cold rain had fallen overnight. Autumn showed its harsher side, hinting at the snows to come. The year was drawing to a close.

Dreary, rainy days always cast him into a somber mood, and recent events made his thoughts more bitter and funereal. At home, the memories of Seimei would surround him. He would finally have time to grieve. Not even holding his wife and little daughter in his arms again would ease that pain.

He had come because of Akogi, a young life extinguished before she could taste it. He had no proof that she was murdered, but his every instinct and what he had learned convinced him that she died horribly. Most likely, she had been held under water until she stopped struggling.

The door opened, and the lady of the River Mansion tripped in, followed by another female. On this occasion, the lady's costume was strictly formal and proper for a ranking court lady of mature years.

Her companion carried a small folding screen, prettily painted with wisteria blooms overhanging a pond with playing *koi*. This she set up between her mistress and Akitada before taking her own seat in a corner of the room.

"A pleasure to welcome you again, my Lord," the lady said from behind her pretty screen and an open fan. "I was disappointed by your abrupt departure the other night."

Perhaps she expected an apology or a comment on his discovery of Sadenari. Akitada ignored her. With his sternest face, he said coldly, "I have been told, Lady Kazuko, that you arranged meetings between Oga Yoshiyo and the girl Akogi. As a result of those meetings, both have died."

She made a startled movement. "Oh, that poor young man," she said softly. "I grieve for him. He was the son I never had. Such a sweet boy. It is a great loss to his father."

"I doubt his father thanked you for introducing him to Akogi."

"But I did not," she cried. "At least not directly. The governor knows that very well. It was he himself who asked my help in the matter."

"Perhaps you'd better explain."

She moved her head impatiently. "I don't understand. Why should I explain to you? And why did you come here with armed soldiers? I belong to the great chancellor's family and live here under imperial protection."

"I serve under special orders from the Minister of the Right. The prefect supplied the escort. As for this visit: during my investigation into local ties to piracy, the case of the murdered child courtesan came up. Since her murder involves the highest-ranking official in the province, I thought it best to look into it." This skirted the question of his authority. He hoped she would be nervous enough not to demand proof.

She did not. Instead, she pleaded with him. "Murder? I know nothing about any murder. Oga is a doting father, and the boy was his only son. He wanted the best for him, but Yoshiyo always had his head in his books and talked about taking the tonsure. That handsome boy!" She paused to shake her head at the shocking thought. "His father has been a guest at some of my little parties and thought I could show the lad what he'd be missing in a religious life. I obliged him. I invited the reigning *choja*, this year's queen of the courtesans in Eguchi, and several other exquisite women. The boy came with his father. He was shy around the women, but he did speak to the young girl who attended the *choja*."

Akitada knew what was coming and waited.

With a small sound of impatience, she continued. "Yoshiyo returned the very next day. Without his father. He asked me to arrange meetings with the young one. I argued. To no avail. There were difficulties. The woman who runs the Hananoya wouldn't hear of it, at least not without being paid the presentation money. He paid it and forgot all about becoming a monk. The two lovers met here, in the pavilion overlooking the river. They made a charming couple, and I thought all was well, but then the young fool went to his father to ask for money to buy her out. He wanted to make her his wife. You may imagine what happened next. The governor raged down here like a fiery dragon. He swept in and threatened me. Me!" She shuddered at the memory.

"I see. What did you do?"

"Nothing. Why should I? Let him deal with his own family problems. He left to speak to the woman at the Hananoya, and that's the last I know of it."

"And then the girl was murdered?"

Again the impatient movement behind the screen. "Not murder. She must have drowned herself in despair."

"From what you say about the young people being deeply in love . . . or at least thoroughly infatuated with each other . . . I think Akogi would have run away to be with him. She would not have killed herself."

Lady Kazuko said irritably, "Have it your way. I told you all I know. And now you may leave and take your soldiers with you."

And that was that.

His next visit was to the Hananoya, the brothel where Akogi had trained. He left the soldiers outside but took Tora and Saburo with him. The owner was a short, middle-aged female whose elaborately twisted hair looked false and who wore an inappropriate and costly silk brocade gown. She smiled, bowed deeply, and asked how she might serve the honored gentleman.

"I have some questions regarding one of your women," said Akitada.

"This insignificant person is at your lordship's service. Nakagimi, the current *choja* resides in this house. Alas, she is not available, but my other young ladies are as pretty and very talented. How may we please you?"

Akitada sat down and waved to Tora and Saburo to do the same. "Send for her. I'll wait."

So her name was Nakagimi. He had been too besotted to ask her.

The Hananoya's owner blinked. Then she bowed. "My deepest apologies, your Honor, but a *choja* cannot be summoned at short notice. She receives invitations, and if she feels like it, she attends."

Akitada raised his voice a little. "You're wasting my time, woman. She will answer questions, not entertain. If you don't bring her, my attendants will do so."

A servant slipped in and whispered something in her mistress' ear. The owner of the Hananoya looked less assured. "My maid says there are soldiers outside. What is this about, my Lord?"

"The girl Akogi. Go get the *choja*."

Perhaps there was fear in her eyes, but she hid it well. "A moment," she murmured and left with the servant.

"That one's a killer if ever I saw one," muttered Tora. "I bet she beats the girls and cheats them out of their money."

Tora had considerable experience with brothels and their inhabitants, much to Akitada's irritation over the years. Now Akitada wished he had been more understanding. He had a great deal to be ashamed of and would have done much to avoid the coming encounter.

The owner returned presently, followed by the young woman who had come so painfully close to seducing Akitada during the party. Nakagimi wore only her thin silk undergown and a loose embroidered robe over it. Perhaps she had been roused from a sound sleep. He was almost afraid to look at her and hoped that in the light of day he would find her vulgar and tawdry. Instead, she looked enchantingly flushed and confused.

She recognized him, flushed a little more deeply, and knelt. "Lord Sugawara," she murmured, "you honor me. I thought you had forgotten our time together. Please forgive my appearance."

Aware of Tora's eyes boring into his back, Akitada said stiffly, "I have come because you may have information about the death of the *shinju* Akogi. I was told that she attended you when you were introduced to the governor's son."

"That is so, my Lord."

Akitada caught a glimpse of trembling lips and steeled his heart. "It must have been irritating for you that a mere child captured the young man's heart."

That made her angry. She bit her lips. "Not at all," she said coldly. Then she caught herself, lowered her lashes, and added more softly, "I prefer older men. Men of your own age, I mean, my Lord."

Akitada cursed the woman inwardly. "I understand the governor found out about the relationship between Akogi and his son and came here to put a stop to it."

She looked at the owner of the Hananoya. "You would have to ask Mrs. Wada."

"Well, Mrs. Wada? What did Lord Oga say to you?"

The mistress of the Hananoya answered calmly enough. "His Excellency asked me to stop future meetings. I agreed and informed Akogi. The foolish girl was very upset. That very night she drowned herself. I blame myself. I should have realized how strong her emotions were."

A brief silence followed, then Nakagimi said flatly, "Akogi did not drown herself."

Her mistress snapped, "You know nothing about it!"

The younger woman flushed with anger. "I know what I know," she said darkly.

Akitada would have followed up on that, but he decided to let it go for the moment. "I understand you are related to the local warden, Mrs. Wada. What is that relationship precisely?"

"He's my husband."

"No doubt that is helpful in your business?"

"The business is mine, my Lord."

"Indeed. But I expect you called on his assistance when the governor turned his anger on you."

"Oh." The *choja* sucked in her breath. She was staring at Mrs. Wada, clearly shocked by a thought that had occurred to her.

"You must tell what you know, Nakagimi," Akitada said. "Akogi was murdered, and we believe the Wadas are implicated."

"Murdered?" She glanced at him and back at the older woman. "I will not stay here any longer. This scandal will ruin my future."

Her reaction was utterly self-serving, and she lost all of her attractiveness for Akitada at that moment. He hated that he had once again been proved correct in his disdain for courtesans and women of the street and rose in disgust.

Mrs. Wada glared at the *choja*. "It's all nonsense. And you cannot leave. We have a contract."

Nakagimi raised her chin. "I'm buying myself out."

Instantly, the women fell into a heated argument over moneys and rules. Akitada broke in sharply, "Enough! You're both under arrest until the matter is cleared up."

They protested. The *choja* cried, "No. I'll tell you what happened. I heard it all. I didn't know what they were up to, but I know she gave Akogi to her husband, and that was the last that anyone has seen of her."

Mrs. Wada screamed abuse and hurled herself at the *choja*, and the *choja* fought back by biting and scratching. Akitada jumped aside in alarm, while Tora strode into the middle of the fracas, seized the women by their flailing arms, and pulled them apart.

"Thank you," said Akitada with a sigh of relief. "Saburo, call the soldiers. They can take the women and the warden to the prefectural jail for interrogation."

Their departure became noisy and ugly, but Akitada was adamant. He was fed up with them. Let the authorities handle the matter.

The warden arrived just as the women were dragged outside with their hands tied behind their backs. He goggled and demanded, "What's all this? What are you doing in my ward? Let my wife and the *choja* go this minute."

The guard officer grinned down from his horse. "Sorry, Wada. We were just going to inform you in person, but you've saved us the trouble. You're all under arrest."

Content in the knowledge that the Wadas had confessed and were safely jailed and awaiting trial, Akitada paid a final visit to Professor Otomo. The house was silent and no one answered his call. The silence seemed ominous and made him nervous.

He found the old couple, seated side by side in the main room of the house, small, shrunken figures in the stiff hemp gowns of deep mourning. The professor's wife was weeping silently, her face wet with tears. She clutched her husband's hand. The professor looked pale but calm. He met Akitada's eyes with resignation.

"Am I under arrest?" he asked.

"Are you guilty of a crime?"

"Perhaps. I don't care, but my wife is innocent. It would trouble me to leave her."

His wife squeezed his hand and smiled tremulously through her tears.

Akitada sighed and seated himself. "What are you doing? Why the mourning? Surely that isn't customary for a former pupil."

The old people looked at each other. Then the professor said, "Yoshiyo was our grandson. We loved him more than our lives."

Akitada gaped at them. "Your grandson?"

"Yes. Our daughter died when he was small. She was the governor's concubine. That was my fault. I should not have permitted it."

His wife said, "Nonsense, my dear. She loved him. And you would not have had Yoshiyo."

Her husband bowed his head.

This came as a surprise, but one that might explain much. "Is that why you lied to me about the Korean girls?"

The old man nodded. "Yes, to my shame. The amulet was my daughter's, and she had passed to Yoshiyo. I knew he had given it to Akogi. When you mentioned the drowned girl and showed me the amulet, I was desperate to keep him from finding out."

"And so you tried to convince me that the girl we found committed suicide because she had been abducted from Korea?"

The professor nodded. "Yes, I had to make up a story to account for the amulet. A man's love for his children and grandchildren, it seems, is stronger than his regard for his honor.   Please forgive me."

They sat in silence. Akitada pondered his own past and thought of Seimei. Seimei, Tora, and Tamako had helped him shed the black despair that had nearly turned to self-destruction. He felt great pity for the two old people.

He sighed and took the amulet from his sash. Placing it before Otomo, he said, "You must have hated leaving this in my hands. I lost a child myself and, in my grief I, too, made mistakes. I cannot restore your grandson to you, but I can at least tell you what happened. Your grandson loved Akogi, and I believe she loved him too much to forget him. In his rage, the governor threatened the owner of the Hananoya, and she and her husband took her young life. They have been arrested and have confessed."

The professor moaned and dropped his head into his hands. His wife cried out in horror. After a moment, Otomo looked up. "This is horrible, but the governor cannot be responsible for it. He would never order such a thing. You must believe me."

Akitada had considered this. "They have accused him," he said, "but that doesn't mean much. Still, even if he gave no orders, he bears responsibility. His love for his son drove him to separate the two young people. Sometimes, excessive love brings death to the very person we cling to."

The professor shook his head. "If so, his punishment has been terrible. We have all been punished."

Mrs. Otomo reached for the amulet and placed it in her husband's hand. "You and I," she said, " we forgot all others when we were thinking only of those we loved. My dear, there must be many things you can still teach the young. Let them be your grandchildren."

Professor Otomo looked at the amulet. With a sad smile, he said, "What is a man to do with a foolish wife?" Then he put his arm around her and drew her close.

Akitada nodded to both of them. "One should always accept a generous gift."

30

Homecoming

The return to a house that no longer contained Seimei was unexpectedly eased by Saburo. He was an odd addition to the Sugawara household, even given Akitada's dislike of spies and Tora's fear of demons.

The evening of their departure from Naniwa, Saburo had approached Akitada in his typically offhand manner. "Well, you're finished here," he said, his face working quite horribly. "I'll say goodbye then." He looked down at himself and stroked his new clothes with his good hand. "You'll want these back, right?"

Akitada had not come to any decision about Saburo, but he certainly did not want his clothes back. "Of course not."

"Oh." Saburo did not look at him. He fingered the fabric of his robe and sighed.

Conscience smote Akitada. There was hardly a creature in this land who had suffered more at the hands of his fellow man than this one. He had even more suffering to look forward to, and neither his new clothes nor his innate intelligence would protect him from being shunned. He said, "If you like, you can come along with us. We can use some help for a while. How long you stay will depend on your behavior. My position doesn't permit my people to behave scandalously or illegally." He paused. "The decision is up to you. What do you say?"

Saburo drew himself up. "I'm aware of your position, sir. As for becoming your servant, I'll try it. I may stay if I like it. Haven't been to the capital in a while. It'll make a change."

And that was that. No word or gesture of gratitude. No bowing or kneeling or fervent promises of loyal service. Saburo turned on his heel and left.

To be fair, on the journey home, he took on the humblest chores without being told, cleaning their boots, looking after the horses at the post stations, carrying saddlebags. He managed to do a great deal of work, even with a nearly useless arm.

Saburo knew his way around horses and seemed to have other useful skills.

Tora told him about the capital and the routine in the Sugawara household. Akitada did the same for the other family members and his own habits. When Tora asked Saburo about being a spy, he answered briefly and with a nervous glance at Akitada.

It was only when Genba swung the gates wide that Akitada had a moment of panic. What would his family make of the horribly disfigured creature he was about to introduce into their midst?

Genba was glad to see them until he saw Saburo. And when Tora introduced him as a new servant, Genba's face fell even more, though he nodded politely. More problems?

But Akitada had no time to worry about Genba's feelings. The main doors flew open, and the children rushed down the stairs, shouting and laughing. Behind them, came Tamako, looking deceptively pale and fragile in her dark robe because they were still in mourning for Seimei. But there was no time for grief either: His daughter Yasuko flung herself into his arms, and Yuki did the same for Tora.

To see his wife again and hold his child was almost more than Akitada could bear. He hugged Yasuko tightly and murmured an endearment into her ear. It was a moment of pure happiness.

Then Yasuko's eyes fell on Saburo and widened. "Who's that man, Papa?"

Saburo hung back, holding the horses, and was now drifting off in the direction of the stables. Akitada called after him, "Come and meet my family, Saburo."

He came, his head bowed until his chin touched his chest. He bowed to Tamako first. "My Lady."

Akitada said, "Saburo has agreed to stay with us and help out wherever he's needed. He has had an interesting life."

He saw that Tamako understood. Her face warmed. "You're very welcome in our house, Saburo," she said, giving the ugly man a smile.

Yasuko asked, "What's the matter with your face, Saburo?"

Her parents tried to speak at the same time, Akitada to explain, and his wife to remind her daughter of her manners. Both broke off, embarrassed.

Saburo raised his good hand to his disfigured cheek. "It got cut, Lady Yasuko. I hope it doesn't frighten you."

"No. I'm not frightened." She studied him with a solemn expression—Saburo bore it patiently—then she smiled at him. "Poor Saburo. I'm sorry you got hurt."

Saburo's face worked for a moment. "Thank you, little lady," he said. "Perhaps, if your honored parents permit it, I'll tell you some good stories some time. I know lots of stories."

"Me, too," cried Yuki, running over. "I like stories, too."

With his household thus adjusting to change, Akitada went early the next morning to present his reports at the Second Minister's office in the Dajokan-cho, the building housing the offices of the great council of state.

He had spared Munata and Oga as much as he could and stressed Munata's help in quelling Watamaro's aspirations. He felt certain they had been dangerous aspirations and urged that the government deal firmly with the fugitive Watamaro and his pirates. Otomo he did not mention at all. He had suffered enough. Oga was another matter because of his involvement in the murder of Akogi, but that crime did not concern the council of state, and Akitada hoped that the loss of his only son was punishment enough for Oga's ruthless handling of the love affair.

In the Second Minister's office, he was not asked to make his report in person. He was neither surprised nor offended by this. His rank was far too low for him to be consulted by a man who stood at the top of the government.

From the Dajokan-cho, he walked to the Ministry of Justice. As he entered and walked down the corridor, the familiar surroundings cheered him until he heard boisterous voices coming from the archives. He put his head in and saw Sadenari, perched on a ladder and surrounded by six or eight of the youngest clerks. He seemed to be regaling his spellbound audience with a highly colored account of his exploits among pirates and courtesans. Sadenari was too engrossed to see him right away, and Akitada took a step inside.

"Hard at work, Sadenari?" he asked.

The other youngsters scattered, and Sadenari slid down, flushing crimson. Akitada merely looked at him, then turned and left.

Fujiwara Kaneie was in his office and received him happily. "My dear Akitada, welcome. Sit down. You've been missed. All sorts of things are in arrears, and I cannot get any work out of the young clerks. Are you all done with that irritating piracy business?"

Akitada bowed, sat, and indicated he was.

"Well, that's good. You're to have some leave, what with the recent death of your old retainer, but if you would just have a peek at a few matters before you take it, I'd be very grateful."

"Of course, sir. You are well, I trust?"

"Yes, yes. Thank the gods. I'll be on my way into the country to have a look at my family estate now that you're back. Getting in a little hunting perhaps. Do you hunt?"

"No, sir. Not lately anyway."

"I'm going to try falcons. The sport of emperors." He laughed. "Very clever birds, I'm told. You just toss one into the air and it chases down your duck or rabbit or whatever and brings it back. Imagine that."

"Very impressive. May I ask what you have decided to do about Sadenari, sir?"

The minister's face fell. "Ah, yes. Silly boy! Sorry he gave you a hard time. I've put him in the archives. Surely that'll teach him a lesson."

Akitada sighed inwardly. The young man was a liability, and Akitada had little hope that he would become a useful member of the ministry, but his exploits in Eguchi had mostly been due to youthful foolishness and an excess of libido. He recalled the young man's humble family and thought it best to leave matters alone, provided he was never saddled with him again.

"By the way," the minister said, "the governor of Settsu . . . man by the name of Oga. You must've met him."

"Yes, I did. What about him?"

"Resigned his office. Says he decided to take the tonsure. Why is everybody in such a hurry to enter a monastery these days?"

"I have no idea, sir."

"Exactly. It's a mystery." The minister pushed a stack of document boxes toward Akitada. "Here are some of the cases you need to have a look at. Handle them any way you see fit. I have the utmost confidence in you. Well, I think that's all. I should be back in another week."

Akitada carried the boxes to his office where his elderly clerk greeted him with a smile and the words, "Oh, dear. More documents? There's no room. His Excellency has been sending everything here for the past two weeks."

Akitada looked around his small room. Every surface was covered with boxes and scrolls, some with small tags attached that proclaimed them to be urgent. He put the boxes in his arms on the floor, and went to sit behind his desk, staring at the stacks that rose before him and threatened to topple in his lap. It reminded him of Nakahara's desk.

The clerk offered, "Shall I clear the desk a little? I can put all those on the floor with the new ones."

Life was back to normal.

The next morning, Akitada rose early and stepped from his wife's room out onto her veranda. It was dawn of another fine day. Their wisteria was not blooming so late in the year, but it looked particularly healthy and lush, with many seedpods dangling among the leaves. Already the small maple had turned completely red, and Tamako's chrysanthemums bloomed lavishly white and golden yellow.

He sat down and thought about his marriage. He had felt shame while making love to his wife last night, shame because he had wanted to bed the *choja* Nakagimi. Even this morning in his peaceful domesticity, his feelings were still ambivalent. He knew he would have taken Nakagimi that night if not for Sadenari's appearance. He had lacked both the strength of character and the wish to resist. As for Nakagimi, she was very beautiful, but there had been a hardness about her that he found repellent. Had he been angry with her because of his own failure?

He pondered this for a while. A bird began to sing somewhere close by.

He had been unfair, he decided. More than likely, she, like Akogi, had suffered a "presentation" when she was still a very young girl. But she had not fallen in love with a handsome and dashing young nobleman. No doubt she had been taken by an older man who had been both unattractive and inconsiderate. She had learned early to look out for herself because no one else would.

He sighed. He must learn not to judge people too harshly. Even Watamaro had gone into his violent and mercenary business with a wish to improve the lot of poor sailors and fishermen.

A rustling of the bed clothes in the room behind him reminded him of the eager and passionate lovemaking he and Tamako had shared. No courtesan could improve on that. With a smile, he rose to get his flute and play for his wife. He walked quickly from her garden to his and into his study. Taking the flute from its box, he returned.

To his delight, the sun had risen over the trees and struck the top of the maple, making the crimson foliage blaze more brilliantly than the most costly dyed silk robe fit for an empress. He put the flute to his lips and played.

Tamako came out and stood listening. He looked at her in her white undergown with a flowered quilt wrapped around her shoulders against the chill morning air. She was beautiful, and he put his heart into the song. She was his beloved, his luminous pearl beyond compare.

When he finished, she came to him. "How lovely," she said, touching his cheek and looking at him with moist eyes.

"Thank you, my dear." He put an arm around her and pointed with the flute. "Look. See how the sun brings out the fire in those maple leaves. I am very happy at this moment."

"I was very happy last night," she murmured with a smile. "Oh, Akitada, I wanted to wait to be quite sure, but I'll tell you now. I think I am with child again."

He pulled her close, his heart full of joy. "I wish Seimei could be here."

"Yes. He wished for another boy."

An heir for the Sugawara name. If they had another son, Akitada hoped he would be a better father to him than he had been to Yori. His happiness faded as he thought of that other father who had caused his son's death by wanting the best for him. He felt afraid.

Historical Note

The time of *Death on an Autumn River* is 1024, nearing the end of the Heian era that predated the period of shoguns and samurai warriors. Though there certainly were wars and warriors, life was more peaceful than in later centuries. The ruler was an emperor and the government was centralized in the capital Heian-Kyo (later Kyoto) but reached across the land via provincial administrations and a well-organized transport system. Most customs and institutions were patterned after those in T'ang China, but contact with foreign countries had been broken off completely in previous centuries, and what foreign trade there was again was still severely controlled.

Japanese officialdom dominated every aspect of the people's lives, but it was no longer in the hands of the best and brightest as in China. It had passed into the control of a single family of the Fujiwara clan. Through marriage politics, senior Fujiwara officials held all the highest positions. They became the fathers-in-law, uncles, grandfathers, and cousins of ruling emperors. By the eleventh century, they encouraged the early abdication of emperors in order to place another, easily controlled, child on the throne. Perhaps the most powerful man of the time was Chancellor Fujiwara Michinaga, who had ruled for many years, either as chancellor or as the father or grandfather of chancellors, empresses, and emperors. By 1024, he lived retired in the Byodo-in, his palace on the Uji River.

The capital was connected to the provinces via a system of roads with post stations and barriers. All travel could be checked on the highways and along river and sea routes. The most important of these rivers was the Yodo because it connected the capital to the Inland Sea, which in turn linked the Western Provinces and Kyushu with the central government. The Yodo also connected with the Uji River, a tributary that came from Biwa Lake and the North-Eastern provinces. Both boats and sea-going vessels carried people and goods to and from the capital. People traveled the Yodo to engage in business, make pilgrimages, and pursue pleasure, sometimes combining them. Famous shrines and temples were on the route, as were port cities and the pleasure quarters of river villages.

Ocean-going vessels of the period resembled the deep-bottomed Chinese junks. They had huge square sails as well as oars and carried goods from the provinces and from foreign countries to the port of Naniwa. This former capital and major port at the mouth of the Yodo River had silted up by the eleventh century, and several other ports developed along the coastline, but the Yodo River continued to play its role.

Because of storms, sea travel was uncertain and wrecks were common. In addition, pirates roamed the Inland Sea. In the tenth century, Fujiwara Sumitomo, a local nobleman with aspirations and a fleet of several hundred ships, raided commercial ships and those carrying tax tribute. Subduing Sumitomo was costly for the government, and in later years, it tended to close its eyes to more modest depredations.

A number of the river towns specialized in the sex trade. Eguchi, the town in this novel, lay near the mouth of the river and was one of the most important of these. According to Janet R. Goodwin's Selling Songs and Smiles: The Sex Trade in Heian and Kamakura Japan, attitudes toward prostitution were on the whole tolerant during this time. Distinctions were made between *asobi,* entertainers who also engaged in sexual relations, and *yahochi*, who seem to have been ordinary streetwalkers. No doubt, both types flourished in the river towns. Accounts in the diaries of noblemen of the time speak frequently of pleasure cruises from the capital to Eguchi and other towns. They mention local courtesans and reigning beauties (*choja*) by name.

Little is known about the administration of Settsu province during this time. It would have had a provincial capital and a governor, as well as prefects in the various districts. All provinces had police forces by this time. Military protection for the officials and their headquarters also existed, but the ranks of the guard were filled with local warriors. The central government appointed governors and assistant governors from among the ranking nobility. District officials came from among the local landowners and frequently served a lifetime, a fact that greatly contributed to the rising power of the provincial warrior class. In addition, there were hundreds of irregular appointees with or without noble rank. Their numbers and ranks were carefully fixed by the intricate bureaucratic system. All officials were annually evaluated. Their primary duties involved collection of taxes, keeping the peace, and enforcing laws. Judges worked in conjunction with the provincial administration. Possibly, sentences were harsher the farther crimes occurred from the capital, but executions were still uncommon. The most serious crimes were punishable by exile.

In the centuries before Japan closed its borders to foreigners, both Chinese and Korean immigrants had been made welcome and settled in the country. Their knowledge of the Chinese language and literature, of Buddhist practices, and of the arts made them respected members of Japanese society. Professor Otomo is such a descendant of earlier immigrants, and like many of them, an academic.

By the beginning of the eleventh century, trade with China and Korea began again on a small scale with special permits being extended to certain merchants only. The court nobles controlled all imports. The taste of the highest-ranking nobles for foreign art and the craving of the powerful temples for Buddhist religious objects made them the prime consumers of such goods, and permits were issued frequently.

The two religions practiced in Japan at the time, Buddhism and Shinto, coexisted amicably, sometimes within the same temple or sacred place. This collaboration was especially useful in the case of death, because Shinto abhorred contact with the dead and required elaborate purification rites before worshipping at a shrine. Hence the taboo tags worn by Akitada after Seimei's death. The funeral rites for Seimei were carried out by Buddhist priests.

Finally, the figure of the ninja-like spy Saburo may seem an anachronism this early in Japanese history, but toward the end of the Heian period, temples and monasteries began military training for monks and lay soldiers in order to protect their lands and defend themselves against rival monasteries. It was in this context that the first "spy" stories appeared.

.

About the Author

I.J. Parker was born and educated in Europe and turned to mystery writing after an academic career in the U.S. She has published her Akitada stories in *Alfred Hitchcock's Mystery Magazine,* winning the Shamus award in 2000. Several stories have also appeared in collections, such as *Fifty Years of Crime and Suspense* and the recent *Shaken.* The award-winning "Akitada's First Case" is available as a podcast. Many of the stories have been collected in *Akitada and the Way of Justice.*

The Akitada series of crime novels features the same protagonist, an eleventh century Japanese nobleman/detective. It now consists of nine titles. *Death on an Autumn River* is the latest. Most of the books are available in audio format and have been translated into twelve languages.

Also by I. J. Parker

The Akitada series in chronological order

The Dragon Scroll

Rashomon Gate

Black Arrow

Island of Exiles

The Hell Screen

The Convict's Sword

The Masuda Affair

The Fires of the Gods

Death on an Autumn River

The Emperor's Woman

Death of a Doll Maker

The collection of stories

Akitada and the Way of Justice

The HOLLOW REED Saga

Dream of a Spring Night

Dust before the Wind

The Sword Master

For more information, please visit
I. J. Parker's web site at
http://www.ijparker.com